inkBLOT

inkBLOT

by

Johnson Naigle

Crossroads Publishing House

www.CrossroadsPublishingHouse.com

inkBLOT
Copyright © 2011, Johnson Naigle
Print ISBN: 9780615509020
Digital ISBN: 9781466129887

Cover Art Design by Crossroads Publishing House

Digital release, July 2011
Trade Paperback release, July 2011

Crossroads Publishing House
P.O. Box 723
Emporia, VA 23847

Acknowledgements

Special thanks to our families and friends who believe in the stories we have to tell, and to you for coming along on the journey.

Dedication

To anyone who has ever wondered just how much
of our online interactions and information
is truly confidential, and what could happen if...

If scars are just tattoos with better stories,
maybe that's why a good story is like a tattoo on your
memory.

We hope you enjoy this story.

.

inkBLOT: the novel

CHAPTER ONE

Ronnie's mind juggled the images on the screen and the faces of those two dead girls.

He rubbed his eyes which stung from being up all night. The two computers he had in front of him hadn't gotten a break either.

Positioning his chair in front of the laptop, he reran the data model. Turning to the inkBLOT server to run another report, he thrummed his fingers against the wooden desk. Nervous excitement gave him a buzz as he waited for the results to pop up on his twenty-two inch monitor.

The screen flickered as the results displayed across the screen.

Ronnie's jaw dropped.

Please don't let this be a dream.

He closed his eyes and opened them again.

"It *is* a match!" He slapped the desk. "A solid match." He grabbed his mouse, copied some information from one file into another, and adjusted the numbers in the algorithm from the data on inkBLOT.

A warm rush of excitement swirled in Ronnie's stomach. The model worked. This wasn't a fluke. It might not be a statistically significant sample yet, but today marked a turning point. He scribbled numbers on a piece of paper, double-checking them against the results on the computer screen.

A swell of pride tickled his ego. All those hours of studying inkblots and the psychology behind them hadn't been a waste of time after all. He tucked his pencil behind his ear and went to another screen.

Running a hand nervously through his hair, he reached for his can of Mountain Dew. Empty. He popped it with his knuckle, sending the can off the side of his desk to the floor.

The black lab snoring under the desk scrambled to his feet, retrieved it, and dropped it into the trash can.

"Score," Ronnie said without even looking up. That was the first trick Rorschach had learned as a pup and he never missed. "Thanks, Rorschach."

The dog yawned, then belly-crawled back under the desk.

"Sorry, buddy. The all-nighter taking a toll on you?" He couldn't remember if he'd fed him, so he took a dog biscuit from the cookie jar he kept on his desk and tossed it to him just in case.

Rorschach snapped up the biscuit, let out a sigh, and went back to the business of sleeping.

A feminine voice seemed to come out of thin air. "What's going on here?"

Ronnie jumped and Rorschach shot out from under the desk with a woof.

"Dang, girl. You scared me to death." Ronnie hadn't heard Tiffany come in, but there she was, propped in his doorway. "What? Are you in stealth mode?"

Tiffany laughed. "Hardly." She gave Rorschach a rub on the ears before she plopped her purse down in the chair at the other desk.

"How long were you standing there?" he asked the tiny blonde.

"Long enough to see you looking right smug about something."

He smiled. "I'm feeling pretty good."

"Well you don't look so good. You've got circles around your eyes as dark as your hair, and man, this whole place smells of garlic from the half eaten pizza still sitting on the table. Yuck. That's not the pizza from Saturday night, is it?"

"'fraid so."

"That's not like you. What the heck's been going on?" The color drained from Tiffany's face. "Please don't tell me the iPad app crashed again."

Ronnie could almost feel her nervous energy from where he sat. "No. No way."

He propped a foot against the edge of his desk. "The changes you made to the app are fine. inkBLOT is up and running without a hitch. In fact, last month's numbers are higher than ever."

"Well, then why do you look like you've been up all weekend?"

"Because I have been." Suddenly he caught a whiff and realized the pizza wasn't the only thing that stank. He folded his arms across his chest to hide the funk. "You won't believe what I've been working on."

"Do I really want to know?"

"Remember the string of missing girls up in Pennsylvania?

"Yeah. They caught that nut. It was all over television. He had all those victims tied up in display cases around his house like a life-sized doll collection." Tiffany shivered. "What a weirdo."

"The last update I heard was that they found the other two girls that were missing buried in the guy's backyard."

Tiffany rubbed her arms to chase the chill. "That's scary. The families knew the guy, too. But wait a minute, what's that got to do with your place smelling like a trash dumpster? Oh, and by the way, you kind of look like you've been sleeping in a dumpster, too."

"Thanks a lot." Ronnie took a comb out of his back pocket and whisked it through his hair. "Better?"

"Yes," she said.

"Good. So, you want to know what that freak has to do with us?"

Tiffany straightened and shook her head. "With me? Not me."

He motioned between the two of them. "With inkBLOT. Which means you *and* me."

She looked skeptical.

Ronnie raised a challenging brow. "The big deal is that inkBLOT matched him."

"Whoa." Tiffany rushed to Ronnie's side, and looked at the screens in front of him. "Are you saying what I think you're saying? This isn't embezzling or some white collar crime. This is really dangerous stuff."

"I know." Ronnie rocked in his chair as he nodded. "It's big."

"You've got to tell someone about this."

He shook his head. "Not yet. When I have a scientifically sound sample, and enough credit for people to take me seriously, then I'll get it in front of the right people."

"But Ronnie, you're saying that the data we've captured is chugging out lists of people who aren't just up to no good, but potentially dangerous. Deadly!"

"That's true," Ronnie said. "And it's getting more and more accurate."

"Yeah, and when the names were attached to less horrifying crimes, I was fine with waiting, but these last couple, they're big. We could save lives."

"Some day," Ronnie said.

Tiffany folded her arms across her chest.

Ronnie sat forward. "They'll shut us down if we tell now. We can't put everyone on a list who MIGHT be dangerous. It would be like putting a percentage of the population under arrest just in case they did something. We can't do that."

"We have to do something."

Tiffany looked frustrated. Ronnie got that. It bugged him to keep all this great work hush-hush too, but who would believe a theory that a couple of teens put together? No one. He knew that. Like everything else in his life, he'd have to wait until the timing was right.

Ronnie softened his voice to soothe her concerns. "Soon. I hope it will be soon, too. That's the plan. For now though, I'm still working on the piece of the model that will tell us what level of crime could occur before it happens. I'm tweaking that."

"Was that guy on the lists I've been checking?"

Ronnie opened a blue folder. "Yep. Right here. Number 51793. He surveyed with us several times. I cross-checked his results against the data you usually run. Can you imagine if we could get everyone to take the inkBLOT quiz? But, and this is rockin', the marker questions we added, they're really helping weed out suspect answers. Now, when people make stuff up, we'll know it."

"This is great. You amaze me. Over and over again." Tiffany's look of excitement turned to concern. "Have you slept at all since Saturday night?"

"No. I've been too amped up to sleep. Once I got it all sorted out, I updated the model and reran the reports to see how the ones we already validated played out. Time flew by. Tiff, all of the data is on the money. This list is getting tighter with each tweak."

Tiffany slapped Ronnie's hand in a high five, and then headed over to her desk. "At least the list of folks on my report that I have to keep tabs on will be smaller. That's a relief."

"We're making progress, Tiff. Real progress."

"I sure feel lame. I sat in my room reading all weekend. You should've called. I'd have been here in a hot second."

He knew it was true, but when everything started coming together he hadn't been able to slow down for anything.

"Well, I'm pretty much done with it for now."

Tiffany powered up the computer on her desk, then turned back to Ronnie. "You probably need to get some rest."

"It's eight in the morning. I can't go to sleep now. I'll be fine once I jump in the shower," Ronnie said. "In fact, that's where I'm heading now."

"Good. Take that trash out while you're at it." Tiffany turned and started working through the files on her computer.

"Hey, this is my apartment."

"Yeah, well I work here, and for a real bargain I might remind you."

She had him there. He'd been in a bad place when his mom left for Florida and never came back. inkBLOT and Tiffany became the most important things in his life. Once they turned the inkblots into a game and set up the portal, Tiffany took over the detailed analysis and advertising which was profitable for them both. They'd become best friends in the process.

She looked pretty today. He stopped in the doorway and turned to say something about it, but feeling corny, he swallowed the words.

CHAPTER TWO

Chelsea Pressman read the front page of THE DAILY
BANNER.

LOCAL NOVELIST FOUND DEAD

By Scott Topper

PORTSMOUTH, VA

Local resident and bestselling mystery
novelist Sheila Monroe had no idea
that while fans lined up to buy her
latest book released on September
23rd, police would have a hot murder
to solve—her own.

A resident of Stratford Apartments
on Hedger Road in Portsmouth
arrived home from the night shift
and discovered the body of the 30-
year-old victim in the stairwell
outside of apartment 324, with a
pink boa around her neck. The

victim had no direct tie to the apartment complex.

Investigations continue to determine if the murder took place in the stairwell or the body was dumped there. At noon today, the cause of death was still undetermined.

Ms. Monroe's latest novel, *Unexpected Threat*, was released last night to record sales. The sequel to *Unexpected Threat* is titled *Don't Look Now*. The back-to-back books have been heavily marketed. *Don't Look Now* will release next month.

Funeral services will be closed to the public.

Anyone seeing anything unusual the night of the crime, or tips that may lead to an arrest, is encouraged to contact the police at 1-555-LOCK-U-UP.

How Chelsea wished she'd written this story. She'd have put a cool spin on the headline. Something people would never forget.

If only I could get a really good story. One that doesn't have to do with lemonade stands and church barbecues. What do I have to do to get a break?

She'd been volunteering for every opportunity that came her way, and her blog had nearly as many followers as the paper had distribution these days. Chelsea grabbed her things and headed to work mumbling about the article the whole way. One day Wadsworth would have to give her a chance with a real story. Something with front page potential. Heck, any page would do if it was a hard hitting news story.

Chelsea'd just sat down in her cubicle when Harold Wadsworth waddled by, craned his thick neck and scanned the sea of cubicles. Wadsworth's gravelly voice rumbled. "Where's Scott? Anyone seen Scott?"

Chelsea felt the green-eyed monster come over her. As hard as she fought to not feel that way, it was inevitable.

She stepped into the aisle. "He's not in yet. I hear he's sick or something," Chelsea lied.

Wadsworth spun in her direction. "I need him to get on this story. Get him on the phone."

What? Am I suddenly the secretary?

"It's important. Time sensitive. Hop to it," he said with a snap of his fingers.

She stared in disbelief. *Tell me he didn't just snap his fingers at me.* She swallowed the thoughts that threatened to escape her lips. She turned and ran her finger down the list of reporter cell phones, and began to dial. As she hit the last number, she pressed her finger down on the release, and waited for a five count. "No answer, boss."

Wadsworth's jaw tensed. His eyes darted, the way they did when things didn't go his way.

Jackpot. Chelsea raced to the editor's side. "What's up? I can cover it for Scott. Give me a chance." She stood facing him, trying not to fidget.

"I ought to give this story to you. At least you're around when I need you," Wadsworth mumbled through clenched teeth.

"I won't let you down." Chelsea reached for the assignment. She'd typed up Scott's handwritten notes enough times over the past two years. She knew she could do better.

The editor started to hand her the details.

Her heart soared. *Yes, the break I've been waiting for.* She reached for them, but just as she touched the printouts, Scott walked in the door and Wadsworth tugged them back.

"Scott. Why didn't you answer your phone?" The editor wobbled past her toward his star reporter, leaving her in a waft of his aftershave.

Chelsea's heart sank. She sucked in a breath and let it go slowly. *So close.*

Scott grabbed for his phone, shrugging. "I didn't hear it ring. Did you call? What's going on?"

Dismally, Chelsea watched the two men walk off, talking about the story. She slinked back to her cube, slapped her assignment pad against her thigh, and plopped down in her chair. She called the charity contact for an interview later in the week and headed out to work on her restaurant review for the Daily Leisure section.

She daydreamed about bigger stories all the way to Antonio's Restaurant. As she approached the front door of the red, white and green building, she looked up at the giant sign.

Suck it up, Chelsea. Every story has the potential for something bigger. Go for it.

CHAPTER THREE

Ronnie's legs peeled away from the leather seat of his new convertible Mustang like a band-aid being ripped off. For a late September morning it was as hot and muggy as a July afternoon and the seat was having no mercy on his legs. The oceanfront was filled with late season beach-goers, locals who'd steered clear of the strip during the height of tourist season.

He wished he'd worn jeans instead of shorts. It was a small price to pay to drive a sweet ride.

Not brand new, but new to him, the black Mustang gave him an instant confidence boost he hadn't expected. Good riddance sensible Toyota. That was only the first step. He'd promised himself tomorrow would be the first day of a new Ronnie. No more nice-guy-finishes-last. No more playing it safe. No more third wheel-on-a-date guy. No more regrets.

Ronnie tugged at the front of his shirt to keep it from sticking to his skin. Perspiring like a prize fighter, he wondered if it was the heat or a warning that this was a mistake. He blew out a breath and rolled his shoulders.

His phone chirped. He silenced it without looking. It was Tiffany. It was always Tiffany. She'd wonder where he was since he was rarely out of the office this early in the morning, and if she knew what he was up to, she'd try to talk him out of it. It's what best friends do, the voice of reason and all.

Fighting the churning in his stomach, he swallowed hard and moved closer to his destination. He eyed the bright neon sign.

The Crown Tattoo.

Getting a tattoo might be a wild thing for the old Ronnie to do, but he wasn't completely crazy. He'd been careful. This one topped the list by a mile. People came from up and down the east coast to Virginia Beach to get tattoos by King at *The Crown Tattoo*. But, the shop got its share of one-timer tourists who get too much sun on the beach, douse the pain with liquor then go home with a permanent souvenir on their shoulder or ankle. That was obvious from the guestbook entries on their website.

Ronnie walked up the block. The shop was well lit and boasted gallery-like images in the windows. Pretty classy. Not what he'd expected at all. He pushed through the heavy glass door. The stack of new twenties out of the ATM felt thick against his thigh.

A rush of cool air hit him as he walked inside.

He stepped up to the long counter that stretched across one side of the storefront.

A big dude tattooed in psychedelic images looked up from his sketchpad.

Ronnie straightened to his full six-foot three. "Are you King?"

Without a word, the man wheeled the rolling stool closer to the counter. A bandanna, not a real one, but one tattooed around the guy's forehead, was so three-dimensional Ronnie had to keep from reaching out to touch it.

Ronnie pulled a slip of paper from his hip pocket and pushed it across the counter.

King examined the graphic, squinting above the smoke from the cigarette hanging between his thin lips.

Ronnie looked around. Artwork covered almost every wall in the tattoo parlor. Colorful sketches and photographs of finished work on skin lined the walls. Some of the work was simple, but most was elaborate. Real art.

Across the room, a heavyset guy with a bleached Mohawk sat in an old barber chair. He was getting a tattoo of a brilliant blue and lime green fire breathing dragon on his bigger-than-a-softball bicep.

The hum of the equipment tickled Ronnie's ears, drowning out what little chatter was going on between the artists and customers in the back of the shop.

An older woman, probably someone's mom, lie face down on a table getting a tramp stamp on her lower back. From the look on that lady's face, she was in a lot of pain.

Ronnie's stomach flipped. Maybe this wasn't one of his best ideas.

"This what you had in mind?" King handed the drawing back to Ronnie.

Ronnie pushed his glasses up on his nose, and nodded.

King frowned. "Can't do it, kid."

"But you said—"

He pinched the cigarette between his fingers, letting the glowing tip fall off like a lightning bug dying in midflight. "I said I do custom work...but I don't do company logos. It's a personal thing. I got standards. A tattoo should be about you. Not a billboard ad for someone else's brand." King turned his back on Ronnie. "Pick somethin' else."

"Wait, but that is me. It's mine. I drew that." The fear he tasted a minute ago was replaced by his dislike for being told no.

"Look. You may have drawn it, and you're a real good artist. I'll give ya that. But that's property of that business owner. Bet you thought I wouldn't know about inkBLOT. I've got a daughter. I can surf the web. I know all about it."

"I own inkBLOT. I built it. I run it. It's me."

King snickered. "Yeah right, and I'm Kid Rock."

"No. Really." Ronnie ran a palm across his chin. "I can prove it. Got an internet connection in here?"

"Cat," King yelled to the back of the shop.

Ronnie watched a high school age girl stroll out of the back in no big hurry. Her coal black hair and the tattooed stars around her left eye made her look like a Kat Von D wanna-be, albeit a much younger version of the famous tattoo artist and television celebrity.

"What d'ya want, Dad?" She leaned against the doorjamb looking bored.

"Bring your laptop. This guy needs to look something up."

She rolled her eyes, disappeared for just a minute, then plopped a hot pink mini on the counter. "You know I hate people messing with my stuff," she mumbled.

Ronnie tilted back the screen and started typing on the tight keyboard. The familiar click of the keys and light of the display was like power to his engine and relaxed him a bit. He pulled up the web domain registration for inkBLOT displaying his name and address as the owner of the company.

"See?" He spun the laptop back toward his judge and jury. Then he took out his wallet, and placed his driver's license and a business card in the middle of the keyboard. "It's me." He lifted his chin, daring King to contradict him now. "Name and address match."

"No kidding. I guess I stand corrected. All right, Mr. Big Shot. Where do you want this tattoo?"

"On my arm. Like his." Ronnie pointed toward the guy with the Mohawk.

"Yeah?" King pulled out a piece of transfer paper and started tracing out the design. "I took that test online once. Your inkBLOT thing. Just for kicks to humor my daughter. The report was surprisingly accurate."

"Cool." Ronnie watched King transfer the image on the tracing paper. Then, the huge man stood. Ronnie was tall but this guy made him feel like a munchkin.

"Follow me. You can take off your shirt and have a seat over there. We'll see where we want to put this."

Ronnie followed the hulk of a man. The back of the shop seemed hospital room sterile. The air smelled of cleaner. He pulled his tee shirt over his head and sat down. His heart raced a little.

King placed the tracing paper on Ronnie's arm and slid it up and down along his bicep, looking for the right place.

Ronnie's jaw set. *If I'm going to change my mind, I'd better do it soon.* He'd weighed all the possibilities. So, maybe getting a tattoo to get a girl wasn't the best reasoning, but he needed a serious image overhaul. There was no question about that, and Chelsea Pressman really dug tattoos. She'd written a whole article about them the week before in her column in The Daily Banner. That's when he'd gotten the idea.

"This is the easy part." King laughed.

Ronnie watched in the mirror. The design looked a lot bigger now.

"I like it." Ronnie lifted his chin. Until now, his attention had been squarely on inkBLOT, but even that had taken a backseat to his interest in Chelsea. The dark haired beauty had his attention from the first time he'd read her column. Her online blogs were fuel to his fire. She was perfect. Perfect for him, anyway. Now, he just needed to convince her of that.

"Look kid. You sure about this? You seem kind of nervous. It's permanent, not something to be taken lightly."

Ronnie nodded. "I'm sure."

"Okay, well here's what I'm gonna recommend. Let's shrink it a little, and raise the logo up like this." King repositioned the template. "You can hide it under a short sleeved shirt that way. I don't want you doing something you're going to regret...your first one and all."

"I'm sure about it, but yeah, smaller *is* probably good." Ronnie took a deep breath and tried to relax while King resized the image and then transferred the purple outlines to his skin.

King moved from in front of the mirror. "What d'ya think?"

Ronnie checked out his arm in the reflection and watched Cat walk out and snag her computer off the counter behind them.

"Thanks," called Ronnie after her.

"Whatever." She spun around and gave him a level stare.

Ronnie turned his attention back to King. "Yeah. Cool." He twisted his arm up and around. "Yeah. Exactly how I pictured it."

Cat leaned against the doorway, gawking at him through her thick black eyeliner. "That's gonna hurt, y'know."

"Be nice, Catherine."

She shrugged. "I'm just sayin'."

King gave her a warning look. "This guy owns that website you love so much. inkBLOT."

She lunged in Ronnie's direction. "Get the heck outta here." She gave Ronnie the once over. "Really?"

King nudged Ronnie. "See. Told ya'. She's obsessed with it. That printout from inkBLOT said she liked being the center of attention and had wings to soar above any obstacles. It was like you already knew my little girl." He snapped a pair of latex gloves on his beefy hands. "You ain't been messin' with my baby girl, have you?" King eyed him as he turned on the equipment and it began to hum.

"No sir," Ronnie said. *That girl will never get a date with him as her dad.*

King cuffed his shoulder. "I was just jokin' around, kid."

Ronnie blinked and swallowed.

"You're RUU?" Cat challenged Ronnie.

"What's RUU?" asked King.

"It's under the logo on the splash page, Dad." Cat rolled her eyes. "inkBLOT powered by RUU."

Ronnie nodded. "Yep. R for Ronnie and UU, double-u, for W Wright."

Cat's prickly disposition switched to friendly. "I thought it stood for 'Are you you?' You know, something deep like that."

"Nope. Nothing that deep. Just my initials."

Cat stepped close to Ronnie, just inches away. "Look." She tugged her jean leg up to expose her ankle. "I did this angel right after I got that first inkBLOT read." Then she spun and cocked her hip out. A tiny inkblot surrounded by a heart peeked over the top of her jeans. "See. I've got the inkBLOT logo, too."

Ronnie swallowed hard. "Wow. You are a fan." He prayed King wouldn't notice the way his heart just amped up and knock him out for ogling his daughter.

It was an ego rush to see Cat so excited about the website. inkBLOT's success had been an unexpected pleasure financially, but he'd never told anyone he owned the site. Being labeled a geek hadn't proved to be a good thing so far in his life. So, he'd figured if people knew he started inkBLOT it would only make that reputation worse. Maybe he had an ace in the hole he'd never considered.

"How many levels have you done?" he asked.

Cat straightened. "I've got the INKpad and everything."

She actually looked kind of pretty when she smiled. "You *have* spent a lot of time on inkBLOT. There aren't too many people at those upper levels yet."

"Oh yeah. My INKpad is totally decked out. I've got artwork, furniture and even the magic 8 ball. I do the daily INKspiration reads, too."

"Cool." Looking at Cat with a mix of gratitude for the flattery, his mind wandered. It had been quite a journey.

She's really impressed with inkBLOT. And to think I just threw that program together that weekend after I realized Mom wasn't coming back. If social services had ever found out, I'd have been thrown in a foster home for sure. Thank goodness Dad's child support checks were still getting mailed to the apartment.

Ronnie never would have made it through the first year if it hadn't been for those checks. A guy can get real resourceful when his back's against the wall.

Cat shifted her hip again and Ronnie's thoughts snapped back into the present.

"Glad you like the site," Ronnie said. "I don't want it to get out that I own inkBLOT, so let that be our little secret, okay?"

"Oh, hell yeah," Cat said.

"Watch your language, young lady." King raised a brow and gave her the stink eye.

"Sorry, Dad." She rolled her eyes and shrugged.

Unless she slipped up with her language, she seemed to have her daddy wrapped around her little finger.

"All the kids at my school think it's the coolest website," she gushed. "This is awesome. I'm so stoked to meet you." She squatted next to the chair, watching her dad start to outline the image.

"Where do you go to school?" asked Ronnie.

"Keller High."

"One of my best friends is a senior at Keller. Tiffany Collins?"

"Get out." She smiled wide. "I know Tiff. We don't like hang out, but she's nice. She's in my art class. I guess it's true that everyone is somehow connected to everyone."

"Small world," Ronnie said. At least the conversation was keeping his mind off the sizzling sting of a thousand angry bees on his arm.

"You said when you set up your appointment that you read about my place in the paper, didn't ya'?" King sank the buzzing needle into Ronnie's skin.

"Yeah. Chelsea Pressman's column." Ronnie sucked in a breath and winced as the needle penetrated his skin deeper.

"Got the article framed right over there on the wall. Ya'll friends?" King never lifted his eyes.

"Yeah," he answered too quickly. "Well, no, not really friends."

King's mouth pulled into a smirk.

Cat said, "Dad's been working nonstop since she wrote that article. Saturday morning used to be our fun day. Now, he just works all the time."

"Was she a customer? Is that where she got the idea to write the story?" asked Ronnie.

King wiped a rag across Ronnie's arm. "You'll have to ask her about that yourself, son."

"What's she like?" he asked.

King shrugged his huge shoulders. "Mostly, she asked questions. I answered them. She's young. Pretty. Seemed bright. She kept angling for a bigger story than I had to give." King dipped the needle in a little white to add some shading and continued.

Ronnie fixed his sights on the rows of designs on the wall across the room. They were arranged by category: animals, military, nature, cartoons and other stuff.

Thumbtacks held pictures of people with fresh ink next to some of the sketches. There was enough skin on that wall to make a guy blush. Boobs, butts, thighs, backs, ankles. A rush of warmth flooded his chest.

The needle dug into his skin. Ronnie gritted his teeth and tried not to move. His mind slipped off to that dark spot.

The place where nothing hurt and all was silent. The place that had helped him survive all those years when his step dad used him to make himself feel like the big man of the house by throwing Ronnie in the closet. The first few times, Ronnie had clawed on that door until his fingers were raw. That's when he discovered the dark spot.

Ronnie shifted his attention to the drawings. An airplane tattoo took him back to his childhood. In his mind's eye, he was a kid again, sitting on the floor drawing a picture of an airplane. His step dad had been a fighter pilot in the Navy, but Ronnie had only ever known him as a fighter. Fighting with his mom, the neighbors and taking the worst of the abuse out on him.

Ronnie had thought he could get on his good side by drawing that picture of his step dad's coveted airplane model. Instead, he'd accidentally tipped the bottle of his mom's calligraphy ink on the carpet. The more he tried to clean it, the worse the ink had smeared.

The memory clicked off like a horror movie, time spun in his mind and there he was all over again. He could almost feel his step dad's hot breath and the fine spray of spit hitting his face as the drunk called him stupid for the gazillionth time. He'd snatched him by the nape of his shirt, and shoved him into the closet for punishment.

But after a while, Ronnie knew every square inch of that closet. Every board, every nail, every shelf, every spider web. His tears had washed and rewashed the woodwork many times over, until he finally found solitude. He'd hidden a flashlight, ink, and paper in the closet just for those occasions. That was when the space became his safe place. That's when he'd become obsessed with inkblots too—blurring ink into designs in that closet. It wasn't so bad, better than out where it was worse.

Mom had given up trying to control her second husband. Husband number one, Dad, was crazy and they fought all the time, but with words. His step dad was crazy *and* physically mean–a bad combination.

Ronnie's muscles tensed at the memory. Even now the memories made him a little sick.

"You need a break?" asked King.

"No. I'm fine." Ronnie shook off the horrible memory and turned his attention to the image on his arm. A symbol of what he'd become. Something no one could take away. Hopefully, it would also help dispel the geeky image a little, too.

The outline had hurt the worst. Now, he was either numb to it, or the pain wasn't all that bad.

"Nearly done," King said as he leaned forward to do the last details. Finally, he pushed back from Ronnie's side and held up a mirror. "What d'ya think?"

Ronnie examined the reflection. The colors were bright in contrast to his sandy brown hair and pale skin. He poked at the tender skin where it was swollen pink. The tattoo looked good. Crisp. Clear. Like high resolution.

King swept a coating of Vaseline over the design and cuffed Ronnie's shoulder. "If you're looking to impress that little reporter with it, I think you will."

His eyes connected with King's stare. *Is it that transparent that I have the hots for Chelsea?* Ronnie shrugged and avoided King's look. It was true he hadn't been able to get Chelsea out of his mind. He'd even subscribed to the regular paper, instead of just the online version, to get copies of her stories. He loved her sharp wit. She was bold and fearless, something he'd never been.

Becoming Chelsea Pressman's kind of guy had become his mission. Maybe for once, he might actually get a real life. Hopefully, with Chelsea in it. A normal life, with weekend plans.

Ronnie counted out a stack of twenties on the counter to settle his tab with King and ended up autographing a picture of his new tattoo for Cat. He posed for a photo for the wall before getting his arm wrapped in cellophane and heading out the door. The skin would take about three weeks to heal, shorter if he took good care of it.

Ronnie climbed behind the wheel of his black Mustang. The car had been a mess when he bought it the other day, but a good scrubbing and waxing brought the paint back to life. The old Toyota his mom left behind was still in running condition, but it wasn't anything that would woo Chelsea, so he'd dipped into his savings and treated himself to the car. The Toyota was in his mom's name anyway, and this was all his.

He caught a glimpse of himself in the rear view mirror. *Sure wish I looked older*. He furrowed his brow and tensed his chin. It didn't help. He pushed up his sleeve and twisted his arm.

He admired the vibrant colors of the tattoo.

"Tiffany is going to flip, and not in a good way." Ronnie said to his reflection in the rearview mirror. "I wonder what Chelsea will think?"

CHAPTER FOUR

Chelsea uploaded her latest column to the shared drive for editing and pushed back from her desk.

Her very own desk.

With a nameplate and everything.

Finally, after two summer internships, and a little nudge from her uncle who was friends with the editor, The Daily Banner rewarded her hard work with a full-time position and cubicle all her own.

The view sucked, but if she tippy toed she could almost see the sky from the window. Thank goodness, she didn't have to sit in the big data entry area at a desk shared by different shifts. She used to spend the first hour of every day reorganizing things in that windowless dungeon just so she could function.

Chelsea leaned back in her chair and smiled at the row of rainbow colored binders lining the shelf over her monitor. She'd spent her whole first paycheck on office supplies. The biggest binder held business cards of contacts she'd made. It had lots of blank pages for the new ones she was determined to make this year. They'd come in handy in future articles and for networking. Last night she'd printed labels for all the binders on her home color printer. The newspaper was too cheap to have a color printer for them to use. Those binders now stood lined up and labeled like soldiers ready for war. Yes, war—and those binders were her army. A battle to the top. To a real career. A career as an award winning journalist whose work appeared regularly on the wire and got picked up by all the big papers. *A girl can dream, can't she?*

She switched two binders to correct the order. *That's more like it.* By size, then in alphabetical order.

Harold Wadsworth stopped by her desk and slipped an assignment in front of her. The balding editor always looked sweaty and puffed like he'd just spent an hour on a stair-climber, something that was highly unlikely by the looks of him.

She glanced over the assignment in hopes for something more interesting than the back-to-school menu and homecoming schedules she'd been assigned last week. No such luck. *Another fluff piece?*

"Thanks," she said to Mr. Wadsworth, faking enthusiasm. "Is this the Juvenile Diabetes Research fundraiser where local celebrities wait tables to raise money?"

He nodded.

"Awesome." Chelsea pasted a bogus smile on her face, but then it struck her. "What if," she said, hopping from her chair and racing to his side. She tugged her blazer straight and tried not to sound desperate, "I not only write the publicity piece, but I offer to be one of the servers and do a follow up afterward?" Her fake smile turned into one of genuine excitement. This could actually turn out to be an interesting assignment.

He stopped, and turned. For a moment he just stared.

She held his stare.

Without a word, he raised his brow. "You know, that's not a bad idea, Pressman. If they'll have you, go for it."

She smiled broadly. One little victory. "Great. I'll set it up." He was already halfway down the aisle of cubes before she could say thanks.

Chelsea swept the notes from her last article to the side and then froze.

The name Sheila Monroe was circled in her notes.

No wonder that name sounded familiar.

Chelsea yanked the notes up for a closer look. Sheila Monroe had been in Antonio's Italian Restaurant while she was interviewing the owner. Antonio had made a big deal of it. He wanted her to include a line about local celebrities frequenting the establishment, but there was no other evidence that it was true. There was no wall of autographed pictures just décor as crazy as Antonio himself.

A spidery tingle of realization raced up Chelsea's spine. Part of that wild décor was the tacky pink boas that hung from the bar and nearly every light fixture in the place.

Chelsea forced herself to get through her assigned stories, but Sheila Monroe invaded her thoughts all day.

On the drive home she realized she was probably one of the last people to see Sheila Monroe alive the night of her murder.

Maybe there's a chance for me to get in on this action, and out scoop Scott. That would be awesome.

Her heart hammered as the plan started to frame up in her mind.

Sheila Monroe had been found with a pink boa around her neck. No one would miss one from the many decorating Antonio's. Had Antonio given her one as a token of appreciation? Maybe he was a fan, or maybe the boa was the murder weapon!

She practically slid to a stop in the parking spot in front of her house. Chelsea ran inside and went straight to her bedroom and reread the article, skimming through it with one finger sliding across the inky page.

Undetermined cause of death. But, if the cause of death turned out to be strangulation—this could be the break I've been waiting for.

She forced herself to take a breath. "Yes!" She twirled in excitement.

"Quiet in there," her father yelled from the other room.

She rolled her eyes. *What a buzz kill. I can't wait until I can afford a place of my own.* Living with her dad was the pits. Ever since her mom went away he traveled more, and when he was home he demanded peace and quiet and perfection in everything. She fell short, no matter how hard she tried. Anyone else's dad would probably be thrilled to know his daughter was the youngest staff reporter at an award winning newspaper. Not her dad. Oh no, he just pointed out every error. He even kept a count of how many other reporters were on the pages ahead of her, like a ranking.

She shook those thoughts from her mind. Dad couldn't dampen her excitement tonight. There were better things to think about. Like a little investigative reporting by someone with a sharper eye than Scott. She'd have to hurry before someone else put it together, though.

***

The next morning, Chelsea dashed to the kitchen and plopped a filter in the coffeemaker to get coffee started for Dad. It was the one thing she was expected to do every morning, and she didn't dare fail to please.

I can't wait until I don't have to do this anymore.

She'd been saving every dime to buy a townhouse. If all went to plan, she'd be a property virgin by spring.

She shoved her feet in her black pumps next to the door, and grabbed her stuff. She closed the door quietly behind her to not disturb her dad. She didn't want to listen to that lecture again.

Once in the car, she called her contact at the police precinct from her cell phone.

"Busby. It's me, Chelsea. Got a second?"

"Got all the time you want, girl," Busby said. He was a first year cop, and spent most of his time still puppy-dogging behind the seasoned guys, but he was a wealth of information whenever she needed it.

"What do you know about this Sheila Monroe case?"

"Not a lot. Detective Davison is down there at the crime scene now."

"Is that right?" said Chelsea, then verified the location.

"When are you going to reward me with a night on the town for all this 4-1-1?"

His flirting didn't go unnoticed. Of course, she'd started it weeks ago when she figured out he could get her details to help her stories. He was playing right into her hands.

"Soon." She'd string him along as long as she could. Once they went out, who knew how helpful he'd be. "Gotta run. Thanks a mil."

Chelsea checked her watch. Instead of parking in the garage in her assigned spot on the J level, she took a metered spot out front to save time. She fed three coins to the meter and forced herself to walk, not run, into the building. Once inside, she slid her dot on the status board from out to in, and then moved an 'on assignment' bar next to her name for the morning. That old timey in/out board made her laugh. When would they update their methods and use an online calendar like the rest of the world?

Pacing herself, Chelsea made the rounds with morning hellos and a little water cooler chat. Once she'd made an appearance, she grabbed her purse and hurried out the door. They'd all assume she was working on the charity event assignment. She'd have to make those contacts while driving, but she could still get it done. She was a great multitasker.

Just as Chelsea pushed out the front door of the building it started to rain. Even though Dad's old black Mercedes 300D was trendy, it was temperamental in wet weather.

"Come on, please start," she said as she patted the steering wheel then turned the ignition. Hearing the motor run was music to her ears. *Looks like this is my lucky day*. She squealed tires as she pulled out onto the damp road and headed for Portsmouth.

Of course, she hit every stop light along the way. She drummed her fingers on the dash. "Come on light, change would ya. I have places to go."

The light turned green, and she accelerated through the intersection heading for the apartment where Sheila Monroe was found dead. A misty breeze blew from the car's open window. Wisps of her hair caught in the wind.

Chelsea's thoughts raced. Someone had to have seen or heard something. The folks in this part of the city were always skeptical of the suits. They probably weren't willing to open up to Super Scott. She'd have a much better chance at getting to the truth from this young hip crowd.

This could be her breakthrough article. She'd leave no stone unturned in getting to the truth. She'd have to do it before Scott caught wind of it though. Who was she fooling? He was probably already on to bigger, newer stories. She fantasized for a moment about the possibility of a series of pink boa murders. A high profile string of stories that could even capture national attention. Her heart raced, and she felt herself grin. She could see herself, one of the youngest women – make that youngest ever– to receive an award for such a huge story.

As she neared the address, police cars lined the block in front of the apartment complex. She parked on the far side of the lot, and headed for the building.

The rain had stopped and steam hung over the walkway in front of her. She focused on the hustle bustle in blue uniforms ahead.

Keep your eye on the prize, she reminded herself.

"Hey lady. You can't go through there," one of the neighbors shouted from the far side of the crime scene tape.

Another one said, "Who the heck do you think you are?"

Confidently, she brushed past, ignoring snide comments. Her sole purpose was getting that story.

The security door on the apartment building was heavy. She stepped through and then held it until it clicked closed.

She scanned the area. Three stories. No elevator. The body was found on the third floor outside of apartment 324.

Scott made it sound as though the body may have been moved to where it was found. What a dunce. Not likely someone would drag a dead chick *UP* three flights of stairs. Did he even investigate the story?

Chelsea raced up the stairs, staying on her toes so her heels didn't make too much noise. Two policemen backed to the wall as she passed them on the way up. She heard them pause, and felt their gaze as they watched her climb the steps.

Then, she came face to face with a tall, bulky policeman. Well, probably a detective since he was in a suit. Either way he was definitely an authority figure.

"Can I help you?" He had that bigger than life kind of attitude and the 'because I said so' tone in his voice.

With an air of confidence, Chelsea stared him in the eye and said, "I need to get up to 324."

"Why? You live there?" He folded his arms across his chest.

"No." She shook her head.

"I can't let you up. It's a crime scene." He stood straight and put one hand on the stair rail, blocking her way.

Chelsea matched his stare. "I'm with the press," she said as she started to push past him.

He put a thick arm out to stop her. "Sorry. Can't do it. Not yet."

She leaned against the wall but was nowhere near giving up. She shifted her focus on him with that look that usually worked on any guy, then ran a hand through her hair and pouted playfully. "I've got a lead on this story. I'm going to write it with or without your help. Please, can you help me?" It was working. He was melting right in front of her eyes. *I haven't lost my touch.*

"Maybe I can get a detective to talk to you," he said with a wink.

She licked her lips. "That would be so great." She reached out and touched his arm. *Yep. Works every time.* "I really need this story."

"Wait here," he said with a warning look.

"I hear ya." She propped a heel against the wall, with her knee stuck out. "I'll be right here, waiting."

He disappeared around the corner.

A moment later, a woman in black slacks and a light blue Oxford shirt came walking toward her. Chelsea took a step back for the woman to pass, but she didn't.

"You wanted to talk to me?" asked the attractive, brown haired woman. "I'm Detective Davison."

Chelsea caught the glimmer from the gold badge hanging from the woman's belt, and the gun. How had she missed that? *Well, I won't be charming my way into any details from her.* This would put her investigative reporting skills to the real test.

"I'm with the Daily Banner. I'm here about the murder. One of my colleagues covered the breaking news last night, but I'm here to follow up." She lifted her press badge, and handed the detective her business card. "I think I may have some information that could help."

"You've got my attention." The young detective tucked the card in her pocket and shifted a notepad to her other hand.

"I was doing an article on Antonio's Italian Restaurant last night. The vic, Sheila Monroe, she was there."

"We don't call them 'vic.' You're watching too much TV." Detective Davison rolled her eyes. "So, you saw Sheila Monroe the night of the murder?"

Chelsea nodded. "At the restaurant."

"Tell me more." The detective jotted down a couple of notes. "Was she dining alone?"

"No. She was there with a man. Tall guy. Dark hair."

"What time would you say that was?"

"It was close to closing time. Antonio couldn't fit me in any earlier. That place does a ton of business."

"Never been there, but I've heard of it."

"Well, then you may not have made the other connection yet," Chelsea said.

Detective Davison raised a brow. "What's that?"

"Antonio's has pink boas all over the place. The owner is as eccentric as his décor." Chelsea could tell she had the detective's full attention finally.

"I think we can work together. Come on," said the detective, motioning her to follow.

Chelsea fell in step behind the detective.

With each step closer to the crime scene, Chelsea's exhilaration climbed, too. The air buzzed with excitement. Bright yellow tape marked a protective barrier between the curious and the evidence.

Detective Davison held an arm out as she came to a stop. "We're almost done here. As soon as my guys clear out I'll take you inside, but you can see from here that although the body was in the stairwell, evidence is clear they were inside this apartment at some point."

Chelsea leaned into the doorway. Pink feathers dotted the chocolate brown carpet in the otherwise nearly empty apartment. There was a sofa, one chair and a coffee table in the living room where there seemed to have been a struggle. A lamp lay broken on the floor beside the table.

"What do you think?" Detective Davison lifted her chin, as if challenging her.

Chelsea closed her eyes for a minute and took in a deep breath, then opened her eyes and scanned the room. "She put up a fight. There are feathers everywhere."

"Nope. Actually, she didn't put up much of a fight at all."

"How do you know?"

"No scratches and the only bruising is that around the neck. We suspect he may have used a date rape drug on her. They'll test for that in the lab, but a lot of those are hard to trace. They dissipate in the bloodstream so quickly."

"I thought they were putting dye in those pills so they were easier to spot when they dissolved," Chelsea said.

"They do, but if she was drinking a sweet, fruity or a dark cola colored drink, she probably never noticed. You didn't see what she was drinking, did you?"

"No. Their specialty is Pink Pomegranate Margaritas. Antonio could tell you for certain. His records are all computerized."

Detective Davison jotted that down in her notebook. "That kind of drink would definitely hide the taste or color of a drug."

"Good to know."

"The victim was found wearing only her panties, and the boa that was used to strangle her. We haven't found the rest of her clothes. You wouldn't happen to remember what she was wearing that night, would you?"

"I think I do." Chelsea gnawed on the inside of her cheek as she reflected on that evening at Antonio's. "She was seated, but I know she was wearing a little black dress. I remember because it looked expensive. Had a classic look to it."

"We found a cell phone lying over there." Detective Davison pointed across the room. "It may have fallen off the windowsill. We're checking to see if it was hers. Maybe we'll get lucky and we can just call the criminal."

"Like that would happen," Chelsea said snickering.

"Oh, don't laugh. You'd be surprised how obvious some cases are. There was a picture on the phone that appears to be the victim wearing a little black dress and heels."

"You know what they say about a little black dress. Good for any occasion," Chelsea said with a snicker.

"Sick, that's really sick, you know that? She was murdered," said the detective with a harsh look.

Chelsea glanced away. "I'm sorry."

Then a grin spread across the detective's face. "I like your sense of humor. Can't take this stuff to heart too much or it'll drive you to tears or crazy and neither one will get you anywhere."

"I heard that. Are there fingerprints on the phone?" asked Chelsea.

"You've got a good investigative mind. I like you. They're working on it," said the detective. "We really aren't sure whether the murderer took the picture, or if it was already on the phone. These days everyone has a dozen pictures on their cell phones. We'll have that information later this afternoon."

Chelsea never felt so alive. "Okay. So, we know the cause was strangulation. The creep drugged her or there would be signs of a struggle here. This was no accident, was it?"

"Looks pretty well planned to me. The semi-furnished apartment has been vacant for a couple of months. Looks like the door was jimmied, but that could have been done anytime. People don't notice much around here."

"I want to write this story. The real story, Detective. That piece that ran yesterday looked like an ad to sell books." Chelsea leaned in closer to Detective Davison. "Between us girls, I need the break. Will you give me exclusive access to this case?"

Detective Davison took a deep breath and looked down her nose at Chelsea. "It's tough being a woman working in a man's world. I know how that is. I've read your stuff though. You're good. Yeah. You help me and I'll help you. Can you give me a good description of the guy she was with that night?"

"Absolutely, Detective Davison."

"Call me Hallie."

Chelsea extended her hand, trying to hold back the smirk. "Hallie Davison?"

"Not like I never heard that before. Yeah. My dad had to sell his Harley to pay for the hospital bills when I was born. Of course, we're Davison without the d. He had a sense of humor."

"Good story," Chelsea said. "I appreciate your help. I'll owe you."

"Yes you will, and I'll take you up on that. Count on it." The detective scribbled a name on the back of one of her cards.

"A deal's a deal." Chelsea took the card.

"Meanwhile, can you catch up with this guy down at the precinct? Give him the description. He'll be able to pull together a sketch for us."

"I'm good to my word, Hallie. I'll get in touch with him this afternoon." With clues in hand, Chelsea headed back to her car feeling exhilarated by the potential of this story. She called Harold Wadsworth's extension at the newspaper office but broke the connection before he picked up. *I can't risk him saying no. Too easy over the phone. Nope, I'm not giving him a chance to do that.*

She replayed her pitch over and over as she drove back to the office. This had to work.

Once she got there, she headed straight to Wadsworth's office and found him on the phone. Chelsea stepped up to his desk, waiting for him to acknowledge her.

Finally, he hung up and lifted his eyes to meet hers.

"I've got a REAL scoop." She pressed her lips together tight to keep herself from grinning like a kid from ear to ear.

"I already told you it was okay to do the fundraiser story."

"Not that. It's bigger."

He gave her an unconvinced look.

"It's the Sheila Monroe story." Chelsea braced herself for what she knew he'd say next.

"That's Scott's story."

She couldn't hide her disgust. "Yeah. Well, he blew it." She slapped her hands against her hips. "There's a LOT more to that story than what he wrote. I happened to see Sheila Monroe in Antonio's while you had me doing that fluff piece. That was the same night she was murdered."

"I'm listening." He leaned back in his big leather chair.

"May I?" She gestured to the fine leather chair positioned in front of his desk.

He gave her a nod.

"Great." She settled into the chair and leaned forward as she unfolded the details she'd gathered so far. Wadsworth didn't look completely convinced. "And, I have the Detective's word that she'll give me the exclusive."

Chelsea pulled in a calming breath. "I know I can do this, sir." She hoped she was displaying confidence, because inside she was pleading and begging with all her heart that he'd go along with it.

"You think so, huh?" Harold Wadsworth drummed his thick fingers on his desk. "You remind me of myself when I was young."

"I'll take that as a compliment."

"Don't. I was a complete pain in the ass." A crooked grin spread across his wide face. "But it worked for me."

Chelsea studied him for a moment. Somehow that comment didn't come as a big surprise. Then, turning serious, she looked him squarely in the eyes.

"You'll have the story in the morning." Chelsea was unable to hide her enthusiasm.

"Tonight," he shot back at her, not hesitating for a second.

"What?" Chelsea stopped in her tracks.

"If you want a lead story, you need to get it done tonight. I'll save a cover spot for you until seven. Not one minute after. If you're late, then it's just next day news." He drummed his fingers on the desk again as if he thought she might back down from the challenge.

"Fine," she said abruptly. In a hurry, Chelsea made her way to the police station to work with the sketch artist. She also reconnected with Detective Davison, rather Hallie, now that they were buds. Hallie had given the address to Sheila Monroe's condo so they could catch up.

Chelsea had to force herself not to speed. The excitement was making her antsy and she almost bumped into the cop car because she whipped into the condominium parking lot too fast.

When Chelsea reached for the door knob of the condo, Hallie swept open the door to greet her.

"Your lead was pure gold," Hallie said.

"Yeah?" Chelsea grinned.

"Oh, yeah. Your sketch came over a little while ago." Hallie raised her phone and turned the image toward Chelsea.

"Yep. That's it."

Hallie took her arm and guided her toward a wall of photos in the author's office. "Look like anyone you know?"

"Oh. My. Gosh. That's him!" Chelsea shouted. Right there, tucked into the corner of a framed copy of the NY Times Bestseller book jacket of *Idle Threat* was a picture of the man Shelia Monroe had been dining with the night of her murder.

Hallie nodded. "Sheila Monroe's agent. We're already rounding him up for questioning. He's staying over at the Hilton. Sheila's assistant told us that Sheila was breaking her contract with this guy."

"That's motive," Chelsea said.

"Could be. We'll see."

"I've got to get back to the office and get started on this article. I'm on a deadline. Will you call me with the rest of the details?"

"You got it. Thanks for your help." The detective answered her phone and waved off Chelsea, then began jotting notes in her notebook while talking.

Chelsea raced back to the office and hit the keyboard hot and heavy.

After twenty-five minutes of continuous typing she sat back and reread what she'd written. This was probably the best writing she'd ever done. Tapping her foot against her chair, she waited for Hallie to call.

The wait was killing her. Chelsea stared at the clock at the bottom of her screen. Twenty more minutes and she'd have to let the article fly, or she'd lose the front page billing. She wasn't going to let that happen.

"Come on Hallie. Bring it to me, girl," she said to the phone on her desk, willing it to ring. Chelsea swigged from a bottle of water, swishing it around in her mouth before swallowing. She hadn't even taken the time to eat, running on adrenaline nonstop.

The Pink Panther tune flooded the space. Chelsea dove for the phone and looked at the caller ID.

Oh good. It's Hallie.

"Yes. Yes. No." Chelsea's breathing picked up with each thread of news. "Oh. My. Yes!" she cried out. "I was right. I knew it!" She hung up the phone and typed in the final few lines of the article.

This rocks! I just know it.

Chelsea hit SEND on the submission. *No turning back now.* It was in her editor's mailbox and in queue for distributions before she make it across the office to his door.

She looked heavenward, praying this would be everything she hoped it would be. She tried to visualize herself getting the recognition in the office she deserved, not treated like the kid who was still taking college courses at night. Maybe Dad would actually utter the words, "Good job," for once.

She could only hope.

CHAPTER FIVE

Chelsea raced home to tell Dad about her day. She burst through the door a little after eight o'clock, but the house was empty. She checked the garage, but her dad's car wasn't there. She pressed the button on the answering machine. He'd left a message. He was working late. Again.

Maybe it's just as well. What if my story didn't make the front page? It could happen. A bigger story could push me off right up until the print run started. That stuff happens all the time. Chances were slim that would happen at this late hour, but if she'd already told Dad and the story wasn't there in the morning, she'd never live it down. Waiting until it arrived in fresh ink on the doorstep was probably a better plan. Things always have a way of working out for the best.

Confidence in her plan didn't make it any easier to get through the night. The excitement was making her stomach swirl like Christmas Eve when you still believed in Santa.

She changed out of her work clothes and into a set of hot pink pajamas even though it was still early. *No point in making a mess cooking dinner for one.*

Taking out a snack pack of microwave popcorn, she set it on a minute and a half rather than push the popcorn button, which usually burned a bag that size. Eating it straight from the bag, she channel surfed from the couch. Not finding anything holding her attention, she went to her room and sat cross-legged on her bed.

Tomorrow might be the day Dad will finally be proud of me.

She pulled her journal out of the white nightstand and started writing.

> Approval is something I've always sought.
> Acceptance is something that can't be bought.
> There are three words I'm dying to hear,
> they're "job well done" whispered in my ear.
> For all my life, I've struggled to
> hear words of praise from Mom and you.
> Mom tried to encourage
> When times were tough,
> through thick and thin,
> but it wasn't enough.
> So now as hard,
> as I might try,
> your compliments just pass me by.
> But today is different, I'm sure you'll see
> 'cause now success is courting me.
> So today your ear I need to bend,
> not just as my father—but as my friend.

She closed the journal and held it close to her chest. "Please don't let me down, Daddy."

Chelsea fell asleep with her journal in her arms.

***

Chelsea woke up squinting against the sunrays that were already peeking between the slats of the blinds. She rolled over, then cringed at the purple ink scribbles all over her pillowcase and sheets. The pen lay next to the pillow, its ink having bled out into an inky mess.

I'll have to do some magic on those. Dad'll have a fit if he sees it. She glanced at the clock.

That will have to wait. The paper!

Chelsea jumped out of bed, ran to her door, and quietly opened it. Tip toeing down the hall, she eased past Dad's room, then sprinted to the front door.

She leaned outside to grab the paper, but it wasn't there. Across the way, the neighbors' paper lay on their stoop.

"Great. Of all mornings for the paper boy to miss our house," she mumbled.

She walked down the sidewalk to the front lawn, and then across the dew laden grass toward the neighbor's house.

Looking both ways, she did her fastest shuttle run ever, snatched up their newspaper, and raced back to her front porch like it was a finish line. A quick glance over her shoulder confirmed no one had seen her.

That was crazy. Hot pink jammies aren't exactly camouflage.

She ducked back into the house, trying to catch her breath while she unfolded the paper on the dining room table. The big letters blazed in front of her. Her title. Her byline. She'd dreamed of this moment.

Chelsea looked toward heaven, smiling. Tears of joy tickled her nose and her heart pounded like a marching band.

"Thank you, thank you, thank you." She gulped back the excitement just as Dad's radio alarm went off down the hall. "Uh-oh. Coffee."

Whirling through the kitchen she got the coffee brewing then slipped into the dining room chair and reread what she knew by heart. Wadsworth had barely cut anything in the editing process. It was perfect.

The headline read BOA CONSTRICTED in huge font.

Now that's a headline that'll sell papers.

She could barely take her eyes off her byline. Her name never looked so good.

THE DAILY BANNER
HEADLINE NEWS
BOA CONSTRICTED

By Chelsea Pressman

PORTSMOUTH, VA

New details have surfaced in the real life mystery surrounding the death of local celebrity, Sheila Monroe.

Friends and family were stunned to learn that the Norfolk resident was found dead in the stairwell of the Stratford Apartments on September 23 in Portsmouth. She had no connections to the apartment complex or any of its residents to their knowledge.

A lead from a source at the Daily Banner was able to give key information which led the police to the prime suspect in this case. Lab tests confirmed alcohol laced with a date rape drug in a glass found in an apartment near the location of the body. A hot pink boa has been determined to have been the murder weapon.

Greed led to murder when Sheila Monroe threatened to break her contract with agent, Dean Morgan. Monroe's lawyer confirmed her intent to end the agency contract with

Morgan (46).

Morgan confessed when brought in
for questioning.

The reclusive Ms. Monroe was rarely
known to leave her apartment,
especially on deadline. She had,
however, been marketing her latest
novel which released on the 23rd, the
day of her untimely death.

UNEXPECTED THREAT, a mystery
set in the resort town of Virginia
Beach, sounds like a premonition
more than a title with the recent
events.

Dean Morgan is being held in the
county jail without bond.

Chelsea's restaurant review for Antonio's Italian
Restaurant wasn't tucked on the inside page like usual either,
but rather on the front page of the Daily Leisure section. That
was a bonus she hadn't expected. Wadsworth must have been
really impressed to reward her with that honor, too.

Things were definitely looking up. The front page of
two sections of the paper in one day. She laid both articles
side-by-side on the dining room table. Tears wet her lashes,
blurring her vision as she tried to read.

THE DAILY BANNER: Daily Leisure
ANTONIO'S – Not Just Radically
Good Italian
By Chelsea Pressman
PORTSMOUTH, VA

If you want to wine and dine somewhere, I've got the place for you. Antonio's Italian Restaurant on Shore Drive is just the spot. Once you enter the restaurant, the soft jazz sets the mood right away. Dimmed lights create the perfect ambiance for sweet eats and sweet nothings whispered in your loved one's ear.

Maybe not the spot for any male sports bonding, but there are touches of décor that distinctly appeal to the ladies. Whimsical furry boas drape through chandeliers and line the bar where bartenders concoct their signature Pink Pomegranate Margaritas. Lace tablecloths add another glamorous touch amidst globed candles and if you come on the right night, a violinist might stroll up to your table to serenade you.

Perusing the menu you'll see such favorites as Sweet Glazed Pork Tenderloin and Spaghetti a la Antonio. Their Cannelloni is to die for and for vegans, there's a super Vegetable Ravioli. If you're a big beef eater, you can order a Steak and Shrimp or Steak and Spaghetti plate. I especially love the Spanakopita Pie with marinara sauce. Try it. You won't be disappointed.

This writer gives Antonio's a 5 Pink Cupcake rating. Call 555-3824 to make reservations for that special night on the town.

What an awesome break. Both of my stories hitting the paper in prime spots on the same day. It'll make those old timers at the paper sit up and take notice of me. Maybe now they'll quit treating me like yesterday's news.

Chelsea knew part of the way she was treated was her own doing. That stupid pink cupcake rating system she made up for her first restaurant review was appropriate for the new cupcake café, but she'd have come up with something better if she'd known it was going to stick. Anything would've been better: forks, napkins, chef hats or anything besides girly cupcakes. She stared at the cupcakes in disgust. Next time I'll be more careful in what I post.

She went back into the kitchen, poured herself some orange juice and a cup of coffee for Dad and carried them both into the dining room.

Dad scuffed into the room in his pajama bottoms and slippers a minute later.

Taking a deep breath, she studied his face for signs of a bad mood. Not sensing a danger zone, she folded the paper back the way he liked it and slid it across the table toward him.

He grunted and pulled it in front of him.

"Good morning, Dad."

He peered over his coffee mug just long enough to give her a half smile.

"I've got news." She leaned forward with a hopeful look on her face.

He drug one hand across his scruffy face. "I just got up. Can this wait?"

"Well, I have to be at work early, and I really wanted to share this with you before you see it for yourself."

He rolled his eyes and put the mug down. "Fine. What are you dying to tell me?" He reached across the table and patted her hand.

She forged ahead even though she'd seen that look before.

"I made the headlines in the newspaper today, Dad." Chelsea paused. Waiting. Hoping that for once he'd come through and throw her a nugget of appreciation. Anything.

"That's great, honey. You know, I always look at your column." He picked up his glasses and slipped them on as he shook the paper out in front of him and started to read.

Chelsea stared at him. He'd completely ignored what she'd said. "Were you even listening? I can't believe you did that."

"Did what?" He smirked and raised both shoulders as though in complete confusion.

"Ignored me. You just ignored me. You're always doing that."

"I wasn't ignoring you." He picked up his coffee cup and took a sip.

"I just told you my writing made the headlines today. Front page, Dad."

"I'm sorry. I didn't realize..." He put down the front page and pulled the local Daily Leisure section out. "Oh yes. Well, another restaurant story. At least it's on the first page."

"Look at the front page of the paper. The front-front."

He did and looked impressed. "So you are," he said.

Her mood soared.

He scrunched his nose as he looked down his bifocals to read the article. "I read about this earlier in the week. Well, one day you'll get lucky and get your own story, dear."

"This is my story. I uncovered the leads that helped catch the criminal. I worked my butt off on that story."

"Do they give you a bonus for that?"

Her heart sank. It's always about money, isn't it? "Well, no, but it's a pretty big deal." Why does he always have to point out the negative? Besides, who ever heard of someone at the paper getting a bonus?

"And you won't see a difference in your paycheck for it, will you? I don't know why you continue to beat your head against the wall trying to write for a paper. I never would've nudged Wadsworth to hire you on if I'd known it was going to be more than high school summer job. You need to get out more. You're worrying me with your one-track mind on this job. You are still thinking about that dental hygiene program we talked about, aren't you?"

Chelsea studied her dad's face. She wished he could be proud of her. "Sure. I think about that certification all the time." *Just not the way you have in mind.*

She looked away, pulling her fingers into tight fists in her lap. Even now that she was twenty-one, it still hurt just as bad.

Will I ever make him proud? Will I ever be good enough?

"I've got to go," she mumbled. The chair screeched as she pushed back from the table knowing she'd never treat her kids that way, if she ever had any. She grabbed her purse and left without bothering to say goodbye. Dad didn't even seem to notice. It was all just another day to him. Why did she think it would be any different than all the times before?

In the car, Chelsea turned the radio off, choosing to drive in silence. Why did she let his response, or lack of one, ruin this?

She slapped the steering wheel. "This is big. I'll celebrate myself."

Every time Scott had a big story, the office celebrated with fresh doughnuts. Hopefully, they'd spring for doughnuts with pink sprinkles on them for her today. Everyone knew they were her favorite.

Scott hasn't got a thing over me now.

She drove through the intersection at the boulevard and Main. That's when she spotted the newspaper box in front of the grocery store. She made a right turn from the middle lane. A car honked at her, the man screaming and shaking his fist.

"Sorry," she said through the windshield in his direction but headed for the newspaper box never slowing down.

She pulled up in front of the Daily Banner box, threw the car in park and jumped out. Each quarter gave her a fit as she tried to shove the 50 cents in the slot. A crisp stack of papers were piled inside. Her name was right there on the top. Awesome!

She glanced around, then snagged five copies of the paper and let the door slam shut as she ran back to her car.

A gray haired lady stood outside the beauty salon door staring at her. The old hag must have seen her steal the extra copies, because she was sure giving her the stink eye.

Chelsea smiled to herself. I deserve these. My name's right there on the front page. Mine! Besides, I couldn't ask for extra copies at work. They can't know that it means this much to me. It just wouldn't be cool.

Eventually, Dad would see this was the turning point, her first footing on that ladder of success. It wasn't luck. She had talent.

Chelsea laid a protective hand on top of the stack of papers, and idled back out to the main road.

CHAPTER SIX

Ronnie drifted off to sleep only to wake up again in an hour, and then every hour, all night long. *This tattoo better be worth it.* Between the aching tattoo and dreams about Chelsea, he was exhausted and wound tight.

He sat up in bed, shaking the last moments of the vivid dream from his mind. *Funny how some dreams seem so real it takes a minute to remember them.*

This time he reached over and turned on the bedside lamp. Rorschach lifted his head from the rug next to the bed and stretched.

"It's okay, buddy. Go back to sleep."

Ronnie grabbed a legal pad from the nightstand and began scribbling notes. After ten minutes, he was certain the idea he'd dreamed was a winner.

He turned out the light and lay back down but his mind raced.

There's no way I can go back to sleep. I've got to get up and work on it while it's still fresh in my mind. This dream was something he could take action on. He resisted getting up for a minute, wondering if it would sound as good once day broke. Dreams were like that. Sometimes they sounded pretty awesome until he tried to repeat them in daylight.

A couple of hours later, Ronnie was pleased that the plan seemed even better after he'd shaken out the sleepy cobwebs. What he jotted down was the perfect way to expand inkBLOT and get a completely new set of demographics. It wouldn't take much work to roll it out either. He could build right off of his current platform.

The notes were nearly an entire project plan and a good one at that. He padded out to the kitchen, and fixed himself a big plastic tumbler full of iced Mountain Dew™.

"ink!," Ronnie shouted as a revelation of the logo came to mind. He could see the lowercase letters with the exclamation point in big, round, black letters. **ink!**

"Oh yeah, this could rock." Ronnie headed to the office and flipped on the light.

Rorschach trotted out from the bedroom, shaking off his own cobwebs so hard it made his tags jingle. He plopped back down on the floor next to the desk with a long sigh.

"You are *so* dramatic." Ronnie rubbed his foot across his back.

Rorschach rolled over onto his back, all four feet in the air. Ronnie kept his foot in motion to pacify his companion while pounding away on the keyboard.

A glance at the clock confirmed he'd been at it nonstop without a break for the last three hours. He was on a roll. The sun began to brighten the morning sky. He stood and stretched out the kinks from the hours of coding.

The newspaper hit the doorstep with a thud.

"Come on," he said to Rorschach, with a slap to his leg. They paraded to the front door together. Ronnie opened it and pushed the screen door open. Rorschach stepped out onto the stoop and dipped his head to grab the plastic wrapped paper in his jaws and then pranced into the kitchen to drop the paper in front of the pantry. Rorschach sat waiting for Ronnie to catch up, thumping his tail the whole time.

Ronnie opened the top pantry door and took a treat from the box on the shelf. Rorschach shifted his weight from paw to paw. Ronnie tossed the doggie bone straight up, and Rorschach snagged it from the air before it hit the floor.

"That's my boy." Ronnie pulled the paper from the wrapper. "Give me five."

Rorschach promptly raised his right paw in the air.

"Blow it up," Ronnie said throwing his hand up and spreading his fingers wide.

Rorschach jumped in the air with both paws up.

"Atta boy."

It was their morning routine, right after the morning walk. A bright spot in each day.

Ronnie opened the paper and scanned the headline.

Awesome. There's Chelsea's name right on the front page! She'd broken a hard hitting story, not the local stuff she normally wrote about for the Leisure section. He propped his left foot against the opposite knee and stood there reading the headline news. It was good.

As he read the article at the kitchen counter, there was a light tap on the front door. Tiffany let herself in, singing out a good morning as she did.

"Hey, Tiff."

"Good morning." She dropped her keys on the table. "Did you get all the backups done so I can start the updates to the database?"

He raised a finger as if to say, hold on a minute.

"Hey, are you ignoring me? Hello-ooooooo?" She stood there, frowning at him.

"No." He looked up for a moment. "Just reading something."

"Must be important." She tapped her foot pretending he'd irritated her.

"Just a sec." He folded the paper and tucked it under his arm. "Yeah. I finished the backups a while ago."

The tiny blonde had a hand cocked on her hip; an eyebrow raised, and was shaking a finger at him.

"What's the attitude about?" he asked.

"I get up at the butt crack of dawn to help you with the database updates and this is the thanks I get?"

She was kidding, he knew it, but didn't all jokes have a little bit truth to them? "Oh Tiff, come on. You know how much I appreciate you. I'm sorry I was distracted. I'll make it up to you. I have something to show you."

Looking in his direction, Tiffany gasped and grabbed her chest. "Oh. My. God. You actually did it."

"What?" He spun back around to face her.

Tiffany's mouth was wide open and her eyes looked like they'd doubled in size.

"What did you do?" Tiffany rushed to his side and pushed the short sleeve of his white tee shirt up. "I can't believe you did that." She slapped his arm. "Is it real?"

"Stop it." He tugged his sore arm back from her.

"It *is* real! You got a tattoo. You did. Oh, man." She slapped his arm again. "I can NOT believe you did that and didn't tell me."

"Ouch," Ronnie recoiled. "Yeah. That too."

"That too? You mean there's more. Who body-snatched my best friend?"

"Funny."

"I thought you said tattoos were tacky when I was talking about getting one."

"They are. On you. Besides you're too young to make a decision for a tattoo."

Tiffany's eyes got bigger. "Excuse me? I'm only a couple of years younger than you are."

"Yeah, well that makes a difference. Besides, it's different for guys."

"Oh…you did NOT just go there," she smirked.

He laughed. "Yeah I did."

"What happened to all that stuff you said about scars being tattoos but with better stories?" Tiffany crossed her arms, fighting him with his own words.

"Yeah. Well that was a crock. I read it on a magnet in a shop down at the beach one time."

"You are too much, Ronnie Wright." She focused her attention on the tattoo again. "Just remember that now for the rest of your life, you can't donate blood. Did you know that?"

"That's not entirely true. I googled it. There are some exceptions and it just so happens that the shop I went to is under strict health regulations so I might be eligible to give blood next year."

"Well, there are still lots of folks who get tattoos who can't donate now, and that's not a good thing. Besides, it's still out of character for you." She reached out and examined his arm again. A smile spread. "It does look pretty cool though. Why didn't you tell me? I coulda' gone with you."

He tugged his arm away. "Because you'd have given me the third-degree. Just like you're doing now."

"Let me see it again."

He rolled his eyes and gave in, letting her get a better look.

"Man, that looks great. It's exactly like the inkBLOT logo. I bet that set you back a few bucks."

"Wasn't cheap, that's for sure."

"Did it hurt?" Her look changed from disbelief to compassion for a moment.

"Oh yeah. You better believe it, and still does, but hey, enough about that. Let me show you what I've been working on all night," Ronnie said realizing he'd never changed clothes either.

"I don't know how it could be bigger news than you with a tattoo!"

"It is." Ronnie led Tiffany back to the office.

When they got to his desk, Ronnie brought up the beta site with the new **ink!** logo he mocked up.

"That's cool. I love the logo."

He went through the screens and explained the business case to her.

When he was done, Tiffany took a step back and shook her head. "You're really wrapped up with this tattoo thing all of a sudden. What's going on with you?"

"I thought it was a good idea. You don't think it'll fly?"

"Heck yeah, it'll fly. People will have this application i-phoned, twittered, blogged, facebooked, YouTubed and every new thing out there. It'll be across the internet in nanoseconds and people will probably crash our server trying to take the test to see what kind of tattoo they'll be. The icons are awesome, at least the ones you've got together so far."

"I'm going to ask the guy who did my tattoo to help me out on the tattoo part. He was pretty cool. He has a daughter in one of your classes."

"You're kidding? You went to *The Crown Tattoo* down at the beach?"

"Yeah. That's the one."

"I know Cat. She looks wild, but she's not. And her dad has won all kinds of awards, you know."

"I read that somewhere," he admitted.

Tiffany pulled up a chair. "I'm sure we can get the current advertisers to prepay for ads before you even launch based on the success of inkBLOT. What's the timeline for ink?"

"A few weeks? I don't think it'll take much time. We can use the same structures, just new images and content. We should be able to launch just in time for the big electronics holiday sales and catch some extra buzz."

"Perfect," she said. "It's a great idea, but..."

"But what? Why the hesitation?"

"What's bothering me...is...this just isn't like you. I mean, you're usually really straight-laced and predictable, and I like that, and this is kind of –"

"Kind of what?" He leaned back in his chair and crossed his arms. "Hey, maybe it's a new me."

She raised a brow.

"A new improved Ronnie Wright," he said with a smile, but Tiffany didn't smile. She was giving him *that* look.

"Is that so? I like the old Ronnie."

He stood from his chair, and did an exaggerated muscle pose.

"Oh lord, no. You're really freakin' me out now," she admitted. "And I thought I knew you so well."

"You do. Quit overanalyzing. What are you now? A 16-year-old Dr. Phil?"

"Shut up," she said, swatting him.

"We're best friends. It'll be fine. You up to the challenge of a new site, or not? I'll need the help." He stifled the playfulness for a second and used a serious tone. "*Your* help, Tiff."

"Of course." She stepped in and gave him a hug. "Maybe you ARE the same old Ronnie."

Man, I hope not. "I've got you fooled," he said, hugging her back.

He wondered if people really could change their underlying structure. One more thing to analyze. He knew he was lucky to have a friend like Tiffany.

She's like one of the guys. If I had a group of guys I hung with besides my gaming buddies. Oh yeah—and she's a lot shapelier. Maybe not really like one of the guys at all.

Tiffany carried her end of the highly technical business of inkBLOT. Ronnie loved that he could be himself around her and feel okay about it, but he yearned to feel normal and have a steady girlfriend like other guys. Tiffany definitely had a biased opinion of him.

The next morning Ronnie tipped his green plastic chair back on two legs while daydreaming on the balcony. He hadn't had a good night's rest since he'd come up with the idea of tattoos as a spinoff for inkBLOT. Maybe that was because the tattoo hurt and itched like crazy, and he wasn't much for taking a bunch of stuff to dull the pain. Pills were something he'd never liked. Of course, he'd never liked tattoos either. Then again, he'd never been interested in a girl like Chelsea.

The only girl he'd ever really spent much time with was Tiff. Just as he'd expected, Tiffany had given him a fit over the tattoo. She knew all of his secrets, and her mom was the only adult who knew that his mom had skipped out. Tiff's mom had agreed to keep the secret as long as he agreed to eat dinner with them three nights a week and keep his grades up. She monitored his report cards. Thinking of his best interests, she'd said if anything went out of whack, she'd turn him in.

He'd never tested her on that, and managed to graduate high school at the top of his class. Tiffany and her mom had even helped him get his business started when he had the idea for inkBLOT. He'd paid back Tiffany's mom her original investment of five hundred dollars in less than two months, and things zoomed from there. He and Tiff spent days in the library researching sales and marketing. Because so much is done via email these days, their customers and advertisers had no idea they were working with teens. Tiffany had a great phone voice, so she handled returning all the phone calls. They could master anything they put their minds to.

inkBLOT had been enough–until lately. Once he got his mind wrapped around Chelsea, he couldn't shake her from his brain, and suddenly inkBLOT didn't seem like all that life had to offer.

He'd planned to wait until the tattoo healed to conveniently cross paths with Chelsea again, but when he heard she was going to be one of the celebrities at a local fundraiser, he didn't hesitate dropping a hundred bucks for a ticket. That same night they'd be auctioning off dinner dates with celebs, and she was one of them. He had every intention of winning a date with Chelsea, no matter what it cost.

He liked the idea of meeting her at the charity benefit. It would show that he had some money in his pocket, something most guys his age couldn't do, and community-focused like so many of her stories. He hoped he had a chance with her. Maybe she wasn't too out of his league. He figured they had to be about the same age.

Tiffany's voice pulled him from the daydream. "Good morning," she sang out.

He went back inside and slid the patio door closed.

She pitched his newspaper across the room, and Ronnie snagged it mid-air.

Rorschach barked.

"And the crowd roars," she yelled and faked a roaring crowd sound. "That's four for four this week." She always kept score. She licked a finger and marked the points in the air. She patted the big dog's head. "Sorry, buddy. I guess you were sleeping on the job again this morning."

Rorschach sat in front of her then pushed his nose under her hand.

"Come on. I know what you want." She headed to the kitchen with Rorschach on her heels to give him his morning treat.

Ronnie opened the paper and checked the front page to see if Chelsea had a story there again. No such luck. He flipped back to the Leisure section.

"Cool," he said as he sat on the arm of the couch.

"What's up?" asked Tiffany.

"Chelsea's article in the Leisure section. Did you see she had the front page story yesterday? She's got to be thrilled about that," Ronnie said.

"Was that what had your attention yesterday?"

"Some writer got murdered over in Portsmouth."

"I heard about that. It was Sheila Monroe. I love her books." Tiffany pulled her long blonde hair up into a casual ponytail, and twisted a band around it twice. "I'm going to go get started. I have all those renewals to process."

He was still reading the article, only half listening to Tiffany. He was dying to see Chelsea, to congratulate her on the big story. He didn't want to look like a big dork though. He needed a good reason to stop by the newspaper.

Advertising wasn't something he'd ever done for inkBLOT, except on the web. Until now, it had been important to keep his connection to the business quiet so social services didn't catch wind and find out his mom left an underage kid on his own, but he was of legal age now. There was no real reason to lay low any more. King and his daughter, Cat, seemed genuinely impressed by inkBLOT. Maybe Chelsea would be too.

That could work. A little trip to the newspaper under the guise of advertising needs would get him an early intro and grease the wheels for the next time he'd see her, at the fundraiser. His mood soared at the thought of meeting her sooner rather than later. It was definitely better than analyzing data all day. He couldn't concentrate anyway.

He went into the master bedroom he'd set up as inkBLOT headquarters. Tiffany was already sitting at her computer with her headphones on, keying away. Ronnie pulled a notepad from his desk and started jotting down notes about potential advertising angles, then typed them up in a spreadsheet.

Rorschach plopped his head in Ronnie's lap.

"I know buddy," he said to Rorschach. "We'll go for a run later. You don't mind a rain check, do you?"

The black lab shook it off.

"I knew you'd understand," said Ronnie, patting the dog's head.

Rorschach ran to the living room, grabbed his squeaky toy and trotted back into the office. He dropped the toy at Ronnie's feet and crawled under the desk.

Ronnie patted Rorschach's head. Aside from Tiffany, Rorschach was probably the best friend he had. Like a Walmart greeter, his loyal dog met him at the door every time he came home. Without fail, he'd be there, tail wagging and tongue hanging.

Rorschach was dedicated to Ronnie. It was like he knew that he'd been rescued.

Ronnie had just started inkBLOT and Tiffany was working a couple of hours on the weekend at her uncle's veterinary clinic when she wasn't helping Ronnie. A local real estate agent had rescued the pup who'd been abandoned in a plastic bin at a foreclosed house. The little guy was up to his own belly in urine and poop. He was skinny and diseased. They weren't even sure they could save him. Tiffany made the little pup her personal project and when the pup was finally well enough, she couldn't bear to leave him to the odds of pet adoption. Considering her mom's allergy to dogs, Tiffany begged Ronnie to take the puppy.

It hadn't taken much arm twisting. Two puppy breath kisses and Ronnie was sold. Besides, he knew how much it meant to Tiffany. She had a heart of gold and he'd do just about anything for her. In hindsight, it was one of the best things that had ever happened to him. He'd never felt that kind of affection in his whole life. Now if only he could get that from someone of the opposite sex.

CHAPTER SEVEN

Ronnie was pumped with thoughts of the chance to see Chelsea at the newspaper. It only took him five minutes to trade in his jeans for some khakis, put on a nice shirt, and stuff his notes in his pocket—ready to go.

"Hey Tiff," Ronnie yelled into the office. "I'm heading downtown. Need anything?"

She pulled her ear buds down. "Nope. Will you be back before I leave?"

"Yeah. I'll only be a couple hours."

"Cool. See ya later." She plugged the glittery earphones back in her ears and chair-danced to the tunes. Even her typing kept beat to the music.

Taking the stairs two at a time, the rush of actually meeting Chelsea almost made him shout.

Ronnie got behind the wheel of his car, revved the engine and headed downtown. It was hard to maintain the speed limit driving the sporty new car.

About twenty minutes later, he walked through the doors of the Daily Banner and wandered through the lobby. The paper shared the tall building with several other businesses. Men and women rushed by with their fancy coffees in hand, juggling cell phones and laptop cases.

Sweat formed under his long sleeved shirt. As he lifted his arms he thought, *Oh great. I'm too hot. I had to wear the long sleeves, didn't I? But there's no way I can let her see the tattoo yet. Not 'til it's healed anyway. That would be uncool.*

The corporate directory showed that printing and distribution services were on the bottom floors and the business and sales offices were located on the top floors of the building. He hung close to the elevators trying to calm down.

Finally, he mustered enough confidence to sidle up to a large group waiting for the elevator. He was dressed appropriately so he blended right in with the others as they crammed into the small space.

Ronnie flinched. *I should have hung back and waited for the next one.*

The elevator lurched. Ronnie looked down. Too close for comfort. The elevator signaled each floor with a bell and his comfort level disintegrated with each ding. On the seventh floor, all but one person got off the elevator. He stepped away from the wall, gaining some breathing space. When the doors closed, he looked up and saw Chelsea standing right across from him.

She's even prettier than her picture in the newspaper.

Worry over the elevator fell away. Ronnie's throat went dry at the sight of the brunette. Professional, but alluring. *She's short. At least a foot shorter than me. I like that.*

Her plum colored suit contrasted with the hot pink top that plunged just enough to show a hint of cleavage.

Ronnie watched her shift her briefcase up on her shoulder while balancing her coffee to keep it from spilling as the elevator made its ascent.

She didn't seem to notice him at all.

He looked at the wall of elevator buttons trying to play it cool, scrambling for something to say. He needed a conversation starter quick. The elevator signaled the next floor with a ding. Time was running out.

"Do you work for the paper?" he asked.

She looked up with one of those 'you talkin' to me?' looks, as though she were seeing him for the first time even though they'd been standing side-by-side.

"I noticed the press badge. Chelsea, is it?" He pretended to squint to read her name on it.

"Yeah, I'm a journalist," she answered, but her eyes drifted away instantly.

"You had the cover story about Sheila Monroe, didn't you?" Ronnie said, hoping that would get her attention.

Her head swiveled back to him.

Yes, it worked!

She smiled big. "Yes. I did write the cover story. 'Boa Constricted.'"

"Loved the headline. Great story, too." He looked at her, hoping he was finding all the right words.

"Thanks." Chelsea looked genuinely happy. Maybe he was getting somewhere.

Ronnie extended his hand for a handshake. "I'm Ronnie."

"Hi, Ronnie." Then, cocking her head to one side, she asked, "First day on the job?"

"No. I was going to check into some advertising for my company."

"You own your own company?" She crinkled one eyebrow as if in a state of disbelief.

That struck a nerve with Ronnie but he forged on, or tried to, but she jumped in before he could tell her the name of it.

"Well, you can follow me. The ad department is right down the hall from my office." She looked like she was sizing him up.

"What kind of business do you have?" she asked as they stepped off the elevator.

"An online business."

"That's nice." She pointed down the hall toward the advertising department. "Right down there. They'll get you all set. Nice talking to you." She waved and disappeared behind a sea foam green wall of cubicles.

Ronnie was tall enough to see that she went into the first cube around the corner. It wasn't much, but at least they'd exchanged names. He headed to the advertising office.

"Excuse me, can you tell me who's in charge of the advertising section?" he asked a woman who looked approachable but breezed by without a word.

From a doorway nearby, a woman emerged. "That would be me," said a cheerful blonde with one of those asymmetrical hairdos. "My name's Stephanie. I'll be happy to help you."

"I'm Ronnie Wright. I'm interested in some advertising."

"What's your business name, Mr. Wright?"

He laughed at that. No one had ever called him that before. "You can call me Ronnie."

"Okay then, Ronnie. Tell me about your business."

Is she flirting with me? "inkBLOT. It's a–"

"inkBLOT? That's *your* company?" She laid down her pen and leaned across the counter. "I *love* that site. The seasonal one you did for Christmas was a hoot. We were all doing that one around here. It was more popular than the Elf Around one, and you know how everyone loves that."

"Thanks."

"I had no idea you were a locally run company. That is so cool. You know, there might be a good human interest story in this. I mean you being local and all."

He shrugged. He wasn't even really interested in the ad now. He'd already gotten what he came for.

Stephanie talked him through the pricing and different rates.

"I'd like it to run in the Daily Leisure section. My surveys are something people do in their downtime. Think that would work?"

"I think it's a perfect fit," she said.

He selected an ad size and format and gave her a brief description of what he'd envisioned. She sketched out some possibilities, and they worked on them at the tall counter together. After about an hour, he was actually stoked about the idea.

Wow, the ad is shaping up. This attention from Stephanie isn't bad either.

They finished discussing details and she promised to send him a draft by the end of the week.

As he left advertising, he saw Chelsea walk across the aisle to a printer. He couldn't help but notice the way she filled out her skirt. *Nice. Real nice.* Stalling for time until she returned to her desk, he went to the water fountain. Drinking slowly, he caught a glimpse of her heading back nibbling a doughnut as she walked. He stood there hunched over the fountain, water splashing his cheek. He got a charge out of watching her lick chocolate from her fingers.

Ronnie lifted his head carefully, trying not to dribble water on his shirt, and ran a hand across his chin. He licked his lips and started slowly toward Chelsea's desk. When he got close to her cube, he took a deep breath and poked his head around the entrance.

"So, this is where a headline journalist does her thing."

She spun around in her chair to face him, wiping a few pink sprinkles from her lips. "Oh. It's you. The guy from the elevator."

"Ronnie," he said, reminding her of his name.

"Oh yeah. That's right. Ronnie." She grabbed a tissue from a box on her desk. "Sorry. Excuse me. They bring doughnuts in for special occasions around here. I can't resist them."

"Pink sprinkles, huh."

"My favorite," she admitted. "Is there something I can do for you?"

For a moment, she looked a little miffed at the interruption.

"I just wanted to say, thanks. I got the advertising all lined up." *Maybe stopping by her cube wasn't such a good idea.*

"Okay. Great," was all she said.

The two-count silence was awkward.

"So, I was thinking," he said. "Would you be interested in dinner or something sometime?"

She shook her head immediately. "Sorry, no can do."

The glow he'd been carrying from having met her fizzled.

She quickly added. "I'm pretty busy with my career. I don't date much."

"You mean a pretty girl like you doesn't date? Come on. You must be beating them off with a stick."

"Well, I didn't say I don't get asked out. I do...it's just that I don't accept the invitations. I go on frates once in a while, but that's it."

"Freights?" He had a look of utter confusion on his face.

"Hello? Yeah. Friendship dates? Frates, you know."

"Oh yeah. I thought you said something else. Well, think about it..." He backed toward the aisle way. "Not a date. Just a celebration for the front page story. More than a doughnut..."

"Look–" Chelsea started.

Stephanie stepped up next to Ronnie. "Hi."

Ronnie turned, thankful for the interruption because he really hadn't played out being rejected by Chelsea in the scenario. That would suck.

"Am I interrupting?" Stephanie reached up and patted Ronnie's arm.

He held back the wince of pain as she touched the tender spot on his bicep. She misinterpreted his flinch as a flex.

"Wow, nice muscles. I'm so glad I caught you before you left," said Stephanie. "I was wondering. Could you sign this? No one will ever believe I met you."

He grinned. *She's cute. And what great timing. Maybe Chelsea will notice her paying attention to me.* He scribbled his name across the bottom of a piece of photo paper that had an inkBLOT and one of the horoscope-type write-ups his site churned out for folks who were willing to spend at least an hour on inkBLOT.

Chelsea folded her arms, and gave Stephanie an odd look.

"Ya'll know each other?" Stephanie looked from one to the other, then back to Chelsea. "I can't believe you've been hiding him from us, Chelsea."

"Actually," Chelsea stood from her chair, "he was just asking me out to celebrate my big story."

"Oh." Stephanie took a step back. "Well, I'm sorry I interrupted. Thanks, Ronnie. I'll talk to you when I get your proofs ready."

"No apology necessary," he said.

"So, Ronnie. How about tonight? What time do you want to pick me up?" Chelsea crossed her arms and shot Stephanie a look.

Stephanie backed out and was gone before Ronnie could answer.

"Seven?" he asked.

"Sounds good. Why don't you pick me up here?"

"Okay. It's a d..." he said, catching himself just before he said date, "...frate."

She handed him her card. "My number's on there if you need to get in touch with me."

Ronnie pulled his card out of his pocket and prayed she wouldn't notice his hands shaking as he handed it to her. "You can reach me on email or text the easiest." He tugged his Blackberry on his hip. "I'm always connected."

"Great."

He wasn't quite sure what to say next so he turned and left before he screwed things up.

At first, he'd thought for sure Chelsea was going to totally blow him off, but she hadn't. It may have been because Stephanie was showing him some attention. That *had* been pretty sweet timing. Whatever. All he knew was he wasn't going to take a chance on blowing this opportunity with Chelsea.

All the way home, Ronnie wondered how to make the night exciting. *Tiffany and I hang out all the time. But this is different. This has to be special. Chelsea looks like a high maintenance girl. She deserves the best. Now if only I can figure out how to do that.*

He stepped out of the car and ran up the stairs to his apartment. Tiffany had already left. That was unusual for her.

Ronnie went straight to the office and grabbed the latest printouts from the website surveys Tiffany left for him. That girl had an eye for detail and her analysis was as precise as his.

It felt funny not being completely up front with Tiffany about Chelsea, and he wasn't even sure why. It wasn't like he and Tiff had anything going on. Chelsea was entirely different. The thought of Chelsea in that cute little skirt sent his pulse racing.

He scanned the printouts for a minute, but he couldn't concentrate. He tossed the papers back on the desk and began Googling for somewhere trendy and fun to take Chelsea to celebrate. He decided to take her to a new Tapas restaurant. All appetizers, how could that go wrong?

Content with the plan, he turned on his gaming computer. He played for a couple of hours, trying to keep himself from going absolutely crazy until time to get ready for his date.

Frate? She could call it whatever she liked, it was a date to him!

Freshening up in the bathroom, he made a swipe with his deodorant and grabbed his shirt. Buttoning it, he switched on some music to clear his mind. A remake of an old song, Witchy Woman, came on and he smiled. *Chelsea has me bewitched, that's for sure.* Stepping into the khakis, he'd barely gotten them zipped when the phone rang.

"Hello?"

"Ronnie? This is Chelsea."

"Hey, girl. I was getting ready to head your way."

"Well…that's why I'm calling. I'm afraid I'm not going to be able to go out tonight after all. There's a breaking story I have to follow. You know what they say, 'Strike while the iron is hot.'"

She can't be doing this to me. "Yeah, sure. I understand." He sat on the edge of the bed, hoping she couldn't hear the disappointment in his voice.

"I'll take a rain check. Give me a call later and we'll set something up."

"Yeah, sure," he repeated. "Bye."

He tossed the phone on the bed and walked out to the living room and sank into the sofa. He almost had a date with the hottest girl he'd ever met. Maybe his luck wasn't changing. Almost, doesn't count.

I guess I should have waited until that fundraiser. I hope I haven't blown it completely.

He called and canceled his reservations.

"Oh well, there goes that." He changed into a pair of sweats and flopped down on the sofa for another boring night. The night drug on. Nothing on television to watch, not in the mood to game, not in the mood to work.

He finally gave up and spread out on top of the comforter. Rorschach curled up on the floor next to the bed.

Ronnie tossed and turned, flipping his pillow this way and that. He must have looked at the clock every hour on the hour. His mind wouldn't turn off.

It wasn't really a rejection, or was it?

Things come up. She'd said she was sorry, but then she didn't try to sync up another date either. Rain check. Whatever.

He wanted nothing more than to get back into that office the next day and try again, but he knew he'd have to wait until the fundraiser now.

How much would a date with a hottie like Chelsea end up costing?

CHAPTER EIGHT

On the morning of the big fundraiser dinner, Ronnie's alarm rang at six in the morning. He slammed the snooze button to get an extra fifteen minutes, almost knocking the lamp off the nightstand.

He'd barely slept a wink. "Man, if I don't get some rest, I'm going to sleep through the whole thing." With that, he punched his pillow, closed his eyes and tried to get back to sleep.

He fell right back to sleep and dreamed about Chelsea. In his dream, beneath a perfect blue sky on crayon green grass, he and Chelsea shared a blanket in a tree shaded park. Her shorts showed her shapely legs and her knit top accented a couple of her best assets. They raced across the grass toward a pair of swings. Just as he pushed her high in the air, he woke up.

Sitting on the edge of the bed, he scratched his head and stared straight ahead. *She is SO HOT. Tonight I have to make that connection with her.*

Climbing out of bed, he tried to focus and that wasn't all that easy on too little sleep. *What is it about her? Maybe it's the whole writer thing. Kind of cool that she's a celebrity in the newspaper. Bringing details to the masses first. She always seemed to have an interesting story. And heart. Yeah, definitely heart. Those community angled stories she writes have a personal touch. They touch me. Well she does, in a way I can't explain.*

Ronnie stretched and twisted from side to side, trying to limber up the aches that had settled in through all that tossing and turning. He flexed his arm, admiring the tattoo. It was looking better each day, but two weeks of bicep curls hadn't made any noticeable difference. He stepped on the scale, like he did every morning. One ninety. The same as it always was. He looked at himself in the full length mirror on the bathroom wall. He raised his shoulders and pulled his arms forward a little, trying to stretch his muscles. *There's no use. I'm just not the workout kind of guy.*

Ronnie dragged his bare feet all the way to the bathroom and leaned toward the mirror, looking at the scruff. He flicked morning sand out of his eyes, and sprayed a dollop of shaving cream into his palms, and spread it across his face.

His mind wandered. He imagined Chelsea shaving her legs.

"I'd like to be *her* razor," he said snickering to himself. He splashed water on his face to wash off the shaving cream and stepped into the shower.

Lathering up, he stood under the heavy spray praying everything would turn out perfect at the event.

He went to his closet and pulled out his only suit. It was still in the dry cleaner bag. He pulled out the blue shirt and striped tie he'd gotten the same day he'd purchased the suit. He knew it all matched because it was what the mannequin was wearing. That was how he did all his shopping. It was fail proof.

Ronnie could practically hear the ticking of a bomb counting down the time until the fundraiser. T-minus twelve hours until 1900. The Mission Impossible theme song played in his mind.

Talk about being obsessive compulsive. All he could think about was Chelsea, but he needed help in that department. He needed a female perspective on things.

Tiffany. Yeah, that's who I'll ask. She's always there when I need her.

He went to the phone and pressed speed dial. She answered on the first ring. Good thing too, because he was about to hang up when he heard her say hello. "Hey, girl. I need your help."

"Sure. What's up? You sound frazzled. We're not having another hacker problem are we?"

"I wish it was that easy."

"So, what's got your wheels spinning?"

Do I come right out and tell her how crazy I am about Chelsea? It even sounded crazy to him. He didn't really know Chelsea. Tiffany would think he was a nut. How much should he say? The more she knew, the more embarrassing it would be if it didn't work out. But Tiffany was his best friend. He took in a deep breath and went for it.

"Tonight's that fundraiser for Diabetes Research. That reporter, Chelsea, is going to be there. I'm out of my comfort zone. Well…you know."

"Is Mr. Cool, Calm and Collected coming unglued?"

"I don't want to make a fool of myself."

"It's a fundraiser. What's there to worry about?"

"I want to impress Chelsea."

"Oh?" she said in almost a whisper.

Tiffany's pause made Ronnie uncomfortable.

She continued, "Well, then you need to chill," Tiffany told Ronnie. "You have to act cool. You know…aloof. Girls always want the guy they can't have. It's more of a challenge or something."

"That doesn't even make sense. How's that going to help me?"

"I know. It's stupid, but I'm just sayin'. I could take the biggest, dorkiest guy in school, and if I went out with him, suddenly at least three other girls would be interested in him. It's ridiculous, I know, but I see it happen all the time."

"Are you saying I'm a big dork?"

Tiffany's giggle across the line made him smile.

"Look, you don't understand. Chelsea's good lookin' and all, but there's something more to her. Something in the stories she writes that...I don't know. There's a connection." *Now, I sound like the biggest dork.*

"What are you now? Some newspaper groupie?"

Dork. Dork. Dork. What was I thinking telling her? I sound like an idiot. "That's not funny." Then he laughed. "Okay, maybe it is a little funny. I know it sounds stupid, but there's more to it. I met her the other day, when I was at the newspaper working on that ad."

"So that's what took you so long. I was wondering."

"She's nice, and there's this sadness behind those eyes of hers. I know that hidden sea of troubles and how it feels, how it looks. She's got it. That deep sorrow. The kind that makes you a fighter, competitive. I'm telling you. I think she and I are cut from the same cloth."

Again, silence from Tiffany's end.

Ronnie waited for her to say something but she didn't. He switched the phone to his other ear.

"Are you still there?" he asked.

"Yeah. I'm here. I'm just not sure what you want."

Ronnie took a deep breath. He'd come this far, no sense not asking for her help now. "This is going to be a big night."

"Okay, fine. So, you have a crush on Chelsea," she snapped. "I got that already. What do you want from me?"

"Well... actually... aside from your advice, I could use another favor."

"You know I'd do anything for you," she said. Her voice softened. "Spill."

"How're those haircutting skills of yours?"

"I've still got my scissors. Got an A last semester, but you know that. Why?"

"Yeah, I know..."

"Wait a minute. Don't tell me you're actually going to let me cut your hair?"

He ran a hand through his hair. "I was thinking it could use some updating. You know, maybe kind of short, and...well, you know."

"Updating? You don't even *have* a style. I've been telling you that for how long?"

"A long time," he agreed. "But I'm all yours now."

"About time you came around. I'll do it. You are going to look so hot. Okay, well let me get to school. I'll come over right afterward and do your hair before I get to work updating those files."

"That works."

"Don't change your mind," she warned.

"I won't." He knew he wouldn't even if he wanted to. He'd paid $100 for a ticket to that fundraiser to get another chance to see Chelsea. He needed to have his look together. If he blew it tonight, it could be his last chance. The tattoo was still too fresh, but long sleeves would cover that. No problem.

Later that afternoon, Ronnie sat in the chair on the balcony with a towel draped over his shoulders. Tiffany came straight from school with her backpack of hair supplies. She sprayed his hair with a misting bottle and clipped and snipped for what seemed like way too long for the amount of hair he had.

He couldn't help but notice that some of the pieces were a lot longer than he expected as they hit the deck around him. It was beginning to make him nervous. He couldn't see a thing she was doing, but his head was lighter and he wasn't sure it was all from the weight of the hair she was pruning away. How much hair was he going to have left? King didn't look bad with a slick head, but he didn't have what it took to pull that bad ass kind of look off. That much he knew for sure.

"I hope you know what you're doing up there," Ronnie said only half joking.

"Shush, and sit straight." She pushed on his shoulders to straighten them. "Quit slumping or it'll be crooked. I've given this cut to half the guys in school. I'm a pro. They love me. Stop worrying. I want you to look great." She pushed a wad of hair from his shoulder to the ground. "What's so great about this chick anyway?"

"I think she could really be the one, Tiff."

"You don't even know her," she mumbled.

"I know. I know. But there's something about her that I can't shake. No matter how hard I try. I dream about her at night. I think about her while I'm working at the computer. It's weird."

"You're OC, man. Obsessive compulsive to the extreme."

"Well, that shouldn't be a surprise. It's in my inkBLOT analysis. You've seen it. You know all my secrets."

"You got that right. Maybe we shouldn't use each other for baseline data." She flipped her hair back from her face. "Yeah. Well, it says you're smart, too. So, don't do anything dumb." She pulled the towel from his shoulders and shook it out over the balcony. "Go. Take a look. See what you think."

He jumped out of the chair and jogged into the bathroom.

At first, he didn't even recognize himself. He'd turned from geeky, wild surfer haired Ronnie, into a more sophisticated look.

"You did good," he admitted as he came back into the room. "I owe you. How about I treat you to a movie one night next week in exchange for the new haircut?"

"Chick flick?" she asked.

"Whatever you want."

"Great." She stepped up behind him with an approving nod, swishing her hand through his short cut. "You're welcome. I'll hold you to that."

"You always come through for me."

"Don't you ever forget that." Tiffany held his gaze for a moment.

"I won't." There was a short awkward silence. Ronnie shook it off and got his mind gearing toward what he still needed to do before fundraiser time. "I've got to get dressed. Are you going to work on those files tonight?"

"I kind of don't feel like messing with them now."

"You okay?"

"Yeah. I don't feel so good all of a sudden, that's all." She packed up her things and shoved them into her backpack.

"I hope you're not coming down with something." He walked her to the door. Running his hand through his hair, he looked at her as she opened it. "Thanks again, Tiffany."

"Yeah, sure," she said, not giving him a backwards glance. After watching it close behind her, he went back to his room to get dressed. With the suit, his neatly styled hair and a mist of FIERCE cologne, he was ready to go.

CHAPTER NINE

Sitting at his fifth red light, Ronnie realized the delay was probably a good thing. Ronnie didn't want to be the first one there, looking all dopey and desperate. The Bridges Restaurant parking lot was packed.

He circled the lot twice trying to find a decent parking spot. On the second pass, he saw Chelsea heading to the restaurant. She looked good in her bright red dress but it had to be a challenge walking in those tall skinny heels across the wobbly cobblestone parking lot.

Ronnie pulled into a spot and sat in the car for a moment, trying to pull himself together. *Don't blow it this time.*

People got out of their cars and headed inside.

It was now or never.

He pushed the car door open and fell in step behind a group of them. The greeters took tickets and put colored wristbands on each guest, depending on their level of support.

Each guest was then assigned to a seating area. Ronnie watched as they issued cards to the couples ahead, rotating across the celebrities. When he stepped up, the grandmotherly looking woman tugged the wristband around his arm and then handed him a seating card for one of the other celebrity tables.

He paused only for a nanosecond. "Do you think I could possibly get a Chelsea Pressman card?"

The old woman pulled her glasses up from the chain where they hung around her neck and gave him a sly grin. "Of course darlin'." She shuffled through the cards and handed him one with Chelsea's name on it. "That's the section over there to the right."

He grinned. "Thanks."

"Good luck, Sugar."

He stepped through the door and was absorbed in the throng of people mingling. He inched his way between couples who'd stopped to talk and made his way to Chelsea's section.

There she was with a camera around her neck and clipboard in hand. Delicate fire engine nails tapped a pen against the clipboard as she checked off tables on the chart, and greeted new customers.

Her smile was perfect.

His blood surged and he hoped he wasn't turning red.

She looked hot. So hot! Cassie Freeze, the weather girl from the ABC affiliate, and John Basham the prime time anchor were serving on either side of her. Not a bad spot to be. The folks in Chelsea's section seemed to be having the most fun already.

Ronnie walked over to Chelsea and handed her his table seating card.

"Welcome," she said with a bright smile and almost the dip of a curtsy.

He leaned toward her and held out his hand to shake hers. "Good to see you again, Chelsea."

She glanced back his way. "Oh my gosh. We. I. Oh, yeah..."

"Ronnie Wright," he said, filling in the blank for her. "I'm sorry you couldn't make it the other night."

"Right. Right. But we'll do a rain check." She led him to a table with an empty seat and took his order. "I almost didn't recognize you. Haircut?"

He nodded.

She gnawed on the cap of her pen. "I love it. Your hair. It's great."

"Thanks." *Yes.* He held back the urge to clench his fist in a fist pump. *That was exactly the response I was hoping for.*

She raised her shoulders and gave him a wink. "You can have a seat right here. Got to get these to the kitchen." She pushed through the crowd, weaving through the tables to turn in her orders. "I'll be back," she called over her shoulder.

The place was jam packed. He was glad to see so many supporting such a good cause. He watched as Chelsea flitted through the restaurant dropping hellos and hugs along the way.

As she passed by, Ronnie leaned back and tugged on her sleeve. "Are you still on top of the world from that cover story?"

"Oh yeah. Totally. I love it. I can't wait until the next one!" She patted him on the shoulder and then ran to exchange her clipboard and apron with the real waitress who would do the actual serving.

The evening's speaker went up to the podium before the salads began to circulate. Ronnie noticed Chelsea looking around for a chair. He got up and motioned for her to sit. At first, she refused, but he didn't take no for an answer and she finally slid into his chair. Ronnie snagged an extra chair from a table nearby. Chelsea scooted closer to Ronnie and mouthed a thank you to him.

"You're really doing great with those stories," he whispered.

"Thanks. I appreciate that so much," she said, cocking her head to one side.

The first speaker stepped down and applause rang through the large restaurant. The microphone was passed to the Diabetes Research Foundation local chapter president for a few words about the important work done over the past year and the current goals. They did a sparkling apple cider toast across the whole restaurant, and everyone broke back out into casual chatter while they waited for the meal to be served.

Past Ronnie's shoulder Chelsea noticed Hallie Davison sitting in prime time anchor John Basham's section. That section was heavy on the female side, not that it was a surprise. John Basham was known for his boyish good looks and was voted the hottest bachelor in the area twice. Chelsea chuckled as she noticed that most of the women could probably be his mom, if not at least an aunt.

"Cougar Mommas," she said just above a whisper, shaking her head.

"What?" Ronnie asked leaning in.

"Oh nothing. I was talking to myself." Chelsea waved in Hallie's direction but that girl's eyes were glued to Basham's butt like a laser. She'd have to wait until John Basham was out of sight to get Hallie's attention. No question about that.

Chelsea turned her attention to the far right of the restaurant. Most of her colleagues were sitting together at a table in someone else's section. That was fine. She could bask in the glow of this gig, and flaunt it that far. She'd done her service and now she was free to dine and visit until time for the celebrity auction at which she was one of the prizes. Wadsworth must have seen her looking their way. He lifted his glass and gave her a nod. She shot him her award winning smile and a wave, just as she saw Basham whisk by.

"Hallie! Hallie! Over here." Chelsea tippy toed and waved her hand high, hoping to get Hallie's attention.

"Who's that?" Ronnie asked.

"A friend. She and I worked on a story together."

Hallie wore a brown knit dress that made her look like anything but a detective. No reason to tell him she was one. It wasn't any of his business.

Hallie finally saw her and waved back, motioning her to join them.

Chelsea got up and weaved her way through the packed restaurant away from the table and Ronnie.

"How's it going Chelsea?" Hallie asked. "That last story was great. Way to go, girl."

"Thanks."

"You staying busy?" asked the detective.

"Busy enough. I could use a good story right about now though." Chelsea stooped down next to Hallie who was still seated. "Anything hot going down at the precinct?"

"Crazy as always." Hallie took a sip of iced tea. "You know, come to think of it. You could help me out. I'm working on a cold case. It could use some press to maybe churn up some new leads."

"Happy to do that. I do owe you."

Ronnie had puppy-dogged along. He stood back looking uncomfortable as the two girls swapped schedules and planned to get together later in the week. Feeling awkward as they talked and completely ignored him, he slipped back into the crowd and made his way back to their table.

"This is good for both of us," agreed Hallie.

"Well, I've got to get back to my section. I'll catch you later." Chelsea turned to leave, but Ronnie had already gone back to their table. Now, he was in deep conversation with several people. As she neared the table she heard them talking about inkBLOT.

What the heck is such a big deal about that company? It's not like he's Bill-freakin-Gates or the facebook guy. Geez.

Chelsea approached the group, but no one seemed to notice her.

"Going to introduce me to your friends?" she asked, wriggling in close to Ronnie.

"New friends, actually. We just met. John, Jennifer and this is Mike and Michelle. This is Chelsea Pressman. She's with the Daily Banner. One of the best reporters they have." Ronnie smiled broadly.

Chelsea raised her chin and extended a hand toward the two guys who shook her hand but didn't seem too interested. The couples dispersed and Chelsea and Ronnie sat back down at the table.

"Quite a night, isn't it?" Chelsea gazed at Ronnie. He really did look hot and he seemed to be quite the local celebrity himself with his popular website.

Ronnie nodded, and then spun around as someone tapped him on the shoulder.

"Ronnie Wright! That is you, isn't it? I want to introduce you to somebody." Stephanie from the advertising department at the Banner grabbed the arm of an impressive looking man in a high dollar suit and tugged him their way. "Ronnie. This is my dad. Daddy, Ronnie owns inkBLOT. Remember? I told you about him."

The man extended his hand. "Yes. You've done really well for yourself young man."

Chelsea shrank back. Stephanie's dad was a big shot. He had more money than some small countries. Stephanie didn't even *have* to work.

"Thank you, Sir." He stood straight and tall. He looked proud of himself, thought Chelsea.

"I had no idea you were a local." The man handed him a business card. "I'd love to talk to you about some options with your business, maybe going public with stock. That kind of thing."

"Wow. Thanks. I'm just doing something I love to do," Ronnie said.

"Keep it up. Seems to be working for you, son."

With that, Chelsea took a closer look at Ronnie, seeing him in a new light. She edged in closer to get his attention.

Ronnie stopped and pulled her into the conversation. "Where are my manners? Do you know Chelsea Pressman? She and your daughter work together over at the Banner."

Stephanie's dad exchanged a handshake with Chelsea then said goodbye to mingle with others.

Ronnie brushed his hands together. "This fundraiser is such a worthwhile cause. I had no idea that diabetes is so widespread. Eight percent of the population has diabetes. I didn't know that. Did you? Amazing."

"Yep." Chelsea scanned the room. She needed to make some new contacts.

Ronnie was surprised by Chelsea's lack of compassion for the cause. It seemed out of character compared to the articles she'd written, but he changed the conversation to other safe territories and was able to get her attention back.

"So, how about those Redskins?" he asked her. That really did it.

Her head whipped around. "Yeah, they're doing great, aren't they? If I had a root beer float, I'd toast to you right now."

"A root beer float? What a coincidence. That's my favorite drink too," he said, as he subtly touched a small section of her hair. "I'll treat you to one sometime."

Finally, dinner was served. Throughout the dinner service the Diabetes Foundation president took the mic to share corporate donations and trivia.

While listening, Ronnie sliced into his steak and Chelsea fidgeted with her chicken and asparagus. She nibbled lightly, but mostly she pushed the veggies around on her plate.

"Don't like greens huh?"

"No, not really."

"Asparagus is good for you," Ronnie said.

"Maybe so, but it makes your pee smell funny."

Ronnie felt himself go red. He looked around the table hoping no one else had heard her. *Did she really just say that? Miss Sophisticated?* "I'll take your word for it. I'm not much on it. Looks too much like twigs to me, and I don't think that pee thing's a theory I need to test," he said, snickering.

"All right, you do that, but trust me I know about asparagus. I once did an article about it and how it even has been known to help in chemotherapy and cancer treatments. It's full of antioxidants, but that pee thing. Oh yeah. I'm not digging that. Nothing that stinky can be good for you."

Does she realize she's saying that aloud?

An announcement was made at the podium for all the celebrities to make it to the front to get ready for the highlight of the evening. The celebrity auction.

Ronnie couldn't help but smile. It's what he'd been waiting for.

Chelsea excused herself.

Ronnie watched her leave in that red-hot dress, and then a big hand clasped over his shoulder.

Ronnie swung around and looked up.

It was King, with Cat dressed in an elegant blue gown at his side.

"Hey man!" Ronnie rose from his chair and extended his hand. "Hi Cat. You look great. Hey, what about those stars? You had star tattoos around your eye last time I saw you."

"Oh yeah, temporary tattoos. Dad draws them on with markers 'cause he'd kill me if I got a real one." She glanced in her dad's direction and rolled her eyes. "No real 'toos until I'm twenty. It's our little promise."

"Well, you look beautiful," he said, and he was glad to hear King had laid down the law with Cat on that. His initial impression was wrong. "I didn't know ya'll would be here tonight. It's good to see someone I know."

King pulled out the chair Chelsea had been sitting in and sat down.

"Yeah. We come to the fundraiser every year. This is the first time they've tried the local celebrity thing. Looks like it's working." King placed a fatherly arm around his daughter's waist.

"Good cause," Ronnie said for like the hundredth time.

King nodded, and looked up at Cat who was still standing next to him. "Cat's momma had diabetes. She died when Cat was just a kid."

Ronnie could see the love for her in the look that passed between King and his daughter. "I guess this has a personal importance to you then."

King nodded. "Yeah. I wish they'd find a cure. So far we've been able to control Cat's diabetes with diet and medication. I hope she never has to deal with injections."

"I didn't know," Ronnie said.

King continued, "On a lighter note, it won't hurt my feelings none to pay for a dinner date with one of those pretty things to help a good cause, if you know what I mean." King elbowed Ronnie and gave him a wink. "Bet I know who you'll be bidding on tonight."

Ronnie felt his cheeks go red. That was exactly what he planned to do. To bid on a date with Chelsea.

"It's okay," King said. "Your secret is safe with me. We'll just look like a couple of supportive local businessmen here to support the cause."

Cat slapped her daddy's shoulder. "Daddy, quit it, you're going to embarrass him. It's not like Ronnie would have to pay for a date. Geez." She shifted her gaze back to Ronnie. "By the way. I *love* your haircut."

Ronnie ran a hand through his gelled hair. "Thanks." He could get used to this. He'd never had this many compliments in his whole life.

A booming voice came over the audio and the celebrity auction began.

One at a time, the celebrities sauntered across the stage.

The DJ played wild music to get the crowd going, and the auctioneer was the fast talking, honest-to-goodness, real deal.

"Three-ee, three, three-ee and three-hundred, three hundred. Give me three, now. Three hundred. What's that mean? Come on! Get me on the table, if you want to sit at one with this purty filly. Get me started. Anyone? Do I hear Two-oo, two, two-oo. Got it. Yes. Two-oo, two and two fifty, two fifty jump in for this one. She's nifty. Yeah! There we go, now we're back where we started. Three-ee, three, three, three hundred. Three hundred. Yes. For Diabetes. Good cause, come on now. All in? All done? Three-ee hu-nd-red? Sold! Done! Right in front here in the red shirt. Thank you, Sir."

The crowd roared. The energy in the room cranked up and everyone started getting into the whole auction thing. People jumped from their seats and waved napkins to bid on their favorite celebrity. Some got so caught up in the bid they were standing on their chairs and increasing bids by a hundred at a time for an evening out with a celebrity at one of the local hotspots in town.

All the dinners were donated by the restaurants sponsoring each celebrity for the cause. The weather girl went for a whopping five hundred and fifty-five dollars and to King no less.

The co-anchors, one female, one male brought in big bucks and one of the local DJs from the morning show went for nearly five hundred dollars, too.

Ronnie was ready. No matter what it cost him he had every intention to be the man of the hour in Chelsea's eyes.

When Chelsea stepped onto the stage she looked a little nervous. He'd never seen her look vulnerable before, but for just a moment it was there. The DJ started playing Black Eyed Peas *Boom, Boom, Pow* and then mixed in some *Hot in Here.* The momentum picked up and the fine dressed crowd went wild.

The auctioneer started out at three hundred dollars.

Feeling like a big dog, Ronnie stood up and waved his napkin and shouted, "Five hundred!"

The auctioneer gave Ronnie a thumbs up, and challenged the audience. He took a deep breath and started talking so fast it was musical.

"Finally! Someone who's not gonna nickel and dime me! This guy in the fine suit can see a good thing when it's right in front of him. Thank you, Sir!" The auctioneer inhaled deep, and then chanted, "Five, five, five. I've got five. I'm looking for fi-ive and fifty. Gimme' five hundred fifty. Let me hear ya'," shouted the auctioneer. "Like the song said it's gettin' Hot-hot-hot in Here. I've got five-fifty, there in the brown. Back to you in the suit, now six, now six, now six?"

Ronnie gave a nod.

"That's it. A man who knows what he wants. I got six hundred, six, six. Now I'm lookin' for seven. Seven. Seven. That's seven hundred."

Three guys in their mid-twenties jumped into the bidding frenzy. Ronnie was going back and forth with these knuckleheads and not liking it much. Irritated he leered in their direction and took the bid up significantly.

"A thousand dollars," shouted Ronnie.

The crowd gasped.

King slapped Ronnie on the back.

Ronnie dared that sharp looking buzz cut college-type to top that. It was more than he'd planned to spend, but it was tax deductible. He'd have to dig into his savings but that's what savings were for, weren't they? For those things you really, really wanted. He wanted this date. The power he was feeling from the auction right now wasn't bad either.

No other takers were willing to compete with Ronnie's generous bid. The gavel came down and Ronnie won the date with Chelsea. Not only that, his was also the top celebrity date bid for the evening.

Chelsea beamed like she'd just been crowned Miss America. She strutted over to the local charity president to shake his hand, and waved Ronnie up to get her picture taken with both of them.

The crowd parted as he made his way to the front. People high fived him as he passed and thanked him for the support. Others called him a lucky dog. He felt like one, too.

The fundraiser was over shortly after that. Apparently using celebrities was the way to go. Businesswomen lavished huge tips on the handsome older celebrity waiters, and the young girls were happy to get their moms and dads to foot the bill for the younger waiters, who were ultra-hot. Those guys hadn't spared any flirtation while waiting on them either. The men liked the female celebs equally well. It seemed to be a winning combination. There was already talk among the organizers of the fundraiser that they'd do it again next year.

Walking Chelsea to the door, Ronnie wished he could give her a ride home instead of having to say goodbye. "It was great getting to know you better tonight," he said.

Chelsea looked up at him and batted her eyes. "Same here, Ronnie. I can't believe you bid all that money on me."

"It was worth every penny."

"That's a lot of pennies. You'd need a forklift to carry all those!" Chelsea winked.

"And for a good cause."

"Yes. Well, I look forward to getting to know you even better," she said.

"Can I walk you to your car?" asked Ronnie.

She nodded so they headed toward her car. He was dying to kiss her goodnight, but something told him not to push his luck. So, he patted the top of her car, and then just stood there in the awkward moment as she drove off.

Ronnie walked to his car with a certain bounce in his step.

She hadn't told him much, but he felt like he already knew her. In time, he'd find out more about her. Now that he'd won that dinner date, a date was a sure thing.

With Chelsea gone, his mind was back on business. Switching gears, he couldn't wait to talk to King about his idea on the tattoo spin-off of inkBLOT. He hadn't considered it until he'd gotten to know him a little better at the fundraiser, but now it all made perfect sense. He liked King's fortitude. It had to be tough to be a single dad. There was a lot more to him than met the eye, and he had a feeling King could use the break and Ronnie surely needed the intellect that King had around the ink industry. As soon as he got home that night, he called him.

The phone rang three times and Ronnie was starting to wonder if King had made it home yet. Finally, on the fifth ring, King answered.

"Hey, King. It's Ronnie Wright. You know, from inkBLOT?" He realized that the old feelings of discomfort he usually felt making calls were gone. Confidence took over and he liked that feeling.

"Hey, Ronnie. Yeah. How's it going?"

"We need to talk."

"What's up man? You're not going to ask for me a loan to cover that uber bid you made tonight, are you?" A hearty chuckle came across the line from King.

"No. Nothing like that. I have something new in mind for inkBLOT, and I think it's gonna be huge. I want to make you an offer."

"Look kid. I like you, but I don't know a thing about all that internet stuff."

"Hear me out. When I was in your shop, all those pictures had me thinking. The way you talked about tattoos having a reason and meaning something really stuck with me. inkBLOT has done great; better than I'd ever dreamed of, but it's time to take it to a new place so I don't start losing members."

"Yeah."

"I want to offer you ten percent of a new spin-off from inkBLOT, called **ink!**. It'll be similar to inkBLOT except you'll go through questions and tattoo images, then we'll give them their tattoo image in an icon to use in gaming or social networking. Dude, this is going to go viral. I know it."

"It sounds good. I think you're right, but if you're looking for an investment—"

Ronnie stopped him mid-sentence. "No. I don't need an investment. I've got all that covered. I need your smarts, your experience and I'll give you ten percent of the action for it. Plus, I'll need your contacts to help me promote it."

"You really think this will work?"

"Heck, yeah. It has to be top secret though. You can't tell anyone about your involvement until we do the launch. Can I come over and show you the prototype tomorrow?"

"Okay buddy, come on over to the shop around three," said King. "Let's see what you've got."

Yes! Ronnie clenched his fists and jumped, then took a breath to sound appreciative but not like a kid on Christmas morning, which is exactly how he felt. "Great. You won't regret it, man."

CHAPTER TEN

Chelsea weaved through the traffic, humming to herself and replaying the evening in her mind. She'd overheard Ronnie's name in conversations all night. Stephanie had traipsed right over with her rich daddy to introduce him to Ronnie. Even he'd seemed impressed. Was she the only one who wasn't all gaga and googly-eyed by a stupid online quiz?

He seems more interesting every time I see him. inkBLOT. Sounds like a dumb computer game but I guess I'll have to check it out. Not only was Stephanie all hipped out over him, but every frickin' body seems impressed by him and that business of his. He made some connections tonight, too. Connections that might help me.

"A thousand dollars," she said out loud. She talked to the dashboard like it was a girlfriend, something she didn't have many of. She didn't have time for all of that. "Unfreakin-believable. Yeah, it was for a good cause but none of the other celebrities brought in *that* kind of cash. He could have bid on anyone, but he'd bid on me." Would Ronnie have bid that much on someone else if she hadn't been up there?

They'd acted like they were doing me a favor letting me be a part of their fundraiser when I called. I'll probably get a personal hand delivered invitation to that gig next year.

Ronnie had to be about her age, maybe a year or so younger. She'd worked her butt off and it sure seemed slow getting to the top so far. How did *he* get so far so young? He probably had a rich dad or supportive mom that gave him the easy way up. Yeah. That would explain it. Unfortunately, she didn't have either one of those.

Ronnie really could hang a suit, too. Most of the guys she knew wouldn't be caught dead in a suit. Tennis shoes and good jeans, okay maybe some khakis, were about as far as they'd go. She barely remembered what Ronnie looked like when she'd met him at the paper a couple of weeks ago, but it must not have been that sharp or she would've remembered him. *Maybe I was a little too quick to blow him off that day.*

Chelsea jammed her foot on the brake, sending her purse crashing from the passenger seat into the floorboard, as her car skidded to a stop at the red light.

"That was close." She let out the breath she was still holding and stretched to reach her purse and pull it back up on the seat. She'd almost driven right through the red light. That intersection was always a pain in the butt. Of course, she'd been barely paying attention.

She turned on the radio and let out a squeal when she realized that Nelly song was playing. The same one from the auction. That had to be a good sign.

Chelsea pulled in front of her house and climbed out of the car. Her trendy high heels were adorable but her feet were killing her. She pulled her shoes off and carried them, letting them swing from her hand as she walked up the driveway humming her new lucky tune.

Dad wasn't home yet. Nothing new there.

She unlocked the door and let herself in. The place always felt so lonely.

Chelsea went straight to her bedroom and put her shoes back in the box they'd come in, even stuffing the paper back in the toes. She tucked them in the empty slot in the organizer, grabbed her laptop and went to the living room. Balancing the laptop on one knee and the arm of the sofa, she waited as it started up. The thing always seemed to take forever. She'd been so tempted to buy a new one, but tucking money away for her own place was way more important.

She clicked on the network connection and googled Ronnie. It was a common name. There were a ton of unrelated links. She scanned the list to one that was an award for a science project at Lidell High School a few years ago.

"I bet this is *my* Ronnie Wright." She had to laugh. Not long ago she wouldn't even give him a real date, today he was *her* Ronnie. If she wanted him anyway.

She did an image search, but there weren't any pictures of him online that she could find. She did locate his address though and zoomed in on it with the online maps. Nothing too exciting there.

Chelsea googled her own name. Seeing it pop to the top of the list was always a thrill. She googled herself several times a day to be sure she stayed at the top. The link to her first front page news story was right at the top.

She enlarged the font on the screen to 200%. "Nice." Her heart was pounding. Funny how something like that could really set your heart rate soaring. Taking a deep breath, she closed the window to check that inkBLOT thing out.

Girls in the break room talked about inkBLOT, but she didn't usually waste her time on that kind of stuff.

Her nails clicked against the keypad as she typed in the URL. The inkBLOT logo filled her screen. Pretty cool logo. Catchy.

She flexed her fingers and completed the free sign-up, and the demographic questions that followed. Finally, she got to the screen to select the option for inkBLOT questions.

There were lots of options.

You could get daily reads and sign up to be alerted when new inkBLOTs were added. It also let you join a group of other users whose inkBLOT profiles were similar to your own. She wondered how many people she knew actually played around with the stuff.

There was even a place you could make up your own images and submit them for consideration. If your design got selected as a future inkBLOT item, you were rewarded with a special flag for your inkBLOT space–rather your INKpad. So many angles. *Ronnie must have quite an imagination to think up all of this stuff.*

She forced herself to quit surfing and go back to the general inkBLOT quiz.

Chelsea eyed the first inkblot. *This one looks like a cross between a monkey and some splattered blood but that isn't one of the choices. Should I select OTHER and fill it in? Maybe it's best to keep some things to myself.*

Selecting an answer, she moved on to the next image. *A marching solider or maybe it's a ballerina pirouetting?*

Chelsea clicked on ballerina and went to the next one.

She laughed. *This looks like somebody's getting it on. No way would they want you to see that. Maybe it's a butterfly.*

She tilted her head to the side. From that angle it looked more like a gate with hedges on each side. *How do people decide?*

Her dad walked in the door and tossed his keys on the table. "What are you still doing up?"

She clicked to another screen and tilted the laptop from his view. "Just finishing up some work," she lied.

"You sure are dressed up."

"This is what I wore to the fundraiser," she said.

"Did you tell me about that?" He went to the kitchen and poured a glass of tea.

"Yes, Dad. I told you about it. You should've been there. Everybody who was anybody was there."

"Not everybody." He called out from the kitchen.

"Whatever," she muttered. No need to replay the events for him. He was in one of those moods. All about Dad. She pushed herself up from the couch and went to the kitchen where she gave him a kiss goodnight. Taking her laptop back to her room, she continued working on the inkBLOT quiz.

There's no sense trying to make Dad appreciate stuff he says he doesn't like. He NEVER changes his mind, even when he's wrong.

Chelsea closed the door feeling nicely isolated behind it. She sat on her bed and tipped the screen back to get a better angle. Picking up right where she left off, she selected the next inkblot choice. Several more inkblots displayed, all in black and white. Then she got the option to get her first read, or go on to the color quiz to get a deluxe read. The deluxe read included feedback on your career.

Well, of course I want the deluxe read!

The last screen of the quiz prompted Chelsea to enter the rest of the details needed to get her report. It would be emailed to her. She itched to get that report. Maybe her success would be sweeter in the future than she'd dared ever dream.

When she looked at the clock, she was shocked that over two hours had passed without her realizing it. She pulled off her dress and hung it up on the back of her door. Then she put on an oversized Redskins tee shirt and crawled into bed thinking about Ronnie. He'd said he liked the Redskins, too. *He can't be half bad if he's a Skins fan.*

***

Meanwhile, Ronnie sat at his desk monitoring the inkBLOT site traffic. Three different monitors displayed real time statistics. One showed number of users, another with bandwidth and the third showed the statistics based on IP address location. Usually, the statistics showed a relatively random scatter across the United States with a few international hits. Today, there were a lot of local hits. That had to be from the ad in the Banner. He hadn't really expected it to have an impact, but it had. Maybe advertising in papers was something he should consider. He jotted down some notes. He'd check the ad cost to traffic increase to see what the payoff was. It might just be worth it.

One local session was still in progress.

He pulled up the log. Some people used fake names, but he recognized most of the names on this log. Cat was one of them. She was a frequent visitor, visiting the site almost daily. That cute girl Stephanie had made a visit, as well as Chelsea.

No way!

His hand shook a little. He blinked his eyes again to be sure he read it right.

She was the local visitor on his site at the moment. Chelsea Pressman. *Yeah baby.*

He sat up straight in his chair and scooched closer to the monitor. In a few key strokes, he was able to see the exact path she was taking through the site.

She was signed in to the first round of inkblot quizzes. Excitement flooded over him at the prospect of delving into her mind. He wondered how she'd answer number seven. It was one of his favorites. He hoped and prayed she'd take the whole test. He followed her responses for the next twenty-five images and multiple-choice questions. She made the selection to continue to the next level.

"Yes." He flinched realizing he'd just shouted that to an empty room.

Rorschach looked up at him like he was crazy, then dropped his chin back to the floor.

Ronnie jotted down the session ID that would enable him to easily take a look at Chelsea's data later. He was too stoked to analyze it right now, besides he probably couldn't be unbiased. He'd wait and see what Tiffany's analysis came up with first, then do his own. Thank goodness, Tiffany was an early bird. He could barely wait.

CHAPTER ELEVEN

Ronnie was already sitting at his desk when Tiffany showed up in the morning.

"What are you doing working this early again? Or are you still sitting there from last night?" She tossed her backpack in the corner and spun her chair around.

"Good morning to you too." He said with a smirk. "Couldn't sleep."

"That's happening a lot lately. You okay?" She tossed him the newspaper, but he missed.

He leaned from his chair to scoop it from the floor where it landed. "Everything's cool. I've been working on some upgrades." He had to keep himself from making fun conversation with her like they usually did every morning. That would only slow her down, and he was dying to see the stats she came up with on record number O832B551.

"How was the fundraiser last night? The haircut go over big?"

"Yep." He ran a hand through his gelled hair and smiled. "It was great. I had a good time."

"Did you impress her?"

"That's not the only reason I went." He knew it was an out and out lie. Originally, Chelsea was the ONLY reason he'd gone, but afterwards he'd been surprised by the uplifting feeling he got from being a part of helping the important cause. Especially after he heard about Cat's mom, and Cat's own battle with the disease.

She dropped her chin and raised a brow. "Really?"

"Okay, well it was a big part of it. Fine. So, shoot me."

"You're turning into such a guy guy."

For a moment, he almost felt less like a geek. Was that such a bad thing?

Ronnie shrugged. "What's so bad about that? I got a date out of it."

She spun around. "Really? With that writer?"

He nodded.

"Hmm." She dropped into her chair and turned away from him.

"Actually, I kind of bid on the date. I didn't really ask her out, but it was for a good cause."

"I saw that in the paper this morning. Some fool paid a thousand dollars for a hundred dollar dinner with one of the celebrities. Is that nuts or what?"

Ronnie looked down.

"You didn't. No. Get outta here! Ronnie Wright, have you lost your mind? Tell me it wasn't you!"

"It wasn't me?" But it came out like a question and Tiffany could spot a lie from him a million miles away.

She jumped from her chair and stood herself right in front of his desk. "What the heck has gotten into that brain of yours? Worms? Tumors? Something is making you go freakin' loco, dude." She popped him on the head, folded her arms across her chest and waited for a response.

Ronnie shrugged.

Tiffany bopped her weight on her left hip, waiting for an answer.

Ronnie knew that look. She wasn't going to let him off the hook. "Look. It's my money. I have it to spend. So I spent some money. It went to a good cause."

"You might be able to fool yourself, but you are not fooling me. A haircut, heck, even that stupid tattoo–that's one thing, but spending a thousand dollars of hard earned cash just to get a date. That was stupid. You're not that desperate."

"Maybe I am."

"Is that why you bought that car, too? Your mom's old Toyota runs fine." She raised a hand and shook her head. "I'm not talking to you about this." She stormed back to her chair and started working on the stats from the night before.

Ronnie should have known she'd blow up like that. He knew her inside and out. She was an "it's the thought that counts" kind of girl, and that came through in her inkBLOT results, too.

The time Ronnie had spent over the past few years studying Rorschach, the Exner system, Klopfer, Kerner and anyone else that had any dabbles in the study of inkblots and the human mind had armed him with a way to see inside someone. Sometimes he knew more about people than they knew about themselves. He'd added his own twists based on personality and temperament testing to the equation. Numerology and astrology rounded out the analysis and were the foundation of the feedback to the test taker. The answers helped supply the right personalized comments for inkSPIRATIONS, too.

The feedback on inkBLOT is what kept visitors coming back to the website over and over again. The more data he gave them, just teensy snippets, the more they wanted.

Each visitor added to his income too, because the advertisers paid based on traffic. Those companies who bought ads were what made his business continue to thrive. Little did people know that their answers made a difference in advertising demographics and analysis. inkBLOT provided that and in a social networking kind of way. The test takers only had one thing in mind – having fun, and so did he, all the way to the bank every week.

It wasn't unusual for people to feel safe behind a computer screen. Being at home also contributed to people letting their guard down. Their real persona showed right through. Shine…or tarnish, whichever the case might be.

Someday Ronnie'd have enough data collected and analyzed to be recognized for the system he'd built. He'd already patented part of the equation to protect it.

Test takers handed over personal information to get silly, worthless gadgets online, and in exchange, he got a sneak peek into their psyches. He probably knew before they did when they were headed for a breakdown. Someday he'd help people with all that information. Part of him wanted to tip them off so they could be lining up a good therapist. But until he had statistical proof there was no way he'd chance people laughing his theories away as nothing.

Ronnie had modeled some of the feedback to help bring awareness to those he sensed were heading for trouble though. He had to. He couldn't sleep with a clear mind if he didn't try to help a little.

Although the scene with Tiffany was awkward, he was glad she'd decided to give him the cold shoulder and get to work. He was dying to see what she came up with on the inkBLOT results from Chelsea's entries last night. She'd kill him if she knew that was the first thing on her plate today.

Thankfully, he wouldn't have to wait long because when Tiffany was mad, she worked twice as fast. That much was a guarantee.

Ronnie flipped through some papers on his desk, but he couldn't concentrate on anything. "I want to update the regional profiles and the 18-24 demographics this afternoon, so if you can process those first it would be great," he said to Tiffany, just to be sure she didn't reorder the work he'd left for her.

"Sure." Tiffany brought up the host management software, put in her password, then clicked into the survey section of the database to download the completed surveys. Transferring the flat file into the other system took the longest. She had it down to a science though. She started the process then pushed back from the desk and went to the kitchen to fix her breakfast.

When she came back with her bowl of cereal, the data was ready, and the cursor flashed on the main menu waiting for her to select the segmentations she'd process today. Ronnie coded the analysis tool, but she was far quicker than him in doing the crunching. Of course, she did it every day.

She ran the initial reports including those by state. The local numbers were way up. That initial advertisement in the Banner was already paying off. The bus would pick her up in thirty minutes, but she had enough time to run the demographics summary and detail reports for Ronnie before she had to head out. The printer started spitting out results, and she inserted the thumb drive for the backup into the USB port to save the extra copy for him to work with from his laptop.

"All done," she said, dropping the reports and thumb drive on his desk.

"Thanks girl." He scanned the detail sheet and tried not to show his elevated interest in the day's information. "You coming by tonight?"

"No. Tonight is the parent-teacher thing. I'll see you in the morning."

He nodded. "That's right. Well, good luck. I appreciate you doing both of these reports before school. You saved me some time."

"That's why you pay me the big bucks, right," she said with a hint of sarcasm.

"Uh huh. See ya later."

Ronnie turned his attention to the papers that lay in front of him. Thumbing through the pages, he found Chelsea's survey stats and took a deep breath before going through them. Since Tiffany only saw the record numbers she'd have no way of knowing from this report that Chelsea was one of them.

He ran a finger down a long column of numbers and indicators.

Okay, what do we have here... adventure loving yet slightly dark individual. Dark? How can anything about her be remotely negative? She's a Gemini. Well, that would explain how some choices show her to be manipulative and others contradicting that as passive. Well manipulate away, baby. I'm putty in your hands; well at least I'd like to be. She's the whole package. The woman of my dreams.

Not only did the test reveal her personality but also her likes and dislikes. He studied the information to see what else he could learn about her. The personality type, astrology and trending made inkBLOT data a real study in character.

A couple of years ago Ronnie had read an article about a con man in the paper. On a whim he searched his database to see if the guy had ever joined his site. Sure enough, he had, and the funny thing was that all the data pointed to the scandal way before it ever happened. That one coincidental checkpoint, turned into a second and third until he couldn't keep himself from trying to find more correlations, and he had. That's when he'd gotten serious about his theories. Eventually he had to ask Tiffany to do daily analytics just to keep up.

This time, though, he knew he was using it for his own personal gain, and although it felt sneaky, he couldn't keep himself from doing it. He wanted Chelsea. He knew in his gut she was the perfect woman for him, and he wanted to make sure he got what he wanted. Sometimes you had to make your own destiny. He'd run her data against his personal data sets before their date. He'd be armed and ready when he saw her next.

inkBLOT's latest improvements leveraged color inkblots instead of the traditional black and white and shades of grey.

It looked like the new elements were a good indicator of the survey takers' emotional life.

With Chelsea so strongly on his mind, he picked up the phone to call her.

"Hi Chelsea. Just wanted to tell you it was fun getting to know you last night."

"Ronnie?" She sounded surprised to hear from him, and that was his plan. She'd just been on the inkBLOT site again. He knew because he'd set an alert to email him, which also hit his Blackberry, whenever she did. It was a great radar system to keep an eye on her.

They chatted about the evening's events. *Okay, so it's small talk but she sounds distracted, or maybe only half interested.*

"Is this a good time for you?" he asked.

"Sure. Yeah. I was just thinking," she said. "I had no idea you were such a hot shot in this town. How have you stayed out of the local papers all this time?"

Hot shot? That's a first! "Lucky I guess. I was calling to see if you might want to get together this week."

"Maybe. What did you have in mind?"

"I thought you might be willing to help me out with something. I need a couple of smart, successful people to test market a new idea for my business. I immediately thought of you."

"Smart and successful. You've got my attention."

He knew she'd like that. "What do you say? I'll fix you dinner and show you the beta version. How about tomorrow night?"

"What's the idea?"

"It's an offshoot from inkBLOT. Instead of inkblots– tattoos. Quizzes like inkblot, but instead of a personality report, it recommends tattoos and what that means about you. It works with the inkBLOT results or stands alone."

"That's interesting. What made you think of tattoos?"

"You did. In a way."

"Me?"

"Yeah. We have a friend in common. King."

"King?"

"Tattoo artist. Owns The Crown Tattoo. Great article by the way. You said you were impressed by tattoo art, and especially those done by King. Don't you remember?"

"Wow. Yeah. I did write that. I remember now. So many styles. Have you ever been in that place? Did you see all those pictures on his walls? So much skin showing in those pictures. What a wild place."

"His daughter said your article did wonders for his business. King was there last night. At the fundraiser. You didn't see him?"

"No, but I'm glad the article helped his business. Hey, do you have a tattoo? You don't seem the type."

"Oh. I'm a type, am I?" He paused for a moment, wondering how she really saw him. "Yeah. I've got one." It felt good to break through the stereotype, like a huge S had just tattooed itself on his chest and nothing but kryptonite could stop him now.

"Cool," purred Chelsea. She sounded impressed.

"I think the inkblots and tattoos are a good connect. It's a win/win situation. He promotes my work and I promote his."

"That might really work, Ronnie. Considering the recent popularity in tattoos, it might be a gold mine."

"That's exactly what I was thinking."

"Maybe I could write an article about the networking done between your business and King's once you get going. There's got to be a story in there somewhere."

"Sounds good to me." He didn't want to screw it up now, so he figured he'd better end the conversation while he was on a high note. "Are we on for tomorrow night?" *Aloof. Tiffany said to act aloof. Man, this is way harder than it sounded.*

"Yeah. You've got my curiosity up."

"Great. I'll pick you up at work around six-thirty. Talk to you later." Ronnie ended the call before she could change her mind.

CHAPTER TWELVE

Chelsea treated herself to a Grande White Chocolate Mocha with extra whipped cream to celebrate her recent success. If Dad wouldn't reward her, she'd do it herself.

As she sipped the frothy drink, she thought about how she'd hoped her dad would've reacted to her volunteering for the celebrity auction. Dad played in fundraiser golf tournaments all the time, but he hadn't been the least bit impressed by her participating in the celebrity auction. In fact, when he heard that she'd put herself up for auction to raise money, he flipped.

You'd think I'd said I was dancing on a pole or something. Dang, it was just dinner. Nope. He hadn't been impressed at all.

After his reaction she hadn't bothered to tell him they'd taken a picture for the paper and everything. She hoped Ronnie photographed well.

Chelsea took another sip and pushed Dad's rain-on-her-parade attitude from her focus. She needed to keep her eye on the prize. It was like her goals were on roller blades, and she was the queen of the derby. The Sheila Monroe story had given her the connection with Hallie at the police department, and that was already opening up new possibilities.

Finally for the first time ever, she was getting attention as a real contributor at the paper, too. It was like suddenly everyone wanted her on their team. One of the reporters even asked if she'd cover for him while he was out on vacation the upcoming month.

She pulled into a parking spot, and headed to the office. *Now, I'm getting somewhere,* she thought as she chucked her coffee cup into the trash can about three feet away. It went right in. *Yep, things are definitely going my way.*

Chelsea pushed through the glass doors and headed for her cubicle feeling like she was on cloud nine. Was it her own confidence or were her co-workers really beginning to look at her a little differently? She sure didn't remember anyone ever acknowledging her as she walked through the office before.

Dropping her purse in her bottom desk drawer, she plopped into her chair. Her computer whirred to life. She brought up her calendar and tasks for the day, while her email loaded. Planning the day was always first on the list. Scanning the calendar, she groaned. *Another team meeting at eleven. I hate those. Wait a second. I'll be recognized in this meeting. This might not be so bad after all.*

She sat a little taller in her chair, feeling better about the day already.

"Hey, great work, Chelsea," Scott said as he walked by.

She got a warm fuzzy just hearing it from her rival. "Thanks, Scott." She wondered if he was sincere.

Wadsworth came up and patted her on the back.

"Chelsea, the Police Chief called me this morning to say thanks. If you hadn't brought together the connection between Monroe and Antonio's restaurant, that might have been a cold case. He said you were a real professional. Good work."

"Thanks for giving me a chance, Sir. I knew I could break that story. The evidence spoke for itself." Chelsea felt validated as a journalist.

Hopefully, this was the end of her being assigned to all the fluff writing, even though the fluff piece and the fluffy boa were exactly what led to that opportunity. The only thing fluffy she wanted in her life anytime soon was a marshmallow fluff crème and peanut butter sandwich. It had always been her favorite celebratory treat when her mom was around. It had been a long time since she'd thought about that. Ever since mom went away there wasn't much fanfare about anything. *Dad's always a grump and every time I visit mom, she's so doped up she barely knows me.*

Chelsea pulled herself off memory lane. She knew better than to dwell too long there, so she forced herself to turn her attention to the big journalism event coming up. *It's going to be awesome. Considering my recent rise in status at the newspaper maybe I'll even be mentioned! I'm going to need a date. It has to be someone important and recognizable, too.*

Chelsea frowned, and rested her chin on her hand. Who did she know well enough to ask to the banquet? Sure, there were a lot of guys at work but she didn't see them as date material. She needed someone who would impress. She started a list of potential candidates. There wasn't much time. She'd have to make up her mind soon.

There's no way I'm going alone.

***

Ronnie rushed through his apartment giving it the once over.

Thank goodness, Tiffany isn't still here logging updates. That could've been awkward. What was I thinking when I set the date with Chelsea for tonight?

The phone rang.

Ronnie dropped his head back and groaned. *Don't let it be Chelsea cancelling.*

He snatched the receiver from its cradle and pressed TALK.

Tiffany's voice bubbled across the line. *Thank goodness.* She wouldn't be by in the morning. She had a dentist appointment she'd forgotten about.

Ronnie hung up the phone and silently gave himself a pep talk before he pulled the door behind him and headed to pick up Chelsea.

Traffic was heavy. He cursed himself for not leaving earlier. A car sat in the right turn lane blocking all the cars that could have turned right on red. Ronnie honked his horn, something he never did. He could see the driver look in his rear view mirror, but the guy apparently had no intention of turning to let the others make up some time. Ronnie tried to stay calm, not to ruin his good mood before his evening started.

Finally, he pulled up in front of the Daily Banner. Chelsea stood near the door. He tooted the horn as he parked, and got out to meet her. Just seeing her made his heart race.

"Right on time," she said as she walked toward him.

He didn't know how he'd managed, but thank goodness something was going right for him.

"Ready?" he asked, gesturing toward his car.

"Nice car. I love sports cars, and black is my favorite."

Of course, he already knew that, but he remembered Tiffany's words. *Act aloof.* "Thanks."

He held the door open for her as she slid into the low ride, then he jogged around to the driver's seat and slipped behind the wheel. "I'm going to swing by Valentino's and pick up dinner. I thought it might be better than me cooking for you."

"Sounds good. I'm starved."

"Good." Valentino's was on the way and it only took a few minutes for Ronnie to come back out with the big bag in his arms. He tucked the bag behind the driver's seat and they headed toward his place.

Chelsea inhaled dramatically. "That smells delicious."

He rubbed his stomach. "I know. I can't wait to dig in. Lunch was a long time ago."

Small talk, Ronnie. No big deal. Compliment her. After all, she does look hot.

"Nice outfit." His heart lurched in his chest.

She flashed a grin back.

He relaxed a little.

They parked in front of his apartment and for the first time he realized how shabby the place looked. He had plenty of money, but after being left with nearly nothing he'd been more than frugal with the money he'd made. *Too late now. It is what it is.*

He climbed out of the car and grabbed dinner.

Chelsea was already out of the car before he could get around to open the door for her, so he led her up the stairs.

"Come on in," he said, as he opened the door.

She stepped in and paused just inside. "Do you live here alone?"

"Yeah." He motioned her in to the living room. "Come sit down. Can I get you anything?"

"Thanks. No. I'm good." She put her purse on the dining room table, her eyes scanning the apartment with each step she took toward the living room. The furnishings were spare, but what was there looked nice. "Holy cow, that's the biggest freaking television I've ever seen in my life," said Chelsea, eyes round with surprise.

Ronnie laughed and shoved his hands in his pockets. "Yeah. I bought that for myself when I graduated from high school. It's a seventy incher. I've got it rigged up for everything from television, DVDs, x-box, my Playstation 3 games and even my computers. That's one good thing about buying your own presents. You always get what you want."

"Rock on. This is awesome. I can't imagine watching movies, sports, anything on this screen. And this couch..." She sank into the sofa, touching it softly with her fingertips. "I love leather."

He couldn't take his eyes off of her. *Chelsea Pressman. Right here sitting in my living room on my couch. What a rush.*

Just then, Rorschach came busting out from the bedroom and let out a woof. He ran right up to Chelsea and shoved his nose under her arm. Of course, it was wet and it left a moist spot.

She took her hand and rubbed the wetness away, crinkling her nose.

"Sorry," Ronnie said. "Rorschach. Stop that." He clicked his fingers and the dog immediately went to a sitting position. "We don't get a lot of company."

Chelsea slid from the couch to kneel next to the dog. "It's okay. I love dogs. I used to have a yellow lab when I was little. What'd you say his name is?" Chelsea continued to pet the dog that was warming up to her quickly, even pawing her for more.

"Rorschach. You know, after the guy who invented the first inkblot test. Get it?"

"Oh yeah, that's cute. My dog's name was Cody." She ran her palm across Rorschach's smart-bump and soft velvety ears. Rorschach went still, ears pinned back, eyebrows twitching in Ronnie's direction.

Chelsea's eyes seemed to dim. "Cody was my constant companion. My parents fought a lot. Cody kept me calm."

His heart ached a little for her. "I had parents like that too. Too bad I didn't have Rorschach back then."

"Oh yeah. I used to snuggle up against Cody until my tears left damp spots in his fur while my parents screamed and argued."

"My step dad was a mean drunk. Never said a kind word," he said. "I hate those memories."

"Oh well. I guess that's where I was lucky, because as long as Daddy wasn't drinking he was the sweetest father you could ever ask for. Still is. I live with him, but I can't wait to get my own place though. He hasn't had a drink in seven years. I used to wonder how he could be two totally different people. Now, I just thank God that he was. At least he did have a good side."

"So, ya'll get along fine now?"

"Oh yeah. It's all good. He's a little demanding, but that's because he wants better for me than he had for himself. No worries there, I intend to be more than he ever was anyway."

Chelsea grew quiet for a moment, then reached out to give the dog another stroke. "Is Rorschach always this timid?"

"No. Actually he's usually a romping maniac. He must be nervous around pretty women."

"Wonder where he gets that from?" She dipped her face towards Rorschach's ears. "Are you nervous around girls, too?" Chelsea smiled a perfect smile, then stood up and sat back on the couch. "If it hadn't been for Cody and my writing I don't know what I'd have done."

"You always knew you wanted to be a writer?"

"Not a journalist, no. I used to write a lot of poetry and short stories. Then I figured out that I wasn't going to make a lot of money writing poems, and decided hard hitting journalism was going to be a better path."

"Poetry, huh? You'll have to show me some of your stuff sometime."

She wrinkled her nose. "Really? You'd want to read it?"

"Sure. If they're half as good as your newspaper work, they've got to rock."

"Thanks. I usually don't share that stuff, but yeah, maybe I will." She shrugged, and then turned her attention to the living room wall. "So what about you? What's with all the inkblot images all over the wall? Occupational hazard?"

"I did those way before I created inkBLOT as a company."

"You made all of those? Like, on purpose?"

"Yep. When Mom first left town with my step dad they were supposed to only be gone three months. She never came back," he said, pausing at the memory.

"Oh my gosh. That's awful."

"At least she paid the rent on this place for almost a year. Then the checks quit coming and I knew that I had to figure out a way to take care of myself. Well, I had the checks Dad was sending and I quit forwarding them to mom and just started forging them to make the rent. Those inkBLOTs were kind of self-imposed therapy. I'm glad now that I saved them. They remind me what can happen when you don't have a plan. I'll never let that happen again."

She stared at the inkblots lined up from one end of the room to the other. All different colors, shapes and sizes. "I don't know what to say."

"Sorry. TMI, right?"

"No. Not at all. Thanks for sharing that with me."

He walked over to the images and pointed to one. "You know you can tell a lot about someone by what they see in an inkblot."

"Yeah, right," she said, rolling her eyes.

"No. Really. Take that one on the right. What do you see?"

She tilted her head to one side, then pushed up her sleeves and took a step closer. "Well, wait a second. Maybe you'll think I'm crazy if I tell you this...these inkblots all look alike."

She was definitely playing the demure card. Funny thing was, somehow Ronnie didn't think she was the type. Seemed pretty straight forward to him.

Why was she acting like she cared what he thought?

Maybe she does care what I think, he mused.

Ronnie motioned her to his side. "Come on. Just be yourself. What's the first thing that comes to your mind? That's what really counts."

She eyed him suspiciously. "I don't know, Ronnie Wright. I think you get more out of this than you're telling me."

He laughed. She was smart, or intuitive, either way she was on to him. "I know. It's easier on the internet. It feels safer. I think that's why the site is so popular. People let down their guards on the internet. Late at night even a normally soft spoken librarian type really lets her hair down when she answers these questions."

Chelsea looked intrigued. "Before I tell you what I see, you tell me more. So do you run everything from this apartment?"

Ronnie nodded toward the door at the end of the hall. "Come here. I'll show you." He grabbed her hand and she followed him to the door. He swung it open and let her step inside first.

"Wow. This is *not* what I expected." Chelsea stepped to the center of the bedroom-turned-inkBLOT headquarters.

A server rack held several processors. Lights blinked showing traffic and connectivity. A bulletin board full of graphs and figures covered one whole wall. Three printers and a wall of monitors churned out stats.

"This is amazing. You do all of this alone?" she asked.

"No. I have one employee. She's been with me since the idea was born."

"You must be doing okay for yourself."

He looked down, feeling a little modest, but not wanting to show his lack of self-esteem either.

"I do okay," he nodded. "Come on. Let's eat. You said you were starved. We can talk inkBLOT while we eat, and then I'll show you the prototype for the tattoos."

She led the way to the dining room table and started pulling items out of the bag, making herself right at home. Ronnie set the table, and she dished out the Italian cuisine on their plates. They ate and chatted about where they'd gone to school, what their favorite hangouts were, and then Ronnie cleared the dishes while Chelsea went into the living room and checked out the inkblot images again.

"How many computers do you have?" Chelsea called in to Ronnie.

"What?" he asked leaning out from the kitchen.

"There's two laptops in here, and what…probably like six computers in the office. You must be a real geek."

Ronnie's throat tightened. "No. I just have different equipment for different purposes. That's my personal laptop. The pilot is on that one, along with some personal analysis that I mess around with separate from inkBLOT."

"Oh." She leaned forward and tapped the screen. The computer screen came alive, displaying a colorful dashboard of charts.

Chelsea looked toward the kitchen. Ronnie was still clanging around. She pulled the computer to her lap and looked closer. It appeared to be personality traits, fears, all kinds of emotions.

He walked into the living room, and his face went flush. "What are you doing?"

Chelsea looked up, startled. "Sorry. I was just curious. It must have been in sleep mode. When I touched the screen it just sort of came to life."

He brushed his hands on his pants and went to sit next to her on the couch. Well, if he couldn't confide in the woman of his dreams, who could he confide in?

Breathing slowly, he looked her squarely in the eye and said, "This is just between you and me. I shouldn't share any of this, but I feel like I can trust you."

"You can totally trust me. This is off the record, and just between us."

Ronnie paused, but only for a second. "The things that people submit to inkBLOT are confidential. I don't sell any of that information and it's very secure."

"Wow, you really know a lot about this stuff."

"Yeah. I do analysis based on the demographics. It's really quite an interesting socio and psychological enigma to be able to get this much data to analyze. I use the sanitized data to test some of my theories on inkblots and my algorithms."

Chelsea ran a hand through her hair. "So, what kind of theories? Are you connected with some Mensa group or something? One of those brainiac think tank things?"

"No. Nothing like that. Independent studies. I don't keep any of these detailed things on the inkBLOT servers. You have to understand. The segments of the population's psyche that remains hidden comes into view with tests like this. This guy here, he pointed to a dot on the far right of a scatter plot, he must have some hidden fetish or something. It shows he might be a twisted character. In real life, he's an accountant. A real conservative guy probably in many respects. Maybe a regular geek otherwise, you know, kinda like me."

Chelsea laughed. "Is that how you think of yourself?" she asked him. "I don't think you're that way at all," she flashed him a big smile, and leaned in closer. "You know I was just teasing you about being a geek, right?"

Ronnie repositioned his glasses and continued to explain the data on the screen. "This woman here has some maternal complex where she wants to mother everybody. She's a social worker and the stats show her to be power hungry too."

"Wow, I bet you see all kinds working with this site, don't you?" Chelsea backed off trying to see the chart a little more clearly.

"It's kind of small. Wait, I'll put it up on the big screen."

"You can do that?"

"Oh yeah." He powered up the plasma on the wall with a remote, pushed a few buttons and suddenly an exact replica of what she just saw was projected on the wall.

"Wow. That is huge! That is one big freakin' inkblot."

"What's it look like?"

"A heart," She raised her brow.

He bit the inside of his cheek when she did that. "I've got almost enough to take some of this to another level."

"This is an amazing study," she said pinching her lip between her finger and thumb. "Someone could do some wild stuff with this data. So if, let's say, my boss did your quiz. You could like tell me everything about him."

"I could, but I'd never do that. That wouldn't be right."

"Oh, of course not. I was just sayin'. Ya know. Someone could."

"Yeah, I guess, but let me show you what I really wanted you to take a look at." He needed to get off that subject. He was tempted to tell her about the crimes he'd been able to predict, and that wasn't something he should share yet.

Ronnie toggled a couple of buttons. The new logo for **ink!** displayed. The brightly-colored image looked just like a tattoo. It covered the screen.

Chelsea leaned closer.

Pride swelled in Ronnie, at least he thought it was pride for **ink!**, maybe it was just being this close to Chelsea. "This is a brand new prototype. You're the first to see it. You can do it as part of inkBLOT and add points to your space, or as a standalone quiz. This isn't inkBLOTs, but ink tattoos. If someone leans toward a certain profile type, it lists the style of tattoo that aligns with their blot profile. I call it cross-hatching. My new use for an old art term."

"What a cool idea. It's all about the image, isn't it? Image is everything no matter how you look at it," she said.

He looked at her sitting there in front of him. Yes, the image he saw in front of him was everything at the moment. He had no doubt about that. Then, shaking his head as though trying to summon some concentration, he turned his attention back to the website.

"There's a lot of cool stuff I can do with this INK path. I'm working with a partner to get the tattoo intricacies down. I had no idea how colors penetrate the skin differently. He's got a lot of study information just in his years of experience to help me start the model. It will take me quite a bit of piloting to get enough data to work out the kinks."

Chelsea raised her hands, fingernails down in front of her chin and made a chipmunk face with her teeth. "Pht-Pht-Pht. I'll be your guinea pig," she said wiggling pretend whiskers.

"Cutest little guinea pig I've ever seen," he said. *Did I just say that out loud?*

He quickly changed the subject. "So you see I have all these stats." He clicked on a folder labeled Stats, and a list of files displayed. "These files contain different demographic spreads so I can help advertisers locate their prime spots, both time and type of quiz, for the targeted group they are marketing to."

"This is so cool. Really powerful stuff," she nodded.

"The patent stuff is more detailed but it's still not personal, just for research. I will admit I have a crazy curiosity about what makes different types of people tick. I didn't take those classes on psychology for nothing. Heck, I've even analyzed myself. Kind of a test study.

"I hear ya," Chelsea said, still studying the images.

"They say that the black and white is what really matters. Color influences emotional choices. I use color only on certain paths of the survey. Red wires some people up and green turns some people off."

"How many people are taking the survey?" she asked him.

"In the beginning it was tens of thousands per day."

"Wow. That's huge. I wasn't getting that it was that big. That's like Google™ big."

He laughed. "It's much bigger than tens of thousands a day now, but it's nowhere close to Google™ big, but it's done well. Since last year, the hits on the site have grown through viral networking. The ad in your paper is the first consumer advertising I've done. When I kick off the beta version of **ink!** I can only imagine how it's going to trace over to inkBLOT with new users there, too. That should send the website visitation through the roof. I'm already looking at new servers for the growth." Ronnie smiled at the thought of the prospect.

"I hadn't thought about that. I guess you'd have to increase the size of your hardware. That'll cost you big, I'm sure," she said.

"I've already worked up the estimates."

Chelsea looked up at Ronnie with a pleading expression. "These images are straining my eyes." She dug around in her purse and then came up with a needy look. "Do you mind going out to your car to see if my glasses fell out of my purse? I only wear them sometimes when my eyes are tired, but I really could use them now."

"Sure thing."

"Thanks."

He got up from the couch and headed for the door.

As soon as the front door clicked shut, Chelsea shifted into MTV Room Raider mode.

CHAPTER THIRTEEN

Chelsea glanced at her watch. She probably had two or three minutes tops before Ronnie realized her glasses weren't in the car and came back up with the news. She ran into Ronnie's office and started scanning the contents.

I've got to find as much as I can about this guy.

A small wooden box sitting on the corner of his desk held several memory sticks.

He couldn't possibly know how many are piled up there.

She stuck one in her pocket. *He'll never miss it.*

Then she opened his desk drawer. *Very neat. Pens and pencils in separate slots.*

The file drawer on his left was locked, but the bottom drawer slid out easily. *Look at all these colored folders. And each of them has their own typed label. Neat and organized. A guy after my own heart.*

Each file was clearly labeled with what appeared to align to the demographics he was talking about earlier, like 18-24 FEMALE, 25-35 FEMALE, and so on.

Her hand froze.

The folders in the back caught her attention. They were labeled: CONVICTED, ACCUSED, SEX CRIME and FINANCIAL SCAMS.

What the heck are you up to, Ronnie Wright?

She knew she was running out of time.

I'll have to come back and check those out another day.

One more look before she left the office. *Mac or PC? PC, not a Mac in sight. Gamer—hobby or serious about it?* She spotted the World of Warcraft mouse pad on his desk. *Gamer.* He seemed the type.

Chelsea ran to the balcony door and peered out to the parking lot. Ronnie was still rummaging through the passenger side of his car. She ran through the living room, skidding around the corner toward his bedroom, Rorschach got excited and started barking and jumping alongside her.

"Shush, you crazy dog." She pulled Ronnie's top dresser drawer open and scoured through them, not even sure what she was looking for.

Chelsea ran back to the living room and plopped down on the couch, half out of breath. Stretching her arms over her head, she tried to look as though she'd been sitting there the whole time while he went to fetch her glasses.

Ronnie came in and gave her the news. "Sorry. I didn't see them anywhere."

The thumb drive in her pocket was begging her to check out what was on it. She had to get the heck out of there and see what else this guy had going on.

"You know what?" Chelsea faked disappointment. "I just remembered something I was supposed to do tonight. I'm so sorry. Can we finish this up another night?"

"Well, yeah. Sure." Ronnie looked bewildered.

She got up and crossed the room. Grabbing her Brighton bag, she cocked her head, looking in his direction.

"Is everything all right?" he asked.

"Yeah. I was just thinking. You're a nice guy. I hate to leave, but I'll make up for it next time, I promise." She laid her hands on his arm and he swallowed hard. She could tell that her touch had him in a tizzy.

He looked at her with a fervent gaze.

"Well, okay. How about I come see you tomorrow night? Eight o'clock at your place?"

"I live at home with my dad, remember?"

"Oh, yeah," said Ronnie.

"I'll treat you to cheesecake," she said feeling bad. "It's my day off and I make the best cheesecake you've ever had. I'll come over here, okay?"

"I love cheesecake. Say no more. I'll be here," he said, happy that things might work out with them after all. He grabbed his keys to take her back to the Banner.

Chelsea was quiet the whole ride. He wondered if he'd said something to offend her, but when he dropped her off she gave him a quick peck on the cheek. Before he could respond she was skipping across the pavement to the private parking garage.

Ronnie rode home feeling optimistic. As soon as he got home he threw himself into the new tattoo project. No way was he going to get any sleep tonight anyway.

He pulled in the file of tattoo images King had Cat email over earlier. Some of them were really hot. Not a bad way to spend some off time. He brought up another picture and cropped just the tattoo from it. Some of those body parts that didn't get picked up were hard to click delete on.

At his desk for another few hours, he documented and created the new tattoo for images for **ink!**. It was exhausting. Bedtime would be sweet. Hugging a pillow for a while sounded good.

Ronnie decided to take a break from the images, except of course, for the image of Chelsea. What WAS it about her?

***

Chelsea couldn't believe her luck. Not only was he hot, but this guy was a freakin' mountain of information. He had no idea the power of the data he had in his hands, at least he didn't seem to. There had to be a killer story in this. What if he's up to no good? Visions of her talking to CNN about the breaking story danced in her mind. Designer suits, heels that made her legs look long enough to get arrested and a smile that people begged to see more of.

She put her hand on her front jeans pocket to make sure the thumb drive she'd shoved in was still there as she jumped in her car and headed for home.

At the next stoplight, she pulled out her notebook and started a page on Ronnie.

> Ronnie Wright
> Apartment —no roommate
> Neat freak
> Home-office
> Successful
> Cute
> Smart
> Leather couch - yum
> Whopper of a television
> World of Warcraft gamer
> Redskins fan
> Wii Playstation 3 AND KINECT in LR
> Dog person – Roarshack (Spelling?)
> Black Lab
> PC Guy
> Organized
> Obsessed with backups?
> Thumb drives everywhere
> Obsessed with inkblots. What the heck?
> ???JUST PLAIN OCD???

The car behind her honked. She glanced in her rearview and then at the light. It had already turned green. She dropped the pen in the console and gunned the engine. Her mind was only on Ronnie. She couldn't shake the thought of him, or was it her fascination with his internet prowess, or the potential of that information and a big story?

Maybe the big story was all about him!

He possessed a certain power with all that information. Could he ever use it for evil?

She laughed at that. No way would a guy like him do anything evil. He was good people. She could tell.

There's something attractive about knowing he has all that power though.

Her body got warm, so she cracked the window.

What I wouldn't give for ALL that information. Maybe it's possible to even change the future.

She pulled up in the driveway next to her dad's new car. *Great.* For once when she didn't want him home, Dad was there. *Now he'll want an update on my day and to give me advice I don't want. All I want is to see what's on that memory stick I took off Ronnie's desk.*

Once inside, she set her things down. Announcers from the World Series of Poker, Dad's favorite show, debated on the television in the other room.

Good. That means I'm totally off the hook. He won't even want to talk to me tonight.

She went into the living room and said hello to make it look like she had made the effort, then gave him a kiss goodnight and headed to her room to supposedly turn in early. Behind her closed bedroom door, she tapped on her laptop to bring it out of sleep mode.

She pulled the memory stick from her pocket. It felt smooth in her hand. She slipped it in the USB port and waited for her system to recognize the new hardware.

It did.

She took in a quick breath.

Her screen opened up to strings of data.

She scrolled up and down and left and right but none of it made any sense. She clicked the X to close the file and tried opening the file with some of the other applications on her computer. None were successful.

Darn, it must be encrypted or something.

She yanked the memory stick out of her computer, and clicked past the warning about not removing it safely.

Who cares? It doesn't work anyway.

She tossed the worthless memory stick in the trashcan and finished changing into her pajamas.

CHAPTER FOURTEEN

Chelsea woke up feeling guilty about taking the memory stick from Ronnie's house. It was all for nothing anyway. Her granddaddy always said nothing good came from stealing, but then again if Ronnie was the big story was it stealing or investigative reporting? In this case, there seemed to be a fine line between the two.

What's wrong with me? How could I have done that to him? And he's so nice. If only I hadn't gotten so wrapped up in the idea of getting a huge story. I hope he didn't realize that I took that memory stick.

She flipped her pillow over, scrunched it under her head and turned over on her side.

Ronnie's the kind of guy I should be dating. Successful and smart. What was I thinking?

She whipped back the covers and groped through the papers in the trash can until she felt the small oval stick. With it in her hand, she got out of bed and tucked it safely into her purse.

Maybe I can return it and he'll never have to know.

She spent the morning at her office, totally distracted. All she could think about was Ronnie. She tried to keep herself busy by spending the afternoon researching editorial archives. They were always ripe with potential article material. Not finding anything, she pulled out the business card to her contact over at the precinct.

She'd call Busby and see if he could tip her off in any good directions. Lucky for her he was working the desk when she called, but he didn't have much. Everyone was focused on the return of the battleship fleet, and the paper already had plenty of people covering that story.

Then, she had an idea.

She direct messaged Ronnie on twitter.

> ::@inkBLOTguy Want to hang out?
> Call me. Can't w8 2cU::

For ten minutes, she sat refreshing her screen, waiting for a response. That was a waste of time.

I guess Mr. I'm-Always-Connected isn't as connected as he advertises.

Chelsea flipped through some of Super Scott's biggest stories to see if they might give her an idea or an angle on a story. She gnawed on her pen cap. Breaking stories seemed to be more right time, right place than anything. Maybe she was spending too much time sitting at her desk.

She pushed her chair back to leave, when the chirping bird sounded from her computer. *Twitter! He'd tweeted her back!*

> ::@StarReporter Sounds good.
> Problems last night. Still working
> them. TTYL around 9:30p???::

Did he know she'd stolen that thumb drive? Panic struck, but then why would he want to chat? It was cool. He didn't know.

"Yes! 9:30p works for me." Chelsea tweeted him back. The she re-tweeted one about the fundraiser.

> ::@inkBLOTguy RT u&me

@FightDiabetes The Diabetes
Fundraiser rocked. Thanks to all who
helped! Esp Top Date – 2Hot
@StarReporter Awesome ::

Chelsea stuck her pen behind her ear and leaned back in her chair staring at her computer screen. It was going to be a long day.

At 9:27 p. m., the phone rang interrupting her online chat with a writer from Charleston. She ended that screen in a hurry. Her plan to appeal to Ronnie's technological prowess had worked. She'd never really twittered much before, but it was coming in handy now. She snatched up the phone and answered in her sexiest voice, "Well, hello there."

"How've you been?" asked Ronnie.

"Good. I've been thinking about you," Chelsea purred. It wasn't a lie. She'd spent a couple hours messing around with that inkBLOT site. She still didn't get why people were so obsessed with it. By creating different login names she'd answered the quiz for real to find out what it would say about the real her. It was fun, but what did they know. It was just a stupid computer app.

"Really? Uh…I mean great. What's up?"

"I know you're busy beyond belief with inkBLOT and all. Was everything okay last night?"

"Yeah. False alarm, but you can't be too careful. One problem like that can wipe everything out."

"I want to apologize. I'm really sorry about how I acted last night, ya know all quiet in the car. I was just so disappointed. I'd looked forward to getting together all day. I hated to cut it short."

"Don't worry about it," Ronnie said.

Chelsea could hear the smile in his voice. She chewed on her bottom lip. People weren't usually this accommodating. Maybe he had an agenda of his own. She dismissed that thought quickly. He wasn't the type, not like the guys she usually went out with that always had ulterior motives, or ended up being just plain flat out losers. Her dad would probably even approve of Ronnie.

"Are you still up for that cheesecake?" Chelsea asked.

"Sounds good. Thanks for tweeting me."

"I won't be late. Promise." She settled the phone back in the cradle.

It must feel so good to be admired by so many like he is. Maybe if I'm lucky, I'll figure out what makes him spark to others. I need that spark.

Maybe she could learn to like a guy like him. And liking could lead to something. Couldn't it? Success and love, could she dare dream that big?

Pick one. Success, for sure. If I'm lucky, I can have both. IF I'm lucky.

***

At seven o'clock sharp, Ronnie watched Chelsea's old black Mercedes pull into the parking lot below. He counted the steps in his head and opened the door when he thought she'd be on the landing.

His eyes met hers. They had a definite twinkle to them. His tongue felt thick and dry. He licked his suddenly parched lips and prayed he wouldn't stutter.

"Come on in, girl," he said, trying to act casual.

She stepped inside and rose up on her toes to give him a friendly hug while balancing the cheesecake she'd made for him.

That sent a swirl of heat through his body.

"You really did make a cheesecake. You didn't have to do that," he said as he took the pie plate from her. "Thanks."

"My pleasure."

He put the cheesecake in the refrigerator. "Follow me. I want to show you something."

"Sure, what is it?" Chelsea followed him to his computer screen and leaned in close, looking over his shoulder. A spreadsheet filled the screen. He showed her how he was separating data into state, gender and category of what survey takers see in the images. "That gives me an analysis of who's taking the tests and what their interests are. I can also tell if any of the ads are helping generate new users in a particular region."

"That's wild. You can tell more about a person by the answers they give, can't you?"

"Sure. It's totally confidential though. I'm using the data to help prove some scientific theories I have." Ronnie nodded slowly with a grin, proud of his accomplishments in the last few years.

"You mentioned something about a patent last night. That's big. Bigger than inkBLOT, right?"

"Much. And much more important."

"That's quite an undertaking Ronnie," Chelsea purred in his ear.

He liked her tone of voice. Somehow it had lost its business sound to it. More personal. He liked that.

"You know," she said. "I had you all wrong."

"What do you mean?"

"Well, I'd assumed since you were so successful and young, that you were a spoiled rich kid. I had no idea. I mean... well, what I'm trying to say, is that I'm really impressed with all of this. That you did it yourself, well, that's huge." Her attention diverted to the screen as he went online and brought the website up again.

"Thanks." Ronnie smiled. Someone acknowledging his hard work wasn't something that happened much, but he could get used to it easy enough. He brought up his own inkBLOT account, the one he used to pilot things or run tests in production. Every option to earn or buy something filled his screen.

"You see, I earned points in every quiz and demographic. With the INKmoney, a user could fill your space with artwork of inkBLOTs, create an avatar, dress them up, decorate your INKpad and even fill your pantry. "

Ronnie loved perusing the back door of folks' INKpads because some of these people had a lot of time on their hands. They went ALL out. It was obvious they'd spent hours on the quizzes earning INKmoney, and hours vamping up their space. It was all good for his business, too!

"Man, what the heck is that?" she asked.

"That's my INKpad."

"Oh. Yeah, I saw that. I didn't create one of those yet."

"It's fun." He wondered what she'd put in hers.

"Your whole screen is full of icons. You've got more icons than I've got shoes! That's a lot by the way." Chelsea inched closer to him as he pulled up the quiz. The first image sprang to life on the screen.

"Look, Ronnie. This inkblot looks like a fairy." Chelsea leaned in for a closer look. "TinkerBell... cute," she said softly.

"What did you just say?"

"TinkerBell. It reminds me of TinkerBell." Chelsea let out a giggle.

"I didn't think of you as a TinkerBell kind of gal." Ronnie looked at her. His heart softened. Chelsea shifted her weight in her chair and for a moment, he felt his attention shift to other things.

She bumped his shoulder playfully. "I have a soft side. Look. There's the wings and it looks like her, right down to her pointy little toes."

"If you say so." He clicked to the next image.

"Now this one looks like..." She wasn't sure what she should say. Actually, she thought it looked sinister but what would that mean to him? She said the first thing that popped into her head. "It looks like a big horse. One of those Budweiser Clydesdale's."

"You think *that* looks like a horse?" Ronnie tilted his head. "I don't see that at all."

She'd just said any old thing to hide her real feelings about the design. It had sparked dark thoughts and she didn't want to trigger distrust on his part. He'd seen it a hundred times. People couldn't fake him out though. He knew the patterns.

"Well," she said. "No, now that I really look at it. It looks like a swirling wind."

"Huh."

"What's that mean?" She leaned back and folded her arms across her chest.

"What?"

"You just said, huh. What'd you mean by that?"

He shook his head. "Nothing. It's just this is one of those designs that almost everyone sees the same thing."

"Really?" She did her best to act as though she didn't know what it looked most like.

"Yeah. Most people see snakes," he said as he studied her face for clues.

That's exactly what she'd seen, but it seemed wrong somehow. Maybe she was reading too much into this.

"I guess now that you mention it. I do see snakes," said Chelsea. "I have a friend that owns a pet shop in town. He has all kinds of snakes. It does kind of look like one coiled up and another climbing. Yeah. I see it." She'd worked in that shop a couple of summers and learned how to handle all kinds of reptiles without cringing.

"Are you afraid of snakes?" he asked.

"No. Why? Do you think that's why I didn't see that in the image?"

He laughed. "No. Lighten up. You're trying too hard."

"Well, I guess if I was in an Indiana Jones snake pit I wouldn't be too thrilled, but it's not like you ever see more than a black snake around here and all they do is eat mice. Are you afraid of them?"

"No. Not at all." Ronnie straightened in his chair. "I used to catch them when I was a kid. They don't bother me. If you pick them up right, even the poisonous ones can't hurt you."

"Good to know." She shrugged. She let the subject drop. He didn't need to know that she'd worked with snakes. It just didn't seem feminine to mention it.

"So anyway, after people submit their interpretations, they fill out a bio to get their report. It includes their name, address, birthday, places of employment, likes and dislikes, fears and goals. It's pretty much all optional except email and age group, but almost everyone fills it all out because that's how you earn points, or INKcoin. For each field and quiz you complete you get the INKcoin to decorate your INKpad."

"How many people actually answer those personal questions?"

"More than you'd think."

"I get it. Yeah. Okay." Chelsea looked as though she found the willingness of people to share such details interesting. "So, they're answering all your questions and taking that quiz just so they can do little online thingies. It's really a lot like on Yoville or Farmville or something, right?"

"Yeah. Kind of like that. I used to just ask for it and no one ever responded, so I raised the bar by adding the other features and man, people just started coming out of the woodwork. It's amazing what people will do to get to the next level, even if there really isn't a big prize at the end."

"I guess it's just the journey they're after. Must be nice. For me, as a reporter, sometimes it's really hard to get someone to open up and give me much information."

"Maybe they're afraid if they tell you too much they are putting their privacy at risk. Like in one of those paparazzi rags. It probably spooks them," Ronnie said. "I don't think they even think about it from their living rooms online."

"My stories are only as good as the people I interview. If they give me juicy tidbits, I might have an exciting article. If I'm short on interesting facts, the article falls flat. Sometimes it's like pulling teeth. Other times, it's hard to get 'em to shut up. Of course, those are usually the stories that don't amount to anything anyway." With that said, Chelsea turned her attention back to the test taking.

While she was working on the inkBLOT test, Ronnie went into the kitchen to answer a phone call. He stayed in there long enough for her to finish the test and have a little free time on her hands. She printed out her test results and looked up as she heard him coming down the hall.

"Well, that was interesting. It's cool how many things you can spot in an ink design," she said as he walked down the hall toward her.

"How did you feel about the images? Did you find them comforting or soothing or did you find them sinister or scary?"

"Why? You ask a lot of questions for a guy."

"Just curious."

"I thought it was all just for fun," Chelsea admitted.

"But that doesn't mean there isn't some scientific basis to it all. Look. Okay, take this one for instance." Ronnie pulled up a screen with thumbnails of a set of inkBLOT designs and answers. A series of graphs and analysis tracked across the bottom. "This woman picked answers that nearly all pertain to money."

"So?"

"Don't you wonder what she's hiding? Maybe tax evasion, or insider trading in the stock market. Maybe she's got a secret stash she's hiding from her husband. And look at this one. Almost all of her answers have a sinister tone to them. What's the deal with that? And look, she's a daycare worker. Ooh. She could be the next child molester. Doesn't that give you the creeps?"

Chelsea shivered. "That would be awful."

"Yeah, I couldn't let that one go. I have to dig a little deeper on it."

"What if you figure out she might be a molester or something?"

"Then I'll know my theory works." Ronnie continued to flip through the reports, citing this person and then that. Revealing more than he should have about each person's idiosyncrasies, where they lived and their employment information. He was on a roll and wanting to impress Chelsea, put confidentiality on a back burner.

"Kind of like somebody who interprets handwriting."

"I guess so. I never thought about it like that. Maybe you're right. So anyway, what ran through your mind while you took the test, hmmm?" Ronnie asked her. He looked at her with one eyebrow raised.

"I'm not sure what to say right now," said Chelsea.

"Why?"

"I don't know if I want you to know what's going on inside my brain." *That was a lie. She KNEW she didn't want him to know what was going on inside her brain.*

"Oh, come on. What's an angel like you got to hide?"

She lifted a shoulder and smiled. "You're so sweet." She looked at him, taking it all in. Kind face, kind eyes, he didn't seem to have a one track mind like a lot of guys. She wanted to trust him. After all, she was a reporter. She had a good sense of people and situations, and things like that didn't escape her notice. This data he was collecting really had her attention. She found the whole thing very interesting. It was kind of like getting an insider interview on people without them even knowing about it. Her mind raced. Surely he felt the thrill of all that power, he had to. She was getting quite a thrill herself, just thinking about how she could get an inside look on some of her friends, or better yet, her enemies.

"Could you look up a specific user? Chelsea tried to hide her excitement.

"I could. I can, but I'd never break a confidence."

Chelsea chewed the inside of her cheek. She'd love to get the inside scoop on a few folks. Super Scott for one. An inside track on him might help her get him out of her way for the next front page story. He'd never be the wiser.

"Oh my gosh," Chelsea said. "I've got to leave."

"Wh-Why? Are you okay? What's the matter? We're just getting a chance to talk and really get to know each other. Did I say something wrong?" asked Ronnie.

"Ronnie, I know the expression carpe noctem means seize the night, but this time I'm afraid I will have to take a rain check, Hon. I've got to go home and work on my column." She pulled her phone from her purse. She flashed it in his direction. "My editor left me a message. They've moved up my deadline. I don't have my computer with me."

"Stay for dinner. You have to eat."

"Deadlines. Sorry, sometimes a journalist doesn't eat every meal."

"Tell you what. You use my laptop. I can lend you a memory stick to save your work."

"Oh, I've got my memory stick in my purse. So, you really wouldn't mind if I used your laptop?"

"Heck no." He grabbed his laptop and pushed it her way. "Here, have at it."

"Thanks. Gosh, this is great. I didn't want to ruin our evening. I'm having so much fun."

Ronnie grinned. *She was enjoying herself! Awesome.* "You work on your story and I'll order something in for dinner."

Not being one to do much cooking, he pulled out a thick stack of menus from a drawer in the kitchen. "This is my specialty, take-out delivery. What do you want?"

"I don't care," she called from the other room. "Whatever you want."

He flipped through the stack and made a decision.

As soon as he dialed the number and started talking, Chelsea opened an old story from her memory stick. She pretended to work on it while toggling his files to the flash drive. She tucked that one in her purse and stuck another into the USB port. She'd probably never get this chance again. She dragged the files to the removable drive. Suddenly panic struck. She started to sweat.

Her mouth went dry. She got a sudden urge to scream out her guilt to Ronnie. Chelsea took a deep breath and calmed herself.

Just then the dinner arrived.

She decided she'd have to make a hasty exit as soon as dinner was over.

They ate and chitchatted, getting more and more comfortable with each other.

Chelsea wiped her mouth and tossed her napkin into the middle of her plate. "I'm stuffed. Thanks for letting me use your laptop, and for the dinner. Awesome."

"My pleasure." Ronnie walked into the kitchen to put away the dishes.

"I've got to go get some rest," she said.

"Already?"

"We'll get together again soon. Promise."

Not wanting her to forget that promise, he asked her. "How about tomorrow night? Like at your place?"

Chelsea hesitated for a moment as if she was thinking things over and said, "Sure. Come on over at seven."

Ronnie was temporarily satisfied but the feeling didn't last long. He wasn't happy about the short evening, but he walked her down to her car, and waved as she pulled out of the lot.

This time when she got home she was thankful to be the only one there. No act with Dad this time. She dashed to her room and pushed her own memory stick into her computer that she'd left on – ready to go. In just a couple of flashes, data filled her screen. This time she hit the jackpot.

Rows and columns went from A to AGK in her excel spreadsheet for thousands and thousands of rows, and in several tabs on the spreadsheet. She selected the tab labeled in blue that said Wright Analysis. A menu displayed with different search criteria. Drop-down boxes allowed for selecting country, regions, even down to states and something called the SCF code. Other filters were allowed on sex, age group, several personality traits and there was also a checkbox for Potential CrimeLink.

What the heck does that mean?

She was practically paralyzed with the sheer enormity of it all.

Chelsea sat back in her chair and stared at her computer. Her palms got sweaty. She brushed her bangs back from her face and selected Male, 18-24, and clicked on Potential CrimeLink = yes. A swirling icon filled the screen and then counted down the processing time completed.

A new screen popped up with a report of individuals' detailed information.

"Holy cow. Is this what I think it is?"

She went back to the selection criteria and did it again, but also selected New York as the state. That's where Sheila Monroe's agent was from. If this was giving her what she thought it was, if that guy had ever taken the inkBLOT quiz his name would pop up here.

She took a deep breath and then clicked to start the process.

"Five, four, three, two and one," she counted out loud. "Bingo." She clasped her hands across her mouth. "This guy must be some kind of Einstein freakin' genius. This is big. Bigger than big. OMG."

CHAPTER FIFTEEN

Tiffany scooted closer to Ronnie, watching over his shoulder as he made updates to the new beta files for **ink!**.

Ronnie deleted the code he'd just entered and started over.

"What's up with you?" she asked.

"Sorry. My mind is somewhere else."

She knew exactly where, too. As long as Tiffany had known Ronnie, he'd been a no nonsense kind of guy. Not one to go nuts about a girl, or anything that might take him off his game. inkBLOT was everything to him, until now. She'd never seen him so distracted. In fact, she'd been trying to distract him for two years now with zero success. It was unnerving her that this chick from the newspaper, that he barely knew, was having this kind of effect on him.

Irritated she got up and went over to her own computer and went back to analyzing the data sets from last night. She shook her hair back over her shoulder and hit the keyboard harder as she typed. The keys were practically smoking.

"What's with you?" he asked.

"You know, Ronnie, you're in a real mood if you ask me. I'm not sure I like the new you." She typed away, trying to ignore the innocent look on his face.

"I was thinking about Chelsea. She came over last night."

Even just the mention of Chelsea's name made Tiffany's stomach churn. "Be careful around her."

"Why do you say that?"

"I've got a vibe about her." If he was going to go all ga-ga for someone, it had better be her. Tiffany had waited long enough, hinted enough times, some day he'd figure out she wasn't just a BF.

"Be nice. Your claws are showing. You're not jealous are you?"

She spun around and glared, but clearly, he'd been kidding. He had that playful grin, the one that pushed a dimple in his left cheek. "Of course not, but did you notice one of the memory sticks is missing since last night?"

"Are you accusing Chelsea of stealing?"

"I'm just sayin'." Tiffany shrugged and kept her eyes on the screen.

"Well, you don't even know her. She's not like that. You probably accidentally stuck that memory stick in your pocket, or..." He leaned down to look under his desk. "It's here somewhere. Give her a break. When you get to know her you'll like her. I promise."

"I doubt it," Tiffany mumbled.

"I'll invite her over one night so ya'll can get to know each other."

"Can't wait," Tiffany said. She had to practically force the words out of her mouth. *What else can I say without looking like a total jerk? Hopefully, he'll come to his senses before it's too late.*

As it got closer to dinnertime, Ronnie got antsy. Tiffany couldn't work fast enough to suit him, and he was being short tempered with her and the speed of the internet, something she had no control over.

"Why are you rushing me?" she asked.

Ronnie shrugged and shuffled his feet under his desk. Why was this so awkward? "I have a date tonight."

"Oh." She swallowed, nearly choking. "I thought you saw her last night."

His eyes stayed glued on the screen, nearly ignoring her.

"So, I guess maybe I'll get to know Miss Wonderful better tonight if I'm still here when she gets here."

Ronnie's eyes went wide. "Well...I...didn't really mean tonight. I mean, well ...I'm going over there tonight."

"I was kidding. Quit panicking." She was just letting him get to her for some reason tonight. Usually, she wasn't one to let her feelings get hurt. "I'm kinda tired anyway. I'll finish this stuff in the morning and let you get ready for your big date." Grabbing her purse, she headed for the door without a backwards glance.

Ronnie looked up and waved goodbye but she'd already left the room.

He glanced at his watch and closed down all the files. Once he secured everything in the office, he headed to the shower. With a towel wrapped around his hips, he brushed his teeth and combed his hair. After getting himself looking as good as possible, he drove over to Chelsea's.

He pulled up to her house right on time.

There were no cars in the driveway, but the house had a two-car garage. *She must park her car in there.* He walked to the door and pressed the doorbell.

Pressing her number on his cell, he waited as her phone rang.

"Hello?" Ronnie heard her voice on the other end and his heart rate picked up. It still did every time he heard it.

"Chelsea? I'm at your place. Where are you?" He looked over his shoulder and down the street in both directions.

"I got delayed. I'm sorry. I'll be there in a few minutes."

"Oh," he said. It would have been nice if she'd have let him know that before he rushed to get here on time. "So, I guess I should just wait here?"

"I'm almost there now."

Ronnie pressed END on his phone and looked toward the house. No one was home, but there were lights on. He was always very conservative about turning lights off when he left a room. His step dad beat that lesson into him enough times as a kid.

He sat on the front porch. Twenty minutes went by. Then thirty, then forty, fifty, fifty-seven. He tapped the face of his watch. Finally, her car pulled in the apartment parking lot in the spot next to him. *It's about time…*

Smiling, Chelsea stepped out of the car.

Ronnie tried to hide his disappointment, but he was ticked and starving.

"I'm so sorry I left you waiting," she said shaking her hair back as she walked up to him and laid a hand on his arm.

His mood softened. "Well, I've been here for almost an hour."

"I'm so so sorry. I swear it couldn't be helped. I'd never leave you hanging without a good reason. What can I do to make it up to you?" she said with a pleading innocence, her eyes wide and mouth slightly parted.

Look at those lips. Suddenly all the irritation drained right out of him, and it was no longer a big deal.

What right do I have to be mad? She'd said she was running late. It happens.

Chelsea reached up and swept a hand across his shoulder as she raised herself to kiss him.

Ronnie was just relaxing into the kiss when Chelsea pushed him away.

"What the—," Chelsea screamed as she jumped to the curb.

An old Buick screeched to a halt right in front of where they'd been standing.

Ronnie jumped on the curb next to Chelsea. Grabbing her arm, confused.

"That idiot almost killed us!" Chelsea yelled, then turned to look at Ronnie. "Do you know her?"

Ronnie nodded, and stepped off the curb toward the car.

"What are you doing? I thought you were going to run us over," he asked Tiffany.

"We've got a problem," Tiffany said.

"How did you find me?"

"I found the address online. You said you were getting together with her." Tiffany leered in Chelsea's direction and got out of the car.

"Oh."

"What's that look for?" Chelsea asked, shooting Tiffany a look that would freeze ice, as she stepped up behind Ronnie with one hand on his arm and the other on her hip.

"I'm not here to talk to you," Tiffany said.

"Why *are* you here?" Ronnie took a step back from Tiffany forcing Chelsea back, too.

Chelsea stepped from behind Ronnie to his side. "Why don't you go home? You look desperate," she said to Tiffany. "What? Are you jealous or something?"

"You don't even know me. Casey or Charlene or whatever your name is. I'm Tiffany, the one he works with. And I just happen to have an important piece of business back at the office that he might want to see."

"Is that so?" Chelsea eyed her.

Tiffany rolled her eyes at Chelsea and turned her attention back to Ronnie. "It's important. You might want to get back home so we can talk."

"Home? Excuse me little Miss Tiffany, but that is not *your* home," said Chelsea. "That's where you work." She glanced at her watch. "And according to my watch, working hours are over."

"Whoa, whoa, hang on now." Ronnie raised a finger to Chelsea, praying she would shush, and then turned to Tiffany. "So, it can't wait huh? Think it's that important?"

"I went back to set up the auto run for overnight and saw a message about a serious virus alert. There was a curious dip in activity for a minute. I hope it's okay, but I didn't want to be the one to make that decision."

Ronnie gazed at Chelsea. "Uh oh. That's not good. I better go."

Chelsea frowned at Tiffany and then at Ronnie. "Great. You go right ahead and leave. Heaven forbid your computer might get sick."

"It's my business, Chelsea. I'm sorry. I need to check it out. It's Friday the 13th. You never know what's going to happen on Friday the 13th."

"Whatever. Your loss."

Ronnie stared at Chelsea as he climbed into his car to back out behind Tiffany. This was a side of Chelsea that he hadn't seen before, but now that he had, it wasn't pretty.

What a screwed up night. First, I spend half of it sitting in the dark on her porch waiting, now this. What else can happen?

CHAPTER SIXTEEN

Chelsea was so wound up she couldn't sleep. Finally, she quit trying. Climbing out of bed, she pulled on a pair of navy blue sweats, grabbed her laptop and quietly eased out of the house so she wouldn't wake her dad. *I am so stressed. If I jogged I could get rid of some of this adrenaline. But there's no way can I do that in the middle of the night. Nope, it's safer if I just drive around.*

She cruised through town for a while. Downtown looked so different in the quiet darkness of the night. Storefronts were dark, and occasionally she'd catch a glimpse of a person huddled against a doorway sleeping.

Not ready to go home, she took the east ramp to the interstate and headed for the oceanfront. She rolled down the window as she got closer to the beach. It was quiet there, too. A few couples walked hand in hand in the moonlight on the boardwalk, but that was about it. Waves crashed against the shore and the water shimmered in the still darkness.

May as well watch the sunrise since I'm already here.

She slid her laptop from the passenger seat into her lap, and pushed the seat back from the steering wheel. While her laptop came to life, things started coming together in her mind.

Everything happens for a reason. I really believe that. Now I just have to figure out exactly why Ronnie and all his information have come to me. Is it him, or the opportunity knowing him brings?

He's nice enough, but maybe it's his story that needs to be told. Can he really be as nice as he seems? Is anyone really that nice?

Chelsea tapped into a hotel wireless and went straight to inkBLOT. As the sound of the waves crashed against the shoreline she entered a fake name to re-take the inkBLOT quiz. The images were different this time. She let herself get swept into inkBLOT like the grains of sand in those waves that were lulling her into a relaxed state. Before she knew it she'd answered all of the questions and was in the bonus area. She had to create a free email account to get the results, but that was easy enough.

While she waited for the results to calculate and make it to her email, she thought more about the questions and the data points. She was smart. She should be able to figure that data out.

Chelsea opened up Ronnie's data file and searched for his name. There it was. She had his deepest secrets right there at her fingertips. Scrolling through the information on him, she read it, reread it, and then read it again. Then, she pulled out the notebook in which she'd started her list about Ronnie on day one and started taking notes. She shook her head as she transcribed the details onto paper. Chelsea liked the power of instant information on the computer, but she was a pen and paper kind of girl.

Scanning the list of data points on the pad, she began circling positive traits and drawing squares around the negative things. *Now, this is really interesting.*

When she looked back up, the sun was already above the horizon. She'd missed the whole darn sunrise. She shut down her computer, tucked it back in her bag and laid it on the passenger seat. As she headed home, the weight of the laptop was making the seatbelt monitor go crazy. After a dozen too many dings, she slid the laptop bag to the floor mat.

The inside of her mouth tugged against her teeth from the smile plastered there. A thrill of enthusiasm tickled her every nerve. Glancing at her watch, she calculated how much time she had before she needed to be home to change for work. There was just enough time to make two of the three stops she wanted to make. The third stop could be on her lunch break later in the afternoon.

Once she made it to work, she got her column in early enough to leave for lunch before traffic went nuts. She ran her errands and grabbed a burger at the drive-thru. While she munched on fries, she tweeted Ronnie:

>@inkBLOTguy Thinking about you.

Ronnie tweeted her back:

>@StarReporter Get together
>tomorrow?

>@inkBLOTguy Wouldn't miss it.
>How about tomorrow morning?

Chelsea's cell phone rang. It was Ronnie. "Hi there," she answered.

"Thought it'd be easier to make a plan on the phone," Ronnie said.

"Sounds good. Since tomorrow's Saturday, do you want to go for breakfast? Around 9?"

"Sure. I'll meet you at Big Sam's. How you been?"

"Good. Crazy busy, I don't know how I can get all this done today, but good."

"Anything I can do for you?"

"Really?" She was right, he *was* a nice guy.

"I wouldn't have offered if I didn't mean it," Ronnie said.

"Well yeah, actually, I had an errand to run, but I'm on deadline. Would you mind going down to the University and picking up a fall schedule for me?"

"You going back to take more classes?"

"Oh, no. Well, maybe. I need it for a story."

"Okay. Sure, I can do that."

"Man. This is so great. I don't know how I can thank you. You know, I kind of need it for tomorrow. Could you go this afternoon?"

Ronnie looked at his list of things to do today. Nothing he couldn't move or pawn off on Tiffany. "Sure. I can make some time in my schedule. I can go around four."

"Perfect. I'll get it from you when we get together in the morning," Chelsea said.

Later that evening Chelsea sat on her bed with the police scanner squawking next to her. It was hard to beat the Banner to the scene of late breaking action, but eventually this scanner would pay off. If Wadsworth wasn't willing to toss her the big stories, she'd make her own break. Dad was out of town and it was nice to be as noisy as she wanted without worrying about somebody getting cranky. With the static and banter crackling in the background, Chelsea updated her calendar with the extra activities she'd planned.

The crackle and slur of the scanner chatter was a little annoying. She couldn't even make out all of it, but she was getting better at it. A shoplifting, several speeders, nothing of interest. She flipped through a magazine and listened. She'd almost decided to give up when something newsworthy finally unfolded.

An accident on the interstate. Police, fire and rescue were all being summoned. She grabbed her purse and ran out the front door, racing to the scene. Luckily, it wasn't far away.

When she arrived at the scene the dizzying blue, red and white lights bounced across the highway making it difficult to focus. She spotted a small brown car in a crumpled heap against the concrete dividing wall. Rescue workers swarmed the vehicle trying to pry the doors open to rescue the driver. Three other cars were pointing in all directions but south, the direction the cars in those lanes were supposed to go.

Chelsea snapped a few pictures, then ran to get closer to the action. She spotted one of her acquaintances on the police force and waved. He gave her a nod in return.

"What happened?" she asked.

He shook his head. "Not sure exactly."

"The witnesses weren't able to tell you anything?"

"They all said the same thing. Everyone was just cruising along, and then this guy crossed the lanes and hit the center barrier wall. The others spun out trying to miss him. Everyone else seems to be okay. Not sure about him."

Chelsea scribbled in her notebook. "Can I talk to the others?"

"Sure." He pointed to a small group of people along the shoulder of the road next to one of the police cars.

Chelsea took pictures of the wreckage and then made a dash over to the other accident victims to get their stories. She gathered all the details she could and then went straight to the Banner office. She transcribed the story and turned it in but it was too late to hit the morning edition. High on adrenaline, she stuck around and worked on another story that was due on Monday. No sense wasting time since she wasn't going to sleep anyway.

It was morning by the time she got home. She was beat, her makeup had worn off long ago but she got ready to meet Ronnie regardless.

He was waiting for her in front of the restaurant when she drove up. He pulled his hands from his pockets and tried to look relaxed, but was anything but. He pulled the University schedule from his back pocket and tapped it against his thigh as he watched her walk toward him.

"Good morning!" she called with a wave.

"How are you this morning?"

"Beat. I was up all night. Big accident."

"Oh man. Everyone okay? I didn't see anything in the paper this morning."

"I missed the deadline. Probably tomorrow's edition. The driver that caused it didn't make it. Three other cars got smashed up trying to avoid him, but they were just a little bruised. One had a broken nose from the airbag. I'm not so sure that's such a great invention. Ever seen what those things do to you in a collision?"

Ronnie shook his head.

"I've seen black eyes, broken noses, bruised up messes from those things. I think I'm glad the old Mercedes doesn't have one." Chelsea's phone rang. "Sorry. Excuse me."

She took the call and talked while she and Ronnie were seated in a booth. "You're kidding me!"

Ronnie opened the menu, but he already had a sneaky feeling his frate was getting ready to be cut short.

Chelsea ended her call and tossed the phone into her purse.

"Everything okay?" he asked.

"Yeah. Well, no. Kind of. That wreck I was telling you about last night. We all kind of assumed the guy had a stroke or a heart attack or something, but it turns out he'd been bitten by a poisonous snake."

"That's weird."

"I know. Good story, though. They've identified the driver. I'm heading over to the guy's house from here to get the rest of the details. Friday the 13th turned out to be bad luck for that guy."

Ronnie tried to hide his disappointment. He pulled the schedule from his back pocket and laid it on the table in front of her.

"What's this?"

"The schedule."

"What schedule?"

"The one you asked me to pick up for you."

"Oh yeah. I totally forgot. Thanks. Was it crowded on campus yesterday?"

"Not too bad."

"It's usually crazy on Fridays. Well, thanks for picking that up. You saved me a ton of time."

They ate breakfast, and sipped on coffee. Chelsea did most of the talking, rattling on and on about the accident. She was eating so fast he wondered how she could talk at the same time. She was definitely in a hurry to get out of there. He could tell without asking that she wouldn't be available for anything the rest of the day. Why ask for the rejection?

Right on cue, she stuffed the last piece of toast in her mouth and washed it down with some juice and said goodbye.

Chelsea headed over to the accident victim's house to meet Detective Hallie Davison. When she stepped through the front door, she stopped in her tracks.

The victim, Fred Crenshaw, was a professor at the University. Chelsea confirmed that much the night before. There wasn't anything special about the outside of this man's house, in fact it was about as average as you could imagine. But once you stepped inside, it was like a whole other world.

Nice place for a professor.

Chelsea ducked to clear the large greenhouse type bushes and trees he had filling his place.

Hallie met her at the entrance. "Wild, isn't it?"

"Like a tropical rain forest. You sure no monkeys or snakes are going to jump out at me?"

"Funny you should say that," Hallie said.

"Why? There aren't a bunch of snakes in here are there?"

"No, but it would have made for an easy open and shut case had there been. Now I still have to figure out where that snake came from."

Chelsea pushed a feathery fern to the side and stepped into the hall. "Talk about bringing the outdoors in..."

"Yes. Crenshaw may have been a Professor by day, but he was most definitely an armchair traveler by night. The guy had an obsession with hunting big game in Africa. Look." Hallie directed Chelsea into the living room.

Pictures filled one whole wall of him dressed in khaki safari attire standing proudly over his prey.

"Wow. Amazing. Ewww. Is that a real tiger head?" Chelsea reached out and rubbed the fur on the toothy beast that flanked one side of the fireplace.

"I think so."

"Weird. You wouldn't think a professor would have a wild side like this."

Hallie shrugged. "I found a stack of printouts next to his computer over here. Delta, Trans Air, U.S. Airways. Prices circled, bad connections or layovers highlighted. He must have been planning a trip for over the winter break."

"He won't need that now. Was he going alone?"

Chelsea walked over and started thumbing through the printouts again. "All of the ticket information was for one. Lives alone. He's divorced."

"I was there at the accident site right after it happened." Chelsea loved the feeling of being the first. "I wonder why he had a snake in his car. He must have been into them. Probably a good hobby gone bad."

"That's what we're wondering."

"I was surprised you were working this case. I didn't know you worked accident cases. I thought you just did homicides."

"You thought right."

Chelsea's heart skipped a beat. "Wait a second. You don't think this was an accident, do you?"

"No way. That guy was bitten by a venomous snake from another part of the world. From Australia. There was no cage in the car, or sack or anything to make me think he was transporting it. Smart guy like that wouldn't take that kind of chance. Someone wanted this guy to die."

Chelsea's jaw dropped. "Poisonous. Oh my gosh." She swallowed hard feeling nauseous all of the sudden. "Just how poisonous was that snake?"

"Very." The detective snapped her fingers in the air. "Like that!"

"I didn't know there were snakes so deadly they could kill a person in an instant."

"It's true."

Chelsea sat down on the couch. "Man. That's scary. Did they find the snake?"

"Yeah. It was dead. It was mangled up in the wreckage with old Fred. Unlike a lot of snakes, this type is very aggressive."

"I can't believe it." Chelsea wiped a bead of sweat from her forehead.

"Thank goodness the snake died, else one of the rescue workers could have been a casualty, too. That's how we were able to identify the snake so fast. Lab tests will confirm the cause of death, but there were numerous bite marks on Crenshaw's leg and abdomen. It's a pretty sure thing."

Over the professor's desk, a bulletin board held an itinerary for a Safari package for the following spring, and an inkBLOT website printout that confirmed his sense of adventure. Chelsea smiled at the connection to Ronnie. Was there anyone who didn't know about inkBLOT?

Chelsea pointed toward the inkBLOT printout. "Have you ever taken that inkBLOT quiz?"

Detective Davison shook her head. "No. I don't mess around with that kind of stuff. Why?"

"No reason. Just wondered. So, you said Crenshaw was divorced?"

"Yes. His ex-wife still lives in town."

"Would you mind if I talked to her?" asked Chelsea. It wasn't like she needed Hallie's permission, but she did need the address.

Hallie wrote the address on a slip of paper and handed it to Chelsea.

"Thanks."

"You'll owe me for this story, too."

Chelsea headed for the door, calling out, "I've got your back," over her shoulder as she wove between the greenery to go have a chat with the ex-Mrs. Crenshaw.

Turned out ex-Mrs. Crenshaw was actually the ex-ex-ex-Mrs. Crenshaw. Apparently, the professor did a lot better hunting wild game than women. The woman had given up on Crenshaw for the same reason as wives number one and two after being warned about his obsession. He was too wild for her but not in the sexual sense. It was wild as in animal hunting wild. Spending vacations in the desert or in mosquito netted swamps was not her idea of a good time.

"Fred always had his head in the clouds. He never wanted to go out or do anything but sit in that stinking camouflage armchair of his, dreaming of the next big adventure. He lived for the next high he would get from some dangerous safari, be it the thrill of the chase or scaling the side of some precipice. If he'd had half that interest in me, or any of the other women he married, he'd have been a catch. No surprise he died from a snakebite."

Ex-ex-ex-Mrs. Crenshaw looked like a snake the way her mouth twisted up just then. There was no love lost between those two.

"He was a bit of a snake himself," ex-ex-ex-Mrs. Crenshaw added.

Chelsea had to hold back a giggle. "Guess you won't be missing him much."

Ex-ex-ex-Mrs. Crenshaw crossed her arms. "Hardly. Good riddance."

Chelsea thanked ex-ex-ex-Mrs. Crenshaw for her time and then called Hallie. She was on her way over to the campus to speak with Professor Crenshaw's peers and to the students from his Friday class.

When Chelsea got to the campus library, Hallie was already there. She was wearing her stern detective attitude with the students, probing for clues.

"I'm sorry to have to tell you this but…Professor Crenshaw was in a fatal car accident last evening," Hallie said.

You could hear the intake from the room. A blonde girl seated to the far right began to sob. A couple of her classmates ran to soothe the shock.

"We're just asking some routine questions," Hallie said. "I'm sorry to have to ask. If it makes you feel any better, it looks like the death was instant. He didn't suffer." Detective Davison paused and the girl who was crying seemed to be settling down a little. "Does anyone know why Professor Crenshaw may have been in possession of reptiles?"

A boy in a striped shirt spoke up first. "He was crazy, and not an easy A or anything, but we all liked him. The Professor even led a Scrabble club on Friday afternoons. He did have a curious obsession with wildlife. It even came out in his Scrabble words."

Another guy spoke up then. "You know, Crenshaw sure seemed ticked when he came into class on Friday. Someone had balanced a purple-haired troll doll straddling the American flag. He kind of flipped. Not sure why. We thought it was funny."

"Do you know who did that?" asked Detective Davison.

Everyone shook their heads and looked at one another.

A pretty blonde girl spoke up. "At Scrabble Club, the professor kicked out Bruce for getting his points and kicks with sex related words. He didn't have many rules but that was one everyone knew not to push."

The striped shirted guy laughed. "Yeah, Bruce had hollered out, 'Hey, is gonad a word?'"

The group of students chuckled and nudged each other.

Detective Davison tried to bring the group back to her attention. "That's when Crenshaw kicked Jackson out?"

The girl nodded. "He didn't leave without a few parting words, including a thirteen-point four letter word that seemed to echo across the corridor. Professor Crenshaw was so wonderful. I can't believe Bruce did that. It was so embarrassing."

Detective Hallie Davison took down the notes and planned a visit to Bruce Jackson. The rest didn't appear to be of any concern.

The timeline of Crenshaw's day was becoming clear. He'd left the campus and had just gotten on the interstate with the accident occurred. Whoever planted the snake must have put it in the vehicle sometime during the day on campus. The university didn't have anything more dangerous than a black snake on the property so it wasn't likely the animal was from there. Detective Davison called in to the precinct to have one of her co-horts investigate to discover where someone could find a snake like that in the area, or even in the state.

Chelsea jotted notes like crazy. With the thoughts from the ex-ex-ex-Mrs. Crenshaw in mind, she wondered if Crenshaw was getting lucky with that little blonde student of his. She sure did seem to go all doe-eyed when she talked about him.

Chelsea tapped Hallie on the shoulder. "Hallie. I'm going to chase down some personal details on the professor while you continue with the investigation."

"Sounds good. I'll call you. Don't worry. I haven't forgotten our pact. To work together as a team. You know, kind of watch each other's back."

"I hear ya. We'll compare notes later," said Chelsea.

"You got something up your sleeve again?"

"Hey, you make me sound like some kind of magician."

"Honestly Chelsea, you're like a reporter and detective all rolled into one. I love it."

"You do what you gotta do to make the front page."

"I guess you do. I'll email you the details. I've also contacted some of the last people to have seen Fred Crenshaw before the crime took place. Some of his students mentioned something about him being on his computer during class. Maybe there's an email or something that will lead us in the right direction. That's hush-hush between us girls, okay?"

Hallie signaled an imaginary lock over her mouth, and crossed her heart. "Abso-freakin-lutely."

As Hallie and Chelsea spoke, just ten blocks away, another bizarre event was about to take place. This one would miss the deadline for the next newspaper coming out, but headline news was headline news and sometimes it didn't happen on the paper's schedule.

Chelsea collected all her notes and submitted her story in time for the next run.

THE DAILY BANNER

SERPENTINE GRIDLOCK CAUSED
BY CAR ACCIDENT
By Chelsea Pressman
NORFOLK, VA
A local college professor died Friday
night in a four vehicle crash on
Interstate 264 eastbound.

The brown 2002 Subaru was traveling
east on I-264 when it suddenly
crossed three lanes of traffic and hit
an embankment and overturned
several times in the area of
Campostella Drive and Brambleton
Road, police said. The crash was
reported about 8 p.m. Three other
vehicles swerved to avoid the Subaru
and had minor damage and injuries
which were treated at Norfolk
General Hospital. One driver had no
apparent injuries and was able to
drive off.

The driver, Fred Crenshaw, 39, was
cut from the wreckage. Ambulance
helicopters landed on the freeway
near the scene of the accident, closing
two lanes of traffic for several hours.

Crenshaw was dead on arrival at
Norfolk   General.   Further
investigation   revealed   that   Mr.
Crenshaw   suffered   numerous

venomous snakebites and died before impact.

Any details that could lead to an arrest should be called into the CrimeLine at 1-555-LOCK-U-UP.

CHAPTER SEVENTEEN

Chelsea stood in front of the mirror counting strokes as she brushed her hair. Mom once told her that a hundred strokes made your hair shiny and glossy. Since Mom had been a model, she knew about those things, so Chelsea took that to heart.

On the hundredth stroke, Chelsea switched her gaze from the mirror to the wall with satisfaction.

All of her best published work, framed article after framed article lined it.

Her eyes rested on the latest one she'd just hung. She'd sprung for a nice frame and even got it double mounted in navy and cream. The frame shop had clipped the headline date and header from the paper and mounted them in a fancy cutout in the mat board above the article. It rocked.

She hoped this morning she'd have a bigger and better something to frame.

Chelsea walked out to the porch and grabbed the morning paper. She closed the door behind her and said a little prayer before spreading the paper out on the table.

Her heart sank.

"It's not fair."

That daggone Super Scott. My story was just as big as his was this time. How am I ever going to get anywhere with him in the way?

Looking at the clock, she knew she had to hurry if she was going to be at work on time. There was no sense in allowing herself to get upset about it now.

Chelsea slung her purse up on her shoulder and headed for the door. As she stepped outside she had the nagging feeling she was forgetting something. She leaned back in and noticed her briefcase on the kitchen table where she'd left it last night when she was going to take out all the old stuff because it was getting so heavy. She ran back and got the briefcase, leaving the papers stacked next to it. She didn't have time to sort through that now.

She ran out to the car and slid in after tossing in her briefcase and purse. Backing out of the driveway, she tried to push the thoughts of that annoying Scott from her mind.

Man, that guy bugs me.

Traffic was heavy for a Wednesday, and she ended up over fifteen minutes late for work. Hoping no one would notice, she left her briefcase and purse in a cube near the reception area out of sight. Grabbing a coffee cup and walking to her cubicle, she hoped no one would think she was just coming in. Once she'd been seen by most of her co-workers, she made sure Wadsworth could hear her talking just outside his office. That way she could get Wadsworth to initial her handwritten time at the end of the day. That would serve two purposes. One, she wouldn't be docked or written up for being late, but second, and most importantly, another chance to chat with Wadsworth and earn some points.

Chelsea meandered past Scott's desk to see what he was up to, but just as she walked up he turned to answer his phone. Standing close enough to hear, she hung around to see who it was.

"No, I'm not too busy for that. Yes sir. I can cover that story, too."

Chelsea leaned back and saw Mr. Wadsworth on the phone. *Great. Scott's going to get another juicy story. I can't believe this.* She glared at Scott, wondering what story he'd been assigned.

"Hi Scott." Chelsea leaned against the wall of his cubicle.

"Hey, Chelsea."

"I was just checking in. I'm all caught up. I can take a story for you if you like."

"I don't think so," Scott said.

Was it her imagination or did he just snicker? "What. You think you're the only one who can write around here?"

"I've paid my dues," said Scott.

"Well, you're not all that. It wouldn't kill you to spread some of the stories around," She slammed her coffee cup down on Scott's desk, spilling coffee and letting her emotions boil over.

"What the heck are you doing?" Scott grabbed a few tissues and futilely wiped at some of the coffee puddling on his desk. "Hey, it's not my call anyway. If you're ticked off, talk to Harry, errr Mr. Wadsworth. He makes the assignments." Scott pulled his trashcan out from under his desk and funneled the rest of the sticky caramel-colored coffee toward it. "Look at the mess you made."

"Yeah, well, it was an accident..."

"No it wasn't. What's gotten into you lately? You've been acting like a whack job. Look, you've ruined my draft."

Feeling bad, she grabbed some paper towels from the kitchen and went back to sop up the coffee from his desk. She didn't mean to let him get to her like that. Even if he was public enemy number one to her, she knew she had to keep her emotions in check at work.

"I'm sorry," she said.

"You got that right." He glared at her.

"That wasn't necessary," she said in response to his snide remark. Once she had it under control she stomped back to her desk, sulking.

The next five hours she sat at her desk and poured her heart and soul into another story. It wasn't a big story but it was well worded and could outshine Super-Scott's work any day. One thing about this town, there just wasn't front page news every day, so you could technically land there for just about anything on a slow news day. This story had every potential of getting there if nothing big happened.

Scott and Chelsea's stories hit the layout editor's desk about the same time. Jill had been at the Banner longer than anyone in their right mind should ever work. She had a team of people working for her, but everyone knew she had the last word on placement of articles and advertising.

Chelsea hung back hoping to see where the articles landed.

When Jill snuck away to the loading dock for a cigarette break, Chelsea rushed over to Jill's computer to peek at where she'd placed their work for the next edition. Chelsea's heart sank. Scott's was first page, top headline while hers was on page three beneath an ad for false teeth.

"I don't think so," Chelsea muttered. She looked around to see if anyone was nearby. Most everyone was gone at that hour, and Jill's desk was in the back corner. Chelsea started hitting keys and dragging and dropping things on the screen, then ran back out and around the corner. *I sure hope this flies. That jealous old hag never liked me anyway.*

Chelsea grabbed her stuff and drove home hoping that her changes to the lineup would stick through the final editing process.

The next morning, Chelsea rushed through breakfast waiting for the newspaper to hit the front porch. As soon as she heard it thump against the door, she ran out to get it.

She opened the paper right there on the front porch to see the first page.

Her face flushed when she saw Scott's byline on front page again.

What is it with this guy? Can't they see that I'm a better writer? She could hear Scott's words echoing in her head. *I've paid my dues. I've paid my dues.*

She had absolutely no intention of waiting that long.

Her frustration bubbled over causing her to slam the paper to the ground and scream out in frustration.

The neighbor's blinds lifted across the street. Chelsea saw them staring.

That's right. Look out your window. I don't even care if you see me. They probably thought someone was being assaulted, and that's exactly how she felt about the layout in the paper she held in her hand.

Chelsea snatched the paper back up and went inside. Her heart pounded and her stomach twisted. Right there on page three, beneath the ad for false teeth, was her story. Only now it had been half-edited to death. Even the picture she'd submitted wasn't used. Jill must have really been mad. She had to know it was Chelsea who had moved them.

The oatmeal she'd eaten for breakfast threatened to come back up. She swallowed the acid taste back down.

Taking the newspaper and refolding it, she slammed it against the kitchen door frame.

"Aaaargh," she screamed as she beat the frame with the paper a half dozen times, leaving inky smears along the high gloss white trim.

Chelsea thought about calling in sick, but she knew that would only work against her. She sucked it up and made herself go to the office.

Once there, she questioned her decision to go in. She had to look normal but she felt anything but. Sitting at her desk, she flipped through archives on her screen, but barely paid attention to them. The assignment she'd been given this week was for the Oktoberfest celebration down at the oceanfront at one of the microbreweries. She wondered what Scott had gotten. She heard him giving instructions to one of the interns. He was getting ready to leave on assignment.

Chelsea gathered her things and slipped out behind him. Maybe she could learn something by watching him. She'd never in a million years admit it to him though.

Chelsea followed Scott across the street to the mall. *What's he doing? Shopping? No, you idiot. He's on a story. He has to be on an assignment, because he has that stupid leather portfolio legal pad in his hand. He carries it everywhere.*

She hung back watching him move through the mall at a leisurely pace. She tracked him from a safe distance until he stopped at the Mall Security office.

Maybe there'd been a robbery!

A moment later, two mall cops came whizzing by on Segways. They must have just gotten them to patrol the mall. Scott shook hands with the mall cops.

Her teeth gnashed as jealousy pushed her buttons. Scott stepped onto a Segway and started zooming up and down the aisle. The two-wheeled people movers looked like a blast. Not only did he get the good stories, now he got the fun ones, too. She stepped back behind one of the kiosks and watched him from the cover of a huge potted palm.

He really thinks he's hot stuff. Look at him showing off.

She grabbed a piece of bark from the huge potted plant and worked it in her hand. The next time he went by she chucked it at him.

It didn't get anywhere near him, but he must have seen it coming because he jerked and the Segway slid from beneath him, sending him flailing across the slick mall floor in one direction and the high dollar machinery in the other. The head of mall security ran over to the machine and two others ran to help Scott.

Chelsea bolted.

She hadn't meant for him to fall, she just wanted to ping him with the small piece of bark. It wouldn't have even hurt more than a bee sting. *You couldn't put an eye out with that small thing.*

CHAPTER EIGHTEEN

When Chelsea passed the editor's office, Wadsworth was sweating bullets. His shirt was wet and his voice loud. She took a step back and leaned in near his half-closed door. She held her breath trying to listen in on his phone conversation.

"Gosh, Scott. That's a tough break," she heard him say. "How will I get the paper out without your cover?" Wadsworth got quiet as he listened to Scott on the other end.

"They took you away in an ambulance? Man, I'm sorry to hear about that. Just messing around, huh?" Wadsworth made a clicking sound. "Uh-huh. Uh-huh. How long will it take you to heal?"

Silence again.

She wished she could hear the other side of this conversation. *Why couldn't he use speakerphone like the rest of the world?*

"Was the Segway insured? Thank God." Wadsworth leaned back in his chair. She could hear it squeak under his weight. "When do you think you're coming back to the office?"

Chelsea crossed her fingers as she lingered, listening.

"Two weeks? Guess it's not as easy as it looks on that Mall Cop movie, huh?" Mr. Wadsworth laughed at his own snarky joke. "Man. Well, we'll just have to get along without you."

Chelsea rolled her eyes. When she heard Wadsworth drop the phone back in its cradle she hustled back over to her desk, hoping like heck that he'd summon her to his office to transfer some of Scott's stories to her.

Two weeks! She hoped he didn't try to hobble in any sooner than that. *It was my fault. I feel bad. Okay, well, not real bad, but a little.*

She couldn't help but smile at the possibilities. *His fall might just be my lucky break!*

Grabbing a pen, she jotted down a poem in her notebook, making sure to not let anyone else see it.

<u>Segway to Success</u>
His Segway to pain
Was my segway to gain
Because it's my time to shine.

With Scott out of the way
It'll be my day
My story and my headline.

An accident came
And made him quite lame
His keyboard is taking a rest.

It's my turn you see
It's a segway for me-
A segway that leads to success!

She tucked the notebook into her top drawer, and then thrummed her pen on her desk in a happy beat.

"Too bad, so sad, Super Scott." She stared at the phone wishing it to ring. The gossip of Scott's fall was already racing through the office. Impatient, she got up and went to Mr. Wadsworth's office to see if she could prod him along.

"Knock, knock," she said as she leaned in the doorway. "I heard Scott was in some kind of accident."

The editor leaned back in his chair, raising his sweat-pitted arms over his head. "Yeah. Bad break. He'll be out of commission for a couple of weeks."

"That sounds serious."

"Yeah for him and for us," Wadsworth mumbled.

"I can pick up some slack if it will help."

"Thanks Chelsea. You're always willing to pitch in," he said. "If you can step up to the plate and cover some of these stories for Scott on top of your other assignments, that would help."

Chelsea's face broke into a huge grin. Then, as if keeping herself in check, she transformed the smile into just a pleasant look. *Careful not to look too happy.* The less you act like you want it, the more likely you are to get it.

"Great. What can I do for you?" Chelsea asked.

"Well. First things first. Scott was working on this story about the new Segways at the mall. That's how he got hurt. Mind stopping over to his place and picking up his copy?"

She cringed. "Sure. My pleasure."

"Great. And take him his laptop. It's on his desk. He might need to work from home for a while." Wadsworth scribbled some directions on a slip of paper and handed them to Chelsea.

"Sure thing." This was not what she had in mind. She turned to leave, sorry for even offering now.

"Chelsea?"

"Yes sir?" She turned and faked a grin.

"When you get back, stop in and see me. I'm going through Scott's assignments now. I'll toss you something good for helping me out. I appreciate a good team player."

"Yes sir!" *That was more like it.*

Chelsea gathered up Scott's things and headed to his house. The sooner she got back, the sooner she'd get her assignment. Scott's house was all the way across town. After a twenty minute drive, she finally came to the entrance to his neighborhood.

Very nice. He must be making a decent salary to live in this area. Someday I'll be living in a neighborhood like this.

She pulled into the driveway behind Super Scott's SUV, walked up to the porch, and rang the doorbell. His lawn and flowerbeds looked beautiful. Every yard on the block was perfect.

Scott's wife opened the door.

Chelsea lifted the laptop like it was a calling card. "I'm from the Banner. Chelsea Pressman. I'm here to pick up and drop off a few things for Scott. How is he?"

Scott's wife stepped to the side and gestured Chelsea inside. "I'm Courtney. Nice to meet you. Scott said someone would be coming by. They've got him on some painkillers. He's pretty loopy." She called to Scott in the other room and he responded with something incoherent. "Sounds like he's still awake. Come on. Follow me."

Chelsea fell in step behind the tall woman. Scott looked like crap. He was sprawled out on the couch with his leg propped up in the air. She suddenly felt very responsible for his accident. A rush of panic made the room spin a little. She steadied herself and stepped closer. "This is a lot worse than I thought. What happened?"

Scott rolled his eyes and let out a deep sigh. "I was doing a story over at the mall about the new Segways they just got. They're ramping up holiday security. I couldn't resist a little spin. Unfortunately, I got off balance and took a spill."

His toes peeked out from the blanket across his lap. They were bright purple.

Chelsea pointed toward his colorful toes. "Oooh. That looks like it hurts."

"As soon as the swelling goes down, they'll be doing surgery. Pins and screws'll put me back together."

"That's serious. Those things must be dangerous."

"Something caught my eye and I lost my focus," he said.

Had he seen her? She swallowed hard.

"I should have been paying attention. It was just a stupid accident," Scott said, then grimaced as he tried to move his leg.

"What did you see?"

"I don't know. It all happened so fast."

Chelsea shrugged and tried to look compassionate. "Too bad." *Thank goodness.* "Well, everyone down at the paper wishes you their best."

He rolled his eyes. "I bet they're all getting a big laugh out of it."

"Don't fool yourself. Piers Morgan pulled that stunt a couple years ago. Remember that? You're just an understudy to the best."

"Really? Piers Morgan took a Segway spill?"

"Yeah. Where you been? Under a rock? He almost didn't make the finale of America's Got Talent that year. It was all over YouTube. Just be thankful no one caught your belly flop on tape."

"Yeah, you're right about that," he admitted. He was already firing up his laptop, and Courtney was yammering on about how he was supposed to be resting and not working.

As soon as Scott handed her his notes, Chelsea got out of there.

Thank goodness, he didn't see me. I'm in the clear, she thought as she climbed into her car to go back to the office.

***

Chelsea settled into her chair and got right to work. She submitted Scott's story and picked up her assignments. Wadsworth had taken care of her just like he'd promised. That was one thing about him. He was loyal to his people. She needed to find a way into that inner circle, and not just because someone was hurt.

Chelsea worked on her story a while, but couldn't get her mind off Scott. It might help to have information on him. She wondered if Ronnie would give her info on Scott if he took the inkBLOT quiz. Maybe she could talk Scott into visiting inkBLOT to pass the time. She could work Ronnie into giving her the details if she asked right, and she sure knew how to do that.

The next day Chelsea checked off the research items on her to-do list, and then went through her mail. She was tickled to receive a thank you card from Antonio for her article on his restaurant. She cut the postmark and return address from the envelope, and carefully taped it to the back of the card. Then, she posted it on her bulletin board with the other cards she'd received.

The card from Antonio's gave her an idea. She flipped through her contact file and found his phone number. After a few quick punches on her phone, she had him on the other end.

"Antonio? How did I know you'd already be hard at work?" she asked. "It's Chelsea, over at the Banner. Thank you so much for the card."

He chortled. "Ahhh, Miss Chelsea. You're a little angel. I'm booked to capacity for the next month. How can I ever thank you?"

"I'm so happy to hear it. That's great! I was calling to see if I could stop by before you opened. I want to get a bowl of that wonderful soup of yours. I have a colleague who took a nasty fall. I thought it would be the perfect pick-me-up."

"For you, Miss Chelsea? Of course. I have a pot on the stove right now."

She laughed at the way he drew out all his words to accentuate his accent. She coordinated a time to pick up a to-go order so she could take it to Scott. A mission of mercy.

Antonio refused to let her pay, which was exactly what she'd hoped. With soup in tow, she headed back over to Scott's house.

There was no answer when she rang the doorbell, so she rang it again. Maybe he was sleeping. She was turning to leave when she heard someone call out. That sound was followed by a series of clunks. He was making his way to the door. He opened the door and leaned on the crutches.

"What are you doing here again so soon?" he asked, grumbling.

She raised the bag. "I brought you soup. I felt bad that you were laid up."

He looked surprised. "That was thoughtful. Come in and put it down on the end table. I can't really maneuver on these things too good yet," he said raising one of the crutches in the air.

"Sure." She slipped under his arm and into the room. "It must suck to hop around on those things. I've never broken a bone."

"Me either. These things are a lot harder to use than you'd think."

"Yeah. You don't make it look too easy," she said with a laugh.

"It does suck." Scott dropped onto the couch with a sigh.

"What have you been doing with yourself?"

"Going nuts already. Surfing the net. Channel surfing. There's not much to do sitting around all day."

"Bummer. Hey, I know something you can do." She nodded toward his laptop. "Hand me that."

He gave her an odd look, but handed her the laptop.

"You got wireless, right?"

"Yeah."

She opened the browser and typed in the URL for the inkBLOT website. She pulled up the registration screen with the demo and turned the laptop back his way.

"Here," she said, handing him his laptop. "This will keep you busy for a while. All the folks at the office have been doing it. Heck, everyone's doing it."

"I'm not into that kind of stuff."

"How do you know? You got nothing better to do. It'll keep you from getting bored," she said. "It's an online inkBLOT test. It's fun. Give it a try."

Turning his attention to the screen, he began clicking through the images and making his selections.

Chelsea glanced at her watch. "Oh gosh, I really have to go."

"Hope you don't mind if I let you show yourself out."

"No, not at all." Chelsea headed for the front door feeling exhilarated by the good deed and the possibility of detailed information on Super Scott. *If he has skeletons in his closet, I'll find 'em. If he has secret phobias, Ronnie will know by that quiz and I can handle Ronnie.*

As she neared the front door, Chelsea noticed Scott's leather portfolio on the side table. She paused and checked over her shoulder. Scott wasn't going to be able to sneak up on her on those crutches. She opened it and peeked inside. Nothing much. Some scratchy notes she could barely read. She was tempted to take it. She slapped the leather portfolio closed and left it, shutting the door securely behind her.

When she got back to the office she made sure everyone knew about the good deed she'd done. For some crazy reason they seemed to treat her nicer because of it.

The next morning, Chelsea saw her story there on the front page for the second time. It really had her supercharged. Bad news for Scott was good news for her.

Chelsea read it again and broke into a little victory dance. Pleased with the end results, she looked at it closely one more time to make sure it was just as she'd written it. Not one change. And the photo, the one of Travis Holden collapsed at the kitchen table with his coffee mug in his hand, she'd taken herself. The caption under the picture read *The Real Mug Shot*.

What a great title.

THE DAILY BANNER
THE MURDERER WAS NUTS
Chelsea Pressman
CHESAPEAKE, VA
Detectives are still looking for the person or persons responsible for the death of Chesapeake resident Travis Holden, age 24, who was found dead in his apartment slumped over his morning coffee. The initial report had been natural causes, but further investigation has ruled that out.

Anyone with information about this crime should contact police via the local hotline at 1-555-LOCK-U-UP.

Too bad Dad was out of town again, not that he'd have made the big deal she'd like him to anyway. She was bubbling with excitement to share her news with someone so she called Ronnie. If anyone would share her excitement that she was in the limelight, he would.

Anxiously tapping her foot on the floor, she twirled her hair in one hand and held the receiver with the other. One ring, two rings... "Crap. Where is he?" Three rings. Finally, an answer.

"Hey Ronnie. I did it. I really did it."

"What's that Chelsea? What's going on?"

"I got my break. The one I've been waiting for. Half the front page, Ronnie. That's what's going on. With my name on it." She spun around in her chair, entangling herself with the phone cord in the process. She fought the corded phone for a moment. *Why do they even make these things anymore?* "Have you seen the front page this morning?"

"No. I hadn't had a chance to read the paper yet, but I'll grab it. Hang on."

She listened as he moved through his apartment. She could hear the door open and close in the distance. Then, the sound of the paper opening.

Ronnie fumbled with the phone. "Wow. You're not just on the front page. You ARE the front page."

"Thanks Ronnie. I knew you'd appreciate my hard work."

"You know it. Congratulations," he said.

"I just had to share it with someone. I still can't believe it. I don't have much time. I've got to run, but thanks for sharing this moment with me."

"I'm glad you called me," said Ronnie. "Want to get together to celebrate?"

"More than you can imagine," she cooed. "We'll talk later."

Chelsea hung up the phone feeling satisfied as she headed to work.

When she made it to the office, it was already buzzing with chatter about her story. Chelsea was on cloud nine.

Wadsworth had looked out for her just like he said. He'd called her with the assignment right after the coroner had announced Travis Holden dead. She was only a few minutes from the address at the time.

Chelsea had been on the scene for about fifteen minutes. Holden's girlfriend had been the one to call 911 to his address. They'd been on the phone when he'd suddenly gasped and then didn't respond. The girlfriend rushed inside the door in a panic and burst into tears. An officer walked her into the living room and comforted her while the rest of the team worked the scene.

It wasn't until later that the police figured out that someone had laced the coffee he was drinking with peanuts. The coffee pot had still been warm when the police showed up on the scene, and the investigation team found a trace of peanut oil on the counter. Someone had to have known about his allergy, and now the police seemed to be looking suspiciously at the girlfriend.

A follow-up with the Big Kahuna-Huna Coffee Company showed no trace of nuts in any of that production lot, nor did the facility handle nuts of any kind in their processing or packaging divisions

What a rush. No wonder Super Scott loves his job. I hope he doesn't rush back anytime soon.

After covering the story, she went back to her office. She'd only been there a few minutes when one of the other writers stopped by and stuck his head inside her cubicle.

"I was going to say congratulations on your story," he said then started laughing at the copies of her article plastered around her cube. "Guess you're having your own little party. Have enough copies?"

"Ten to be exact." *If you don't toot your own horn, nobody else is going to do it for you.* That was her new motto. She looked at one of the copies and smiled.

Chelsea liked this feeling. She hoped ol' Scott took his time getting better so she could keep getting a steady stream of hot stories to keep her on this ego high. No way could she go back to social columns and lunch menus after this.

CHAPTER NINETEEN

The ink hadn't gotten cold on her last article and Chelsea was already chomping at the bit for the next big story. Ronnie had been leaving messages and tweets for her, but she really didn't have time for that kind of playing around right now. She was intent on making fast progress, and she wasn't about to lose steam now.

Chelsea jumped up from her chair and jogged to the break room for another cup of coffee. She'd found that if she kept the coffee going until around two in the afternoon she could skip lunch and spend the extra hour working on her story to make the deadline.

Wadsworth stepped up behind her in the break room.

"What is it with you these days?" he asked, then snorted mucus in the back of his throat.

She held back a shiver at the disgusting sound.

"You seem to be losing that soft touch that everyone loved about you."

"I thought you were happy with my work," she challenged.

"I am. I just don't want you to lose that ability to write the human side of the stories, too," he warned. "Readers have been writing in. They've noticed you've traded in the state fair and fashion shows for crimes and police reports. They miss you."

She'd been getting emails from all the Martha Stewart types, too. It rubbed her the wrong way. The last thing she wanted was to write that drivel again.

"Don't take this the wrong way, Sir, but I don't miss those stories. I feel like I've finally found my niche." Chelsea lifted the coffee to her lips.

He nodded slowly and placed a thick hand on her shoulder. "You're doing a great job, Chelsea."

Her heart raced. She swallowed hard to keep the tears from coming–she could feel the tingle in her nose hinting that tears were on their way. Then the air in the room shifted. She could feel the 'but' coming.

"*But* be careful, young lady. Don't burn any bridges. You still owe your fans from your old column, too."

She cocked her head to one side. "What are you saying?"

"I got a phone call from a woman that wrote in to you. She was paying you a compliment and you blasted her in your response. Please, don't let that happen again."

She looked down. "I'm sorry. Yes sir. I'll be more aware."

"That's my girl," he said, then handed her an envelope. "Here. A little something to celebrate your recent success and to thank you for the extra hours you've put in to keep things afloat while Scott is out."

Her jaw dropped. She reached out to accept the envelope. "Thank you, Sir."

She waited until he left the room then when she was sure no one else was around, she peeked into the envelope. Tickets to the movies. A smile spread across her face. She inhaled the scent of success. This would definitely impress Dad. She folded the envelope in half and tucked it into her blazer jacket. Her first extra perk at the paper.

***

Chelsea stepped into the empty elevator. As soon as the doors closed, she twirled to release the excitement she was feeling.

Like gambling, drinking or sex was to some people, she'd found her fix in writing stories that hit the headlines. She'd overheard someone whispering at work, calling her an attention junkie. They were probably just jealous. They should be.

She'd let Ronnie get a little out of reach lately. He didn't even sound all that ga-ga for her when she called him last. The big annual Mid-Atlantic News Awards Dinner was being held locally this year. She knew she had to line up a date. Ronnie would be the perfect date for it. The guy can hang a suit, and everybody knows about inkBLOT now, even the girls down in payroll who usually spend their time talking about their kids and tee ball. *Guess I'd better give him a buzz so he'll know when the dinner is coming up.*

Pulling out her phone, she called him. When he answered the phone, she plastered a huge grin on her face. It was a tip she got from a story she did on a local call center earlier in the year. If you smile on the phone, people can tell. It sure seemed to work.

"Hey, Ronnie. What are you doing next Friday night?"

"Chelsea? I thought you'd written me off. You haven't returned any of my calls lately."

"I've been busy. So, do you have any plans next Friday? I need a date for the News Awards dinner. Between us, I think I have a chance to win one this year."

"I know you've really worked hard for it."

"So-oooo, will you be my date?" she asked.

"Of course."

"Cool. It's Friday night at the Cavalier Hotel down at the oceanfront. Black tie dinner. Pick me up at 6:30?"

"Sounds like a date," he said, jotting down the date and time on a notepad.

"So, what else do you have going on this week?"

Ronnie sat down on the couch. This felt more like it. "I'm going to be locked away for the next couple of days working on the release of **ink!**."

"I guess Tiffany will be there."

She sounded annoyed, and Ronnie liked that. "Actually, she's working on some project for school, or something. I'll be on my own to get it done."

"That doesn't sound like much fun."

Ronnie laughed. "It's fun for me." Tiffany was probably the only one who understood that about him. Speak of the devil, she'd just walked in.

"Well, I'll let you get back to it. I'm really looking forward to Friday."

"Me too," Ronnie said, ending the conversation. Then tossing the phone in the air, he caught it behind his back. "Yes."

"I'll be right back," he said to Tiffany as he hurried straight to his closet and pulled out the black suit he'd bought to wear to Tiffany's grandma's funeral in the spring. He'd drop it off at the cleaners in the morning.

***

Tiffany could tell by the sappy sweet phone talk that he'd been talking to Chelsea.

He came back in the room and grabbed the newspaper from the desk. "Look. She did it again."

What? Does he think I'm going to share his enthusiasm? Puh-lease.

Tiffany rolled her eyes.

Ronnie said his goodbyes and hung up. "What was that look for?"

Tiffany wondered how dense Ronnie was sometimes. "Really? Front page, again? Don't you ever wonder how Chelsea is the first one on the scene of every crime lately?"

"She's working hard. Give her a break."

"Hey, I'm just sayin'. You know there was this true crime story on television the other day. A man had been accused of leaking his own company's trademark secrets to get a buzz going. He was guilty, too. How cold is that?"

"Maybe it proves Chelsea is a good reporter."

"I doubt it. That chick is no good. I can smell it from here."

"What are you insinuating, Tiffany?"

"Who, me? I'm just making an observation."

"Sounds like you're trying to start rumors."

"Rumors? This is you and me talking. Best friends. Don't tell me you don't find it a little bit odd that she shows such a thrill over these crimes?" She walked over to stand next to him.

"That's not fair. You don't even know her."

"I know she sure picks up the phone to celebrate every time she covers one, doesn't she?"

"Tiff, she's just passionate about her career. This is a big deal for her."

"Where's the fun in someone else's misfortune?" Shifting her weight from one foot to the other, she put one hand on Ronnie's shoulder as he turned back toward his computer. "Something's not right with her."

Ronnie searched for an explanation. "Maybe it's kind of like doctors who have to learn to emotionally separate themselves when surgeries don't go well to keep sane."

"Doctors don't care?"

"No, that's not what I mean. I mean in order to keep on operating, taking those life and death chances, they have to protect their hearts to a degree. If not, they'd have it ripped out every day they go to work."

"Good point." Tiffany pulled her hands to her hips. "But I'm telling you, there's something up with her. Keep your eyes open."

"Keep my eyes open? Why do you say that?"

"Everything is not always as it seems," she said. "Just be careful, and don't do anything dumb. That includes stuff like getting tattoos." She swatted his arm.

"Still harping on that, are you?"

"Sure am." She handed him the files she'd just printed. "I think you did it for her."

"Did what?"

"You heard me." She lifted her chin. "I think you got that tattoo to woo her. I saw that article she wrote about them."

Ronnie shrugged. "That would be crazy."

"Call it whatever you like. You would know."

She was right.

"Here's the next batch of stats," she said and she walked past him to the door. "Keep your eyes open. Eventually you're going to know what I'm talking about."

Ronnie leered in her direction. "Thanks. I think I can take care of myself."

Tiffany didn't need to know Chelsea hadn't even been returning his calls until today, or that now that they had spoken, he'd be her escort for the big award dinner. No sense in getting Tiffany any more riled up than she seemed to be.

CHAPTER TWENTY

Ronnie was so stoked from talking to Chelsea that he worked straight through the night. The first time he checked the clock it was four in the morning. He'd almost finished what he thought would take him two days, so he grabbed a Dew from the refrigerator and kept at it until he heard the paper hit the stoop.

Rorschach must have heard it too, because he raced Ronnie to the door. When Ronnie opened it, Rorschach lunged for the paper and ran with the paper in his mouth straight to the kitchen. His tail thumped against the pantry.

Ronnie tossed Rorschach his treat and carried the paper back to his office.

Chelsea had the cover story, again. "You go girl," Ronnie said out loud.

He'd hoped she'd call, but every time the phone rang it wasn't her. Finally, he tried to call her but it went to her voice mail. Every hour he tried to call but got no answer. She must have been out on assignment. When he finally reached her it was after dark and she was on her way to another story. She couldn't talk.

***

Chelsea pressed END on her phone and grabbed her keys, wasting no time getting to the next scoop. Hallie had come through again. This friendship with Hallie was golden.

Two people had just encountered a near miss with a spiked pumpkin. Emma Cleaver and Spade Rollings had called the police after they answered a knock at the door and a pumpkin was hurled at them. Clearly shaken from the near miss, they hadn't even noticed that two spikes had been pushed into the rind. The police were the ones who'd noticed that.

When Chelsea got to the scene, Hallie waved her through.

Hallie said, "This town is getting weirder by the day, isn't it?"

"You got that right." Chelsea scratched the back of her head as she glanced over Hallie's shoulder, looking at the busted spiky pumpkin parts all over the place. "Can you get fingerprints off a slimy piece of busted pumpkin?"

"We've gotten them off stranger things," admitted the Detective.

Emma's cat huddled in a corner, still trembling.

"Where are the folks who had this hurled at them?" Chelsea asked Hallie.

Hallie pointed toward the kitchen where Emma and Spade sat giving their recollection of the events to an officer.

"That must have been a huge pumpkin. Look at all that. It would make a lot of pies, wouldn't it?" Chelsea joked.

Hallie stared at her. "This really isn't time for jokes, Chelsea. This could have been very serious. Someone with a pretty sick mind planted those spikes in that pumpkin. That took some planning."

"Sorry. You're right." Chelsea held back any further comment.

"They say they didn't see anyone, but they did hear a flute off in the distance," Hallie said.

"A flute?"

"Isn't that the weirdest thing you've ever heard? I always liked the Pied Piper story but this puts a whole new evil spin on it." Hallie shrugged.

Chelsea tried to hide her excitement over the story. *With Halloween around the corner, people will gobble this story up.* She chuckled at her own pun – gobble – goblins – Halloween.

Hallie backed up and gave her another look. "You're really diggin' this, aren't you? You're one twisted sister."

A nearby police officer shot them both an accusing look.

"Can I talk to them now?" asked Chelsea.

"Sure. We're about done here." Hallie tucked her notepad in her pocket and gathered her things.

"Thanks for calling me. Want to meet for coffee in an hour at that coffee shop by the precinct?"

Hallie nodded. "Yeah, thanks. That'll be good."

Chelsea went into the kitchen and sat in one of the cheap metal chairs across from the couple and began asking her own questions. The young couple quickly pushed their nerves aside when they realized they were going to be part of a news story. Slade wanted to be sure she knew he was a drummer, and Chelsea was happy to include it in the story.

Anything to keep that human angle the editor wants, she thought as she tucked her notebook back into her purse.

***

Chelsea drove over to the coffee shop. The detective and one of her partners were already sitting in a booth with coffee and homemade apple pie. Hallie waved her hand toward the guy behind the counter. "Another?"

The waiter walked around the counter with another plate of pie and a cup of coffee.

"Thanks." Chelsea beamed.

"You sure are full of energy," said Hallie.

"I think I stumbled onto something." Chelsea rubbed her hands together in excitement and then pulled her notebook out of her purse. "I have a feeling some of these crimes are connected. I've been reviewing my notes."

"What do you have there?" Hallie tugged the notebook out of Chelsea's hands and started reading her notes. "How did I miss that?"

Chelsea shrugged. "I don't know."

"I'll be." Hallie Davison reread the notes.

Chelsea explained to them both. "When that Slade guy mentioned that he'd had a fear of pumpkins as a kid, I almost laughed. I guess he could see it in my face because he started explaining how it wasn't all that unusual. Kind of like when people are afraid of clowns. He said his inkBLOT report mentioned that similarity. Well, that's when it all clicked."

Hallie nodded. "That professor had an inkBLOT printout on his bulletin board in his apartment. I remember that now."

"And I noticed one at the peanut guy's place, too. Did I mention that at the time?" Chelsea shrugged. "Probably not. It didn't seem important then."

Chelsea shoveled in her last bite of pie, and swigged down her coffee. "I've got to get over to the paper and turn this story in."

She left Hallie and her partner sitting with the wheels in their heads spinning.

THE DAILY BANNER
PIED PIPER PUMPKIN ASSAULT
Chelsea Pressman
VIRGINIA BEACH, VA
Emma Smith purchased the perfect pumpkin for Halloween. She'd planned to use it as a decoration,

carve an eerie Jack-O-Lantern on All Hallows' Eve and then bake a pie and toast the seeds—using the bright orange fruit to its full fall potential.

She hadn't, however, expected someone to use her own pumpkin to nearly knock her unconscious. On Thursday night, Emma was at home at 105 Collinswood Street with her friend, Spade Rollings, when there was a knock at the door. When Spade opened the door, the pumpkin came hurtling toward them, grazing Spade and knocking Emma to the ground like a bowling pin.

Although the person responsible for this attempted assault had fled, flute music was heard in a gradually fading tone as the attacker fled the scene. It was like Halloween and a twisted version of the Pied Piper nursery rhyme all rolled into one.

Upon further investigation, amidst the seeds and pumpkin pulp, sharp rods were found. Not just a common Halloween trick, but a dangerous and potentially deadly deed.

Anyone with information on this bizarre incident please call 1-555-LOCK-U-UP.

Down at the news department, the strange stories kept flooding in.

Chelsea took the call at the news desk from Trent Sniders and set up an appointment for him to come in. It had been a while since she'd seen him but if it meant a good story, she was game. Besides, she'd felt bad because it seemed that ever since they ran the story she did on his appliance warehouse business in the Daily Leisure section, he'd had a run of bad luck. Brand new appliances were catching on fire. Now he was getting harassing phone calls accusing him of endangering people on purpose. The local television station was riding that story for all it was worth. Besides he was hot.

Trent had called the police about the harassment because it was starting to freak him out but they weren't taking him seriously.

Chelsea couldn't say no to him. They'd almost been an item there for a little while after she'd built him up as the Appliance King in her series of articles on him and his business. Now she couldn't deny it was a bit of a kick to watch his kingdom crumble, and see him squirm.

He showed up on time for the appointment. At least he was always punctual.

"Can you help me?" asked Trent, as he sat across the table from her in one of the small conference rooms.

"Can I?" she repeated. "Yeah, I probably could. Will I – now that's the real question."

Trent reached across and put his hand on her arm. "Come on, Chels. I don't know where else to turn. I didn't mean to hurt you."

She leaned back in her chair and crossed her arms. "You should have thought about that a long time ago."

"You don't want to help me. Fine. I guess I deserve that."

"I'll think about it. That's all I can promise." Her foot twitched.

Trent got up. "I deserve a break." He slumped a little as he walked toward the door.

"Trent," Chelsea called after him. "Don't worry. I'll probably write the story. Give me a couple hours to research some stuff. Stick by your phone at home. I'll call later."

"Thanks."

Chelsea stood up. "Oh, and before you go. Would you mind taking a mailer over to the Fed Ex office so it goes tonight? I missed the pickup."

"That's clear across town in the opposite direction." He caught the look in her eye. "Fine. Fine. Go get it."

***

Trent went to the Fed Ex office and dropped off the mailer. It had taken him more than an hour to get back across town. As soon as he got home he went online to see if he could figure out what was causing the fires on those appliances. If Chelsea was smart enough to research, he was too. He'd seen a couple of myths about that kind of stuff before. After three hours straight, he shoved away from the computer. Bloodshot eyes told the tale of too many late nights worrying over all of this. He really hoped Chelsea would help him. He didn't know who else to turn to. *Call, Chelsea, please call.*

His cell phone rang, startling him.

"Hello?" But no one was on the other end of the line.

"Hello. Who's there?" Nothing but silence. "Chels?" Trent's heart pounded. He swiped at the sweat that formed on his top lip. *Maybe she'd changed her mind.*

He started to hang up, but something made him hang on a bit longer to listen closer. It started as a titter. Then the caller burst in raucous laughter.

"Who is this?" Trent's voice rose. "Chelsea? Is that you? Are you messing with me? It's not funny." He lifted a blind and looked out the window.

Then more laughter. He hung up. The phone rang again and he picked it up but didn't say anything. Insane laughter again. His pulse raced. The image of a disheveled madman came to mind. He pressed End and laid the phone down again with a loud snap.

The next fifteen minutes produced more irritating laughing calls. Teasing, Taunting.

Why bother calling the cops? They don't believe me anyway. Thinking that a cup of noodles would help soothe his nerves, he turned to the stove. He flipped the knob, but the pilot didn't ignite. The phone rang again. He grabbed a lighter out of the junk drawer next to the stove to light the pilot. Trent tried to resist but what if it was Chelsea? He answered and there it was again. Laughter. Irritating and taunting.

"Stop torturing me. Stop calling here."

He heard a muffled giggle as he ended the call.

He took a step back with the lighter still in his hand. The phone call had strangely ignited the stove. The memory of a shrill laugh ran through his mind seconds before the flames overtook the whole room with him in it.

***

Hallie called Chelsea about the explosion. With the address clutched in her hand, Chelsea raced to the scene. The fire truck passed her as she pulled to the curb. Hallie met her outside of the house.

"Thanks for calling," said Chelsea.

"I thought you could use the story." Hallie shoved her notebook into Chelsea's hand. "Take a read. I need to go chat with someone. I'll be right back."

Hallie rushed off and Chelsea began scanning the notes.

- *Victim at home.*
- *Male. Sole proprietor. Single.*
- *Reports of harassment recently filed.*
- *Good neighbor.*
- *No one saw any visitors or heard anything prior to event.*
- *Victim found with lighter in his right hand / cell phone in his left.*
- *Check into reports that some cell phones actually ignite stoves due to some malfunction or faulty mechanism.*
- *Check with detective for any correlation between phone calls and the explosion.*
- *Smoke alarm had no battery.*
- *Study itemized list of phone calls made at that time period. Police called the number. It was one of those disposable cell jobs.*

Chelsea saw Hallie crossing the yard and heading to the house. She jogged up to her and went inside with her.

The whole place smelled. The smoke burned her nose. She instinctively covered her nose and squinted as she and Hallie walked toward the kitchen.

Trent's kitchen was burnt to a crisp.

Char and soot were everywhere.

The stench of burned flesh had been almost unbearable when they got close to this part of the house. He'd been caught in the inferno. Not a simple smoldering stove fire like the others that had tormented his business lately, causing sales to dip because of the faulty appliances. This one had raged out of control.

Flesh, food, insulation, all melded into a thick gross smell that made her gag. Forensics people had been nearby, getting fingerprints and examining Trent's telephone. Another one had studied the make and model of the stove. Once white, now gray and black. Her mood felt strangely the same way.

THE DAILY BANNER
WHAT A GAS

Chelsea Pressman

VIRGINIA BEACH, VA

Investigators found that while the dials on Trent Sniders stove were not turned in the on position, something triggered it to ignite. A gas leak caused an explosion that took the life of the local man known to many in the area as the Appliance King.

Trent had been an accountant at Tremble and Tremble for twelve years before becoming the Appliance King.

A memorial service is planned for Trent on Friday night at 7 p. m. at Stuart Funeral Home. Anyone with information about this incident is encouraged to call 1-555-LOCK-U-UP.

CHAPTER TWENTY-ONE

Tiffany read Chelsea's latest article with interest. She didn't care what Ronnie thought or if she hurt his feelings at this point. He was her best friend and this nagging feeling about Chelsea wasn't going away. No one fell into this many newsworthy crimes in this short a time span. She was going to prove or disprove that, once and for all.

Tiffany regretted lying to Ronnie about being busy, but this was for his own good. She started a search on the internet of all the stories Chelsea had covered since that Boa Constricted story. She printed each one and thumb tacked them to her bulletin board in a row. Each headline was a little more provocative than the last.

She read them all, trying to glean the tiniest details and understand the timing of the events. She logged each story date and the date of occurrence in a spreadsheet, and then added a column for the date the article actually ran and its location in the paper. A column to the right calculated the number of days from start to finish. The Gantt timeline showed where there were gaps or overlap.

Tiffany logged all the times she's been aware that Chelsea and Ronnie had gotten together, including that stupid auction. *A thousand bucks. That still makes me crazy.*

"My, my you've been busy Ms. Pressman." Tiffany tapped her pen against her lips. She pulled her hair up into a ponytail and then twisted it, securing it with the ink pen. She pondered her best course of action to fill in the details. Hours of online research helped her prepare a pretty detailed plan on how to investigate and analyze events. That and a couple CASTLE episodes. She'd even found a resource to get a GPS to track everywhere Chelsea went, and tiny cameras if she needed to go that far to prove her point.

For now, she needed to know how many of these incidents were truly coincidence.

Tiffany pulled her feet under her, Indian-style, on her bed and kept working her magic on her laptop. She started a matrix of every key player in each story and then started Googling for any interactions between those people and Chelsea, or any connections between the people involved.

After two hours of Googling and reading articles and posts, Tiffany wasn't any closer than when she started. There had to be a connection somewhere.

She'd driven her mom to work in the morning so she could use the car. Maybe she should check out a couple of these so called incidents herself and see if she uncovered anything new.

Tiffany grabbed her purse and keys and headed over to the Appliance King warehouse. It was only a couple of miles away, and as good a place as any to start.

Electric glass doors automatically opened as she approached the Appliance King's warehouse. Washers, dryers, stoves and refrigerators were stacked on huge metal shelves to the ceiling. A forklift sounded off as it raised its lift to satisfy another order. The place was hopping.

A huge bouquet of flowers sat on the counter at customer service. Tiffany leaned in to read the note. It was a sympathy card for the passing of Trent Sniders.

The short red-haired woman behind the counter peered above her glasses in her direction and then walked over to help her.

"Hi," Tiffany said in her most business-like tone. "I'm interested in purchasing a stove, but I'm afraid I'm not sure where to start. All I have is this style and model number from my husband." Tiffany pushed the legal pad page toward the woman.

The woman pulled her glasses down and read it. She was quiet for a moment. "Oh honey, I'm sorry but we aren't carrying this model anymore. Didn't you hear?"

"Hear? About what?"

The woman leaned forward on her chubby arms and spoke just above a whisper. "Honey, the owner of this place. He went up in smoke, an explosion. We've pulled that entire model right off the sales floor until we can figure out what happened."

"Lord, no. I'm so sorry. I didn't know." Tiffany feigned ignorance.

"It was in the paper and everything. Plus, I just found this article about something similar happening over in Great Britain last year." The woman handed an article to Tiffany.

Tiffany glanced over the article that was frighteningly similar. The story mentioned three connected incidents with the same model and make that had exploded at the same time in different locations. The theory was a cell phone call ignited the disaster.

"Looks like this one in Great Britain was intentional"

The red head nodded. Her painted on eyebrows shooting up in an exaggerated way.

"You don't think the explosion that killed your boss was an accident?"

"Well, he did break up with that young little hot-head not all that long ago."

"Oh, really? Who was that?"

"Never got her name. I tried to stay out of Trent's business. She came in a few weeks ago though. They were fighting. Loud and nasty, too. She was a nasty little thing. Pretty is as pretty does, you know. And snobby if you want my opinion."

Tiffany pulled the picture of Chelsea out of her purse. "This wouldn't happen to be her would it?"

The redheaded woman's eyes popped wide. "Yes! That's the little snip." She tapped the picture with a bright red manicured nail. "I wouldn't be surprised if she was behind it in some way." She looked over her shoulder and then back at Tiffany. "Between us girls, I never liked that little lady at all."

"Between us, I'm not her biggest fan either. Sorry I got you all sidetracked. I guess I'll have to get my husband to come with me and pick out another model stove."

"Oh honey, I'm the one who got you all wrapped up in the gossip. You bring that husband of yours and see me. I'll hook you up."

The lady handed Tiffany a card, and Tiffany took that as her opportunity to get the heck out of there.

Next stop, the university.

Tiffany asked around and even tracked down a couple of the students, but no one there remembered anything helpful. She tapped the steering wheel as she drove, trying to think of another way to connect the dots.

While researching Chelsea's earlier work, Tiffany had come across the article Chelsea had written about the tattoo shop. Maybe Cat could help her crosscheck names against King's customers.

Tiffany pulled the huge Buick in front of the tattoo shop. Thank goodness it was a weekday and not many people down at the oceanfront. She'd never have been able to parallel park this boat. Tiffany saw Cat walking out to meet her as she got out of the car. She must have seen her tweet.

"I thought that was you," said Cat. "Saw the tweet. What's up?"

"Hey. I was hoping you could help me with something," Tiffany said, crossing her fingers. "I think a friend of mine might be in over his head."

"What's up?"

"You know Ronnie Wright, right?"

"Yeah. RUU from inkBLOT. I know him. Nice guy. Hot, too."

Why is everyone lusting after my Ronnie all of the sudden?

Tiffany shook the frustration and continued. "Yeah. I know, well, here's the thing. I think Chelsea Pressman is up to something with all those stories she's been writing, but I can't seem to get Ronnie to see her for who she really is."

"You like him, don't you?"

Tiffany cast her glance away. "Yeah, but that's not the point."

"Yeah it is. I'm in. He's a nice guy. What do you need me to do?"

Tiffany pulled out a printout of the matrix spreadsheet with all the information from Chelsea's stories. Victims, places, all of that. "Can you crosscheck these victims to your Dad's customer database?"

"Sure. Won't take but a minute. I have it all computerized. Come on in."

They went inside and Cat led Tiffany to the back room since they really weren't supposed to be in the shop, being underage and all.

Cat slid behind her dad's desk and clicked on the customer button. A quick search only brought up and validated what Tiffany already knew. That Ronnie got a tattoo on September 23rd.

"Are you sure?" asked Tiffany.

Cat nodded. "That's all I see. Are you sure Chelsea is up to something? I mean, I don't mean to hurt your feelings, but maybe she's just working really hard. She seemed like a real go-getter when she did that story on the shop. Maybe you're a little jealous over her relationship with Ronnie. He *is* hot."

Tiffany took a deep breath to compose herself. Then she shook her head. "It's not just that. I'm missing something."

Cat spun the chair around. "Okay, well what made you think she was up to no good?"

"I don't know. Everything." Tiffany crossed her arms and looked down. "Okay, so I admit I might be a little jealous, but I swear she stole a memory stick off my desk a few weeks ago. It was gone right after she'd been there and then back after another one of her frates with Ronnie. I also found a connection between her and that guy that died in the explosion. It wasn't mentioned in the article."

Cat pushed her black hair behind her ear. "What's on those memory sticks?"

"She couldn't get anything off of it. I encrypt those myself. I'm really careful about the inkBLOT data. There is way too much personal information in those files to let it get out. I mean, Ronnie is using it for his research. It's totally confidential. His studies may change our future, but in the wrong hands it could be disastrous. That wouldn't be good."

Cat raised a brow. "Have you looked at those files for anything on Miss Chelsea?"

"No. I hate to break that confidence." Suddenly, Tiffany jumped up from the stool next to Cat. "I gotta go. I need to check something. What if she was trying to make a story out of Ronnie? With the wrong twist, she could ruin him!"

Tiffany pushed past Cat, waving to King as she rushed out the front door.

Cat ran out to the curb. "Keep me posted. Call me if I can help."

CHAPTER TWENTY-TWO

Ronnie adjusted his tie and positioned the Windsor knot. It had been a perfect week. **ink!** would go live in just two days and tonight he'd be attending the Mid-Atlantic News Awards dinner with the prettiest girl he'd ever met.

He splashed aftershave into his palms, rubbed them briskly and slapped some on his face.

"Now or never," he said.

He rubbed Rorschach's head, and grabbed a rawhide out of the cookie cabinet for him. He tossed it in the dog's direction, grabbed his keys and headed out the door.

Traffic was light for a Saturday evening. He pulled onto the boulevard so he could stop by the florist and pick up the flowers he'd ordered for Chelsea. Win or lose, he had every intention of making this a special and memorable night for her.

The florist already had the flowers pulled from the cooler when Ronnie walked in. They'd arranged the bunch of Calla lilies and palm leaves into an elegant bouquet with a flowing satin ribbon. He'd selected the Calla's because they stand for beauty and the palm leaves for success. He knew how important success was to Chelsea. He paid for the flowers and headed back to his car. He was right on schedule. He didn't have time to spare, but he'd get there on time.

Ronnie got in his Mustang and laid the flowers carefully across the passenger seat.

With one quick turn he was back on to the boulevard.

He barely cleared the stop light as it turned yellow, but he was cutting close on time.

As he glanced in his rearview mirror, flashing blue lights bounced in the reflection.

"No way." Ronnie slapped the steering wheel. "Dude, it was yellow!" The lights pulsated like veins in his forehead. He prayed the cruiser would pull around him and move on, but no such luck.

Woop, woop.

Crap. Looking in his rearview mirror, he knew he was busted.

Ronnie pulled his car onto the feeder road and rolled down the window.

The police officer got out of the patrol car and took his sweet time walking up to the driver side door of the black Mustang. Ronnie fumbled through the glove compartment, looking for his registration card.

The advancing officer was getting close. Finally, he found it sandwiched in the pages of his owner's manual. This would be his first ticket. He looked up at the cop who wore no expression at all.

Maybe if I say something funny, it'll lighten the mood. "It's a beautiful day in the neighborhood," Ronnie said hoping for the best.

"Don't tell me. You're Mister Rogers?" The officer laughed at his own joke as he plucked the license and registration from Ronnie's hands.

Oh great. He might be laughing but I'm not. I'm really screwed now.

Ronnie fidgeted with the seatbelt as he waited for the man to speak again.

"You need to replace your right tail light," was all the officer said.

Phew, is that all? Hopefully, that would mean a warning. "Thank you, Sir. I didn't know. I'll get it taken care of right away."

The officer peered into the car. "Looks like you've got a big date tonight."

Ronnie smiled as he glanced over at the bouquet on the passenger's seat. "Yes sir."

The curmudgeonly old guy finally broke into a big smile. "Don't worry. This will just take a moment." He walked back toward the police car, and Ronnie slid down in the driver seat in an attempt to avoid the bouncing blue lights blinding him. He let out a long sigh of relief.

What he didn't know, was that at his apartment across town, things weren't looking nearly as bright.

***

Tiffany pulled up in front of Ronnie's apartment, disappointed that he had already left. As she approached the stairs to the second level, she noticed a man and a woman knocking on Ronnie's door.

"He's not there," she hollered up the stairwell.

The woman turned and stepped away from the door. "Do you live here?"

Tiffany shook her head. "No. I work here. Are you looking for Ronnie?"

The woman nodded.

Tiffany noticed the pistol on the man's hip that stood behind the woman.

"I'm Detective Davison," she said, flashing a gold badge.

"Is something wrong?" Tiffany looked at them both, neither cast a hopeful smile in return. She almost swallowed her gum on the inhale. "Oh no! Ronnie's okay, isn't he?"

"He's fine."

"His mom?" Tiffany's mind started spewing possibilities like a volcano.

"I'm sorry I didn't mean to alarm you. We have a warrant for Mr. Wright, and access to his apartment."

Tiffany looked puzzled. "A warrant? Is this a joke? Like one of those TV shows?" The look on their faces made it clear it wasn't a joke. "There must be some mistake. I mean, Ronnie is like the most decent guy I know."

The officer raised a brow. "Do you know where he is?"

"You must have just missed him. He's got a date. Some news awards ceremony down at the Cavalier Hotel," said Tiffany.

"Can you let us in?" Detective Davison handed the warrant to Tiffany, and gave the other detective the orders to head to the Cavalier to pick up Ronnie.

"I don't know if I should. Can I call my mom to come over? We live nearby." Tiffany's heart was pounding so hard she could barely hear her own words over the throbbing.

CHAPTER TWENTY-THREE

By the time Tiffany's mom got to the apartment, Detective Hallie Davison had three cars on back-up to help her sort out the situation. Tiffany and her mom stood to the side as the detective unleashed her team on Ronnie's apartment. Not thirty seconds later a rookie jogged up to the detective, anxious to please.

"What do you think of this?" he asked shoving a green three ring binder toward his boss.

Hallie flipped through it with interest. "Good work, Busby. Where'd you find this?"

"It was under the chair in the living room."

Tiffany interjected. "That's not Ronnie's."

"Is it yours?" The detective raised a brow.

"No, but Ronnie doesn't do much on paper and he never uses binders or anything like that."

Tiffany's mom put a protective hand on her daughter's shoulder.

The detective flipped through the pages. "It lists people's names, job and work addresses and inkblot interpretations. What's the obsession with all the inkblots?"

Tiffany's mom interjected. "I know it might seem a little odd, but the kid is truly brilliant. He's been studying that type of psychology for as long as I've known him."

"Interesting." The detective's brows pulled together as she read on. "There's some very personal information in here." The detective handed the binder to Tiffany. "Look familiar?"

Tiffany's jaw dropped open. "Well, yeah, it's our report, but I'm telling you. We never print that stuff out. Never! Everything we do is online or on encrypted memory sticks. The only two people that have access to this are me and Ronnie."

"I see." Detective Davison straightened. "How much do you really know about this young man?"

Tiffany said, "We're *best* friends."

Tiffany's mom nodded. "He's a good boy. He's smart and he hasn't had an easy time of it. He had every right to turn out bad, but he didn't. He's a good kid. Really. I can vouch for him."

"What do you mean he's had a tough time of it?" Detective Hallie Davison looked eager. She jotted down notes, and Tiffany's mom nervously looked around, regretting opening her mouth.

Tiffany crossed her arms and leaned into her mom's shoulder.

Detective Davison let out a deep breath. "Do you know where Ronnie's mother is? The lease is in her name, but we can't locate her."

"What's this all about?" asked Tiffany's mom.

"We have reason to believe Ronnie Wright may be behind a string of crimes, including one that resulted in a death. His website, inkBLOT, seems to be the common denominator."

"NO. No way," Tiffany cried out. "Mom!"

"Calm down, honey. Detective, there's obviously been a mistake. My daughter and Ronnie have put their heart and soul into that company, and they've done very well, but Ronnie would never do anything to hurt anyone. He's got a heart of gold, and he's using that data to prove psychological theories. I'm telling you he's a good kid. You're wrong."

"Hmm. Well, the neighbors are always surprised in cases like this." Detective Davison was feeling this string of cases coming to closure in a hurry and she was glad of that. This town had never had so much action. And although it had been exciting, she didn't like someone being up to no good in her territory. Thank goodness, Chelsea had pointed out the inkBLOT connection. She wondered how long it would have taken her to make the connection without Chelsea. It hadn't taken long to check out the lead. All the victims had visited and participated in the inkBLOT survey at some point. It was the only common denominator.

It didn't matter now though. Everything was coming together, and the chief would be happy, too.

Busby rushed up, excusing himself for the interruption. "Found something else. An address book. It's kind of girly looking. Maybe he's in touch with his feminine side. It was under his mattress."

"That is NOT funny." Tiffany glared in his direction.

Detective Davison put the address book in a sack and scribbled a code across it, to cross check it to the log she was creating. She eyed Tiffany. "Can you tell me when this report was run?"

"Yeah." Tiffany looked at the report code in the top right corner. "This was a couple of weeks ago. I don't know how anyone could have gotten this. The few things we do print, we shred immediately. I don't get it."

"But you can confirm that this is a report from the system owned by Ronnie Wright. Is that true?"

"Well, yeah, but it's not that simple. I keep telling you." Tiffany's brows furrowed. She glanced at her mom who gave her a nod. "Yes. It's from our database."

Detective Davison nodded slowly. "I'm sorry, dear. Sometimes we don't know people as well as we think we do. The names on this report–they list someone from every one of the cases we've been working for the past month. We've also placed him near the scene of at least one of the incidents."

Tears welled in Tiffany's eyes.

Tiffany's mom held her daughter. "Excuse me, Detective. May I take my daughter home?"

Detective Hallie Davison nodded. "I'm sorry. I can see this is hard for you. I've got your information. I'll check back with you later if I have any other questions."

Tiffany and her mom turned and left the detective and her crew to the apartment.

***

Just as the officer was about to hand Ronnie his improper equipment ticket, his police radio squelched and took his attention away from Ronnie.

The officer stepped back and turned his back to listen closer.

Ronnie sat there wishing he'd hurry the heck up. Chelsea would kill him if he was late picking her up for the banquet.

The officer called for the dispatch to repeat the last call.

Details of the APB came back across the radio and the officer compared the information to the driver's license still in his hand. The suspect was the same one he had detained right in front of him. The one getting ready to pull away.

The officer stepped back up to the car and hooked a finger in Ronnie's direction.

"I need you to step out of the car, Mr. Wright."

"What?" His heart climbed somewhere up in his throat. Trembling, he began to pull his keys from the ignition.

"Hands where I can see them, Sir," the cop shouted.

Why is this guy suddenly going all Bad Cop on me?

"Hands where I can see them. Okay left hand out the window. That's right. Now undo the seatbelt with your right hand."

Ronnie followed the instructions carefully. Like a bad Simon Says game, he prayed he wouldn't screw up and get shot in the process.

The policeman pulled the driver's side door open and ordered him out of the car, his gun steadied at the ready. "Step out of the car."

Ronnie dipped his head and slid out of the driver's seat with both hands out in front of him.

"Put your hands over your head."

The officer spun him and pressed him up against the side of the car. Ronnie's throat constricted and the buildings and surrounding traffic seemed to swirl and go silent.

"What's going on?" Ronnie asked.

Frisking him, the cop had no idea why he was bringing him in except it was an APB for armed and dangerous. Looks. They could be deceiving. This was the part of his job he hated. He'd seemed like a nice enough kid. Sometimes the nicer looking guys did some of the most heinous crimes.

"What is this about?" Ronnie took a deep breath, hoping to shake the bad dream feeling that was pushing down on him.

"You tell me."

"You said a broken tail light."

"An APB just came out for you."

"For me? This is a mistake." Ronnie's went up an octave.

"Go ahead and act innocent. They always do. The suspect always knows, no matter how innocent they act."

The officer put a hand on top of Ronnie's head and pushed him into the backseat of the cruiser.

Ronnie slumped in the back seat. His mind reeled. *Had they found out? Did they know that his mom had left, that he'd forged her name for so long he could do it without thinking?* He'd thought now that he'd turned eighteen he was in the clear.

The officer got behind the wheel and looked at Ronnie in his rearview mirror.

Ronnie's mind slipped away momentarily from the problem at hand. *The flowers will wilt. Chelsea will be mad.* Such a trivial worry in light of things, a form of mental escapism. He was a master at that.

The ride to the police station was long and quiet.

The officer was glad there was a separation between himself and the young man in the backseat. He couldn't see anything on this guy's face that resembled guilt or remorse, but you never knew what was behind someone's motivation. He looked again.

All the officer saw was confusion and at that particular moment, he almost felt sorry for Ronnie.

CHAPTER TWENTY-FOUR

Tiffany sprawled across her bed hugging her dampened pillow, wet from the tears she'd shed for Ronnie. He'd been allowed one phone call from jail and he'd called her. That had to mean something. He didn't know much, so with her mom on the other extension, they filled in the blanks where they could for him.

Mom had gone to the police station to find out if there was a way to post bail, and see what she could do to help.

Tiffany glanced at the clock again. The minutes were creeping by.

That detective acted so convinced that Ronnie was guilty. That is SO wrong.

But what if…

Could Ronnie have done something like that?

There's no way they can convince me that could be true.

She turned over and held the pillow against her.

Chelsea's got to be behind this somehow. I knew she was bad news. Did Ronnie give the information to her? He seemed so impressed by her front page stories. Maybe he was trying to help her.

Tiffany stared at the articles she'd plastered on her wall. She'd almost told the detective her suspicions about Chelsea Pressman, but held her tongue after realizing how confident the detective seemed. She hadn't wanted to make things worse.

She needed proof. That's what she had to have in order to get their attention. Anything less would just look like she was trying to help a friend.

Tiffany got up and pulled the Dictionary off the third row on her bookshelf.

Not just any Dictionary, but the one she and Ronnie hollowed out to store offsite system and data backup for inkBLOT. They came up with the backup plan after his apartment flooded and nearly wiped out their backups. So far, the police hadn't messed with the inkBLOT servers, but if they did she'd have to work fast to keep the system up.

Tiffany fired up her laptop. She popped the thumb drive in the USB port, entered her password and pulled in the data. The encryption service kicked in and finally the file was open. She started scanning through the data—searching for any clue.

CHELSEAPRESSMAN

"I knew it!" *She DID take the inkBLOT quiz!* Tiffany checked the date. Chelsea took the quiz right after she met Ronnie. Why hadn't Ronnie mentioned it? Okay, it didn't really prove anything, but enough coincidences were seldom a coincidence. It was somewhere to start.

Tiffany ran the deep analysis algorithm against Chelsea's data points, then scrolled through the results. *This chick is one self-centered twisted sister.*

Too many of Chelsea's responses seemed evasive. She was hiding something. Too bad she hadn't learned how to use the new methodology Ronnie had put together. She'd be able to know how many of the answers were suspect. Some images revealed wicked thoughts but on the flip side, many of them were also angelic. It looked to her that Chelsea was trying to game the information.

It's as though two different people took this test. Chelsea's hiding something. Does she have a split personality, or is she just a big fat liar?

Tiffany took a deep breath. She'd never messed with Ronnie's cross-hatching pipeline, but she was desperate. It only took her three times to guess his password. This program did some cool stuff that matched IP addresses and special cookies that linked entries that were made from the same computer and possibly the same people.

Tiffany scribbled some notes on a small pad, then pulled all the exception data for the same periods when Chelsea was on the site.

The cross-hatching pipeline finally spewed out several sessions. It wasn't uncommon for people to log in as themselves and fake answers, and then make up a pseudonym to see what the system had to say about their true feelings. She and Ronnie were able to usually tie those records back together.

Bingo.

She had it now.

Sure enough, following each of Chelsea's sessions in her own name, a second on the same IP address came through. *Why hasn't Ronnie checked this out? Is he that hung up on this girl? His algorithms are usually right, too. This girl is trouble.*

Tiffany dialed Cat's cell phone.

"You're not going to believe what's going on," said Tiffany when Cat answered the phone.

"What?" Cat's voice went up two octaves. "Are you okay?"

"They arrested Ronnie. They think he committed those crimes Chelsea wrote about."

"No way."

"Way. I told them he'd never do that, but I can't prove it. I've *got* to find a way to clear his name."

"How are you going to do that?"

"I have no idea, but I thought you might help me. I thought we could brainstorm."

"Shoot."

"Remember the pumpkin incident in the paper the other day? There was something about a flute being played as the assailant ran away. I wonder if I can find out who may have owned that flute. They found it. It was really expensive. Don't you know the guy who owns that music shop in town?"

"I do. Want me to go with you?"

"I don't want to waste any time coming to get you. Can you call and let him know I'm coming and that I need his help?"

"You got it," said Cat.

Driving to the store, Tiffany rehearsed what she'd say.

I've got to ask the right questions. It's not like I'm a policewoman or detective. I'm just a friend following a hunch. We'll see where that takes me.

The shop owner had already talked to Cat when Tiffany walked through the door.

"Cat said you need my help. Something about a fancy flute?" said the owner.

"Yeah. That flute the police found after the incident across town last week. You probably read about it. Some people almost got whacked with a pumpkin that night?"

"I remember that," he nodded.

She pulled out the article. "See here. They talk about a flute. It seemed pretty special. I was hoping you might know who a flute like that might belong to around here."

He reached behind him and pulled a folder out. He shuffled through it and then pushed a picture toward Tiffany.

"Who's this?" she asked the music shop manager.

"He's one of our best customers, Joe Griggs is his name." The shop owner pulled an article down from the wall. "Here's an article about him. He's the only guy around here that would have a pricey piece like that."

"Is that so?" Tiffany studied the picture. "Interesting. He looks like he could pick up a chair and hurl it at you. He doesn't really look the classical music type." She couldn't remember when she'd ever seen such a muscular looking musician. Those music types weren't really known for hanging out in a gym in their spare time.

She started to read the article, but the byline caught her attention first. Written by Chelsea Pressman.

The store owner laughed. "I'd have to agree with you on that. He's an odd duck, but he's a real talent."

"And he's local?" Tiffany cut her eyes at the shop owner.

"Yeah. I think it said that in the article." The manager's eyes narrowed a bit, probably wondering where Tiffany was going with this information. "Why do you want to know?"

Ignoring the question, Tiffany jotted down the name and once the owner left her side, she slipped out of the store and went back to the car. She locked the doors, suddenly feeling a little nervous about the kind of people she was encountering.

She pulled out her phone and texted Cat.

::Cat: I need your help. Can you get away?::

She waited, hoping Cat would be watching for the text and respond.

Becoming impatient she texted Cat again.

::Think RUU is over his head. Need ur help::

Cat texted her back.

::Meet me @ the shop::

Tiffany pulled away from the Music shop and headed over to 17th street to see Cat.

Walking into the tattoo parlor, Tiffany felt a wave of nausea. *Was that burning flesh she smelled?* It had to be her imagination they weren't branding people, well not like that anyways. The photos of tattooed bodies caught her attention though. Ronnie had always been against getting them. What could have possessed him to have one put on him? *Must be that woman*, Tiffany thought. *She's not worth the time of day.*

King completed the finishing details on a guy who was getting a cross tattooed on his right arm. Looking over his shoulder at her, he waved hello with his free hand.

Tiffany waved back while she tried not to stare at the customers as she waited on Cat.

One of the other tattoo artists came over and started chatting. "What can I do you out of?" he asked.

"I'm waiting on Cat, but while I've got you I'm also looking for information on Chelsea Pressman. She did a story on this shop a while back. Did you talk to her?"

"The boss did the interview, but I talked to her while she was waiting. What do you want to know?" He grinned and gave her a wink. "I could probably guess about her measurements."

Perv. "Okay, she's hot. I get it. Can we get past the looks?" Tiffany said. "Did you notice anything unusual about her? Did she seem cold or calculating to you?"

"Like I said, when you think about her measurements, she can't possibly be cold. I think hot would be more like it. I loved every minute of our interview that day."

"Well, I can see that I'm getting nowhere fast with you," Tiffany said. "Thanks. I'll just wait for Cat over here."

"Okay, all kidding aside. Yes, now that you mention it, she did have an aloofness about her that was kind of freaky. She asked a lot of questions about people who came in here. She came back a couple of weeks ago, too. King wasn't here. She was asking questions about his partner on that new **ink!** website. You hear about that? It's going to be released soon.

It's going to be the hottest online thrill to hit the web in a long while."

"Yeah. So she asked questions about Ronnie?"

"Yeah. The kid that owns inkBLOT. You know him?" The tattoo artist looked impressed.

"Yeah, I know him very well. As matter of fact, I also know that Ronnie's been arrested. I'm trying to clear his name."

Just then King sidled up to them.

"I'm trying to help Ronnie," she repeated to King.

"Cat told me," King said. "I know that kid didn't do anything bad. He's not the type. Let me know what I can do."

"I'm Tiffany. His best friend. I go to school with your daughter."

"Oh, okay. You're the one that works with him on inkBLOT. He's talked about you."

"Yeah. That's me."

"You let me know what I can do. No limits."

"Sure thing. All I know is, I smell a skunk and I think her name is Chelsea," said Tiffany.

King laughed. "You have more than that business in your heart for that boy, don't you?"

"I didn't say that. I know he's innocent. And like I said, we're best friends."

"Sure kid. I have a daughter. I know that moping puppy dog look."

"Well, it doesn't matter."

"He's a good kid. So are you, but this doesn't sit right with me. Ya'll need to let the cops do their job.

Tiffany took in a deep breath and steadied herself. "I know it sounds crazy, but we'll be careful and we're just checking some things out. I can't just let Ronnie sit in jail, and I can't bail him out. I was hoping Cat would come with me, kind of back me up."

"I'm not going to stop you, am I?"

The girls looked at each other.

"Well, I'm glad you told me. Here's the deal." King pulled the two girls closer to each other, standing them right in front of him. "Take out your phones."

They both pulled out their phones just as he asked.

"Dial me. 282-8866. It spells the number 2 and the word tattoo, in case you forget, Tiffany."

His phone rang.

"Save that number, right now."

The girls nodded.

"You keep me in the loop. Okay? Call me and check in. I'm serious."

"I will. Thanks," said Tiffany.

He hesitated, but just for a minute. "You girls be careful. You're going to have to pull in the cops. It won't do Ronnie any good if you two get into trouble, too."

Cat bounced up next to Tiffany right about then, and gave her dad a kiss on the cheek. "Thanks Daddy."

He looked at her seriously. "I mean what I said."

CHAPTER TWENTY-FIVE

Chelsea straightened her dress in the full-length mirror. She'd just finished having a phone conversation with Hallie who'd told her they'd arrested Ronnie.

Timing. Why is my timing always off?

I can't believe Hallie had to go and arrest Ronnie tonight. Now I won't have a date on my biggest night. This really sucks. Thank goodness I haven't told anyone he was going to be my date.

While she'd be winning an award, he'd be sitting in a jail cell.

What a shame. Wasted genius sitting behind those bars.

A tiny bit of remorse tugged at her, but only for a moment. She shifted her thoughts to the stories she'd written and the attention they'd brought.

Framed copies of them were lined in a perfect row above her desk. A growth chart of sorts: from short, fluffy pieces to long front page headlines with pictures. Regardless of how dark and sinister the subject matter, it was worth it.

Notebooks of research from the internet, and handbooks on specific subjects lined the bookshelf next to the desk. Thank goodness for her Kindle. Now she could download a book and scan it in a moment's notice. As a writer, one had to stay informed.

If I show up at the awards ceremony alone, folks might think I couldn't get a date. Loser. I need a date, and fast.

She grabbed her address book and scanned it, then opened the drawer and took out a stack of business cards.

But who?

She flipped through them. It was last minute, but she needed someone who would draw attention and add to the excitement, but not detract from her.

She shuffled through the cards, shaking her head, and then paused.

"Perfect. He owes me. He even said so himself." The article she'd done on his business had generated a lot of revenue. Surely, he'd do it.

He'd better own a suit. A guy that age has to have at least one suit.

Chelsea picked up the phone and dialed the number on the back of the business card. His personal cell phone number.

"Yyy-ello," the deep voice came across the line.

"King. It's Chelsea. Chelsea Pressman from the Banner."

King's brows shot up. "Well, to what do I owe this pleasure?"

"I need a favor. Sorry, it's short notice. My date for the awards dinner tonight, well, he got sick so I need a date. If you can go, it's black tie."

Sick? Liar. He knew Ronnie had been looking forward to taking her to that event. Tiffany was right, she was no good. Well, it wouldn't hurt for him to spiff up and keep an eye on her.

"What time does it start?"

"In a few hours, but I need to be there early. Can I leave your name at the door? They'll seat you at my table."

"Sure." King grabbed a pen and piece of paper, and took down the address and said goodbye.

King hung up and called Cat to tell her about the phone call. Now they'd have eyes on Chelsea while they tried to figure out what exactly was going on.

***

Chelsea peered out of the window from the back of the Mercedes, imagining people in passing cars were wondering what famous person was behind the dark glass of the fancy stretch limo. She'd rented it herself, paying extra for the uniformed driver.

Her cell phone rang, distracting her from the view.

Unknown Caller.

Popping open the flip phone she pulled it to her ear. The voice on the other end startled her.

"Chelsea!"

"Ronnie? Wha...Where are you? I thought you'd stood me up. I finally had to leave without you else I'd be late."

"I'm in trouble. Chelsea, you've got to help me."

The limo pulled in front of the grand entrance of the Cavalier. Photographers from the other affiliates lined the walkway.

"Ronnie, it's not a good time. I'll have to talk to you after the awards."

"No. Don't hang up. Wait. Chelsea, you've got to help me. They're accusing me of serious crimes I didn't commit. I only get this one call."

He sounded desperate and she hesitated as the uniformed driver got out of the car and circled around, then pulled her door open and she snapped her phone shut without a goodbye.

Chelsea took a deep breath and stretched one leg out the door letting her dress hike a little so the four-inch heel of her designer shoe played lead to her exit.

She stood curbside and gave a backwards glance at the limo pulling away. She ran a nervous hand across her dark hair that she'd twisted up into a rhinestone-crusted clip, and adjusted the straps on her long burgundy gown. It hugged every curve, and she knew it.

"You look great tonight, Chelsea," one of the photographers called out from the sidewalk as he clicked a photo. Of course, she'd told him to be there. She stopped and smiled over her shoulder in his direction until the flash went off. She gave him a wink in thanks.

Chelsea handed her invitation to the doorman and left instructions to let King in when he arrived. She'd have preferred to have her escort with her, but the limelight all alone wasn't half-bad either. She held a smile and reminded herself not to fidget as she entered the grand lobby. Her heels clicked as she made her way down the long corridor of black and white marble tiles. The brilliant chandeliers made her feel even more elegant.

It looked like the Emmy Awards – red carpet and all. Pretty big deal for this town. Familiar faces from the fundraiser turned and gave her a nod. Everyone was dressed to the max. Even Emily Thompson from the classified ads department had on a plunging halter back dress. Emily usually looked like a frump, but tonight even *she* looked pretty.

Dinner was the first thing on the evening agenda. A glance around the noisy cluster of well dressed industry professionals confirmed her expectations. By the look of the cleavage in the crowd, there were more miracles in the bras than you'd see at a healing service.

The dining room was filling up. Elegant tables draped in white tablecloths and filled with fine china and gold ware sparkled under the chandeliers. Gold trimmed place cards indicated the preferred seating. It was nothing short of elegant.

Chelsea mingled with the others, weaving her way through the crowd in an exchange of small talk, while looking for her place card.

She hoped it would be at a place that garnered the right prestige. Close to the stage might mean she was the winner tonight.

"I know I'm here somewhere," she mumbled, starting to feel uncomfortable. Others seemed to find their seats and dive into deep conversations with others at their tables while she continued to wander among tables further from the stage.

Finally. She breathed a sigh of relief, then looked at the place card to the left of hers. *The owner of Benchmark Publications! That has to mean something.* She'd never met him in person, although she'd admired pictures of him at the office. A bachelor, an attractive one at that, he had a reputation of catching the eye of many women at these functions.

Maybe I shouldn't have called King after all. Wonder if it's too late to cancel with him? She glanced at her watch. *Darn. He's probably already on his way.*

She spotted the owner of Benchmark Publications on the other side of the room wooing a cluster of young women. Tall, thin and blond, his eyes scoped the room in spite of the enamored audience in front of him. Then, his eyes met hers. He smiled and held his glass up as if to toast her as the current object of his attention.

Chelsea gave him a nod and motioned to him that his seat was next to hers. She watched him excuse himself and start making his way through the crowd toward her.

For a brief moment, she felt a pang of sadness. *Too bad for Ronnie.* She shoved aside thoughts about Ronnie and set her sites on the suave owner of Benchmark heading her way. He sidled up to Chelsea and placed a hand on her bare shoulder.

"I've been impressed with your work. I wanted to meet the personality behind the pen." He extended his hand, then took her hand in his and kissed the back of it.

"It's nice to be recognized for my hard work." She withdrew her hand, feeling the blush redden her cheeks. "Thank you."

He grabbed the back of her chair and pulled it out for her. "Allow me."

Sitting, her eyes followed the circumference of the table to the faces of those already seated. They included the accounts manager, the head of the graphic arts department, and some from the editorial department. To her left, Ronnie's place card had already been replaced by one that read Guest of Chelsea Pressman. Her shoulders dropped as she read the one on the other side of that one. Scott's place card. *Just my luck. Maybe I'm NOT a sure win tonight. Who's going to win the coveted journalism award? Me or Super Scott?*

More importantly, would she be able to look gracious if she didn't?

"I see we're at the same table," Scott muttered as he approached the table in his walking cast.

She tried to restrain her real feelings, but she knew her smile was coming across only half-baked.

His brows furrowed at the gesture.

"We don't have to be. You could sit back there," she said gesturing to another table. Scott looked uncomfortable but didn't put up a fight. Instead, he smiled and guided his wife to the chair next to him.

The ting of a fork against a crystal glass brought the room to attention.

"Can I have your attention please?" The voice came over the microphone and all heads turned toward the podium.

King pulled out the chair next to her.

"Thank you," Chelsea mouthed his way. She wondered if the pounding was visible through her clothes. She had to win this coveted trophy.

James Thurston, publisher and owner of several newspapers, stood before the crowd of journalists. Looking immaculate in his black tuxedo, bald head shining under the bright lights that were focused on him, he looked at the expectant crowd.

"It's great to see all of you assembled here tonight. It brings me great pleasure to reward and recognize the hard work of those who make it their livelihood to report life as we know it. Whether it be warm your heart human interest or stop your heart cold stories, the latest breaking news affects the life of everyone around us. Of course, in a perfect world, we wouldn't have the latter but unfortunately it is a fact of life and it's also noted that those stories are what really sells papers. Human nature dictates that. Maybe not the best commentary on mankind, but we're always fascinated by what may not always be the most positive of events."

A waiter dropped his tray, spilling a pitcher of tea on a guest. Attention turned to the frantic rushing around, cloth napkins being used to mop up the spill from her lap and other guests who also caught some of the splash. Thurston hesitated a moment then plodded forward with his speech.

"Who's trying to upstage me?" he said, laughing. A round of laughter passed through the crowd as if on cue.

"There's always a mad dash for the big headline. Although what we bring to the masses may not always be good news, we do bring important information to help people avoid becoming a victim. Sometimes we instill some conscience in someone who has thought of committing a crime. For those we report as guilty, well, they paved their own path."

With that, he gestured with his hand across the room. "So without further ado, we will now recognize those who met the challenge of reporting stories that really raised an eyebrow. Stories that will be remembered for some time to come."

He's looking at me! He is. Chelsea held his gaze, and responded back by flashing one of her dazzling smiles his direction. She hadn't been using those white strips for nothing.

As Chelsea glanced toward Scott, it was obvious he too had seen the exchange and his face displayed a discomfort that could only have been produced by deep seated envy.

Chelsea pulled her hands into her lap.

Scott crossed his legs at the knees, swinging one foot with obvious irritation.

"The writer who is being honored tonight has risen through the ranks in record speed. The stories have captured local and national attention."

A silence fell across the room. Chelsea swore she heard Scott bristle.

"Congratulations, Chelsea Pressman."

Applause filled the ballroom.

"Join me up here, Chelsea."

Chelsea stood and steeped for a moment in the feeling of all eyes on her.

The clapping continued.

She dropped her eyes in what she hoped looked like sincere surprise and appreciation.

She pulled her shoulders back and lifted her chin, heading for the stage. She and Mr. Thurston exchanged some words off-mic and then Chelsea stepped to the podium and accepted the heavy crystal trophy. She surveyed the room, daring anyone to resent her getting the award.

"Thank you so much. I didn't expect this." She put a hand over her heart and shook her bangs from her face. "I've been on the fulltime staff for only a couple of months." Chelsea held the trophy in front of her, fingers running over it, feeling its smooth contours, memorizing each dip and curve with her fingertips. It would earn a prominent spot on her mantel at home where she could look at it often and remind herself that she had finally won the approval she so desperately sought.

She set the trophy down on the podium. "Gosh. This is heavy!" She wiped her sweating palms together. "I'd like to thank Harold Wadsworth for supporting my ambition and trusting my talent. The attention these stories have gathered has been exciting and I'm glad the Daily Banner was a part of bringing justice to the victims and punishment to the guilty."

Chelsea took a poetic pause, wiping a tear from her chin.

"It's hard to see the less attractive side of humanity, but things like the Diabetes Research Fundraiser help us balance those things. My position at the Daily Banner opened that door for me this year, and it was an exciting event to be a part of. This means the world to me. Thank you."

The crowd clapped and Chelsea swept through the tables back to her seat.

Scott looked at Chelsea from where he was sitting. He'd watched her expression move from cocky, to compassionate, to grateful, within a matter of seconds. The classes he'd taken in college on psychology had him always analyzing nuances in speech and body language.

As Chelsea walked back to her seat, she made a mental note to thank Ronnie. In ways he wasn't aware of, she had him to thank for much of this. Just how much he'd helped her, he had no idea. Too bad she'd be thanking him while he sat behind bars.

Following the awards, all of the table guests moved to the hall to mingle with those who had been sitting in the audience. She mingled and accepted congratulations from people she knew, and some she didn't, but the most important person on her list, her father, was nowhere to be found.

By ten o'clock, limos were lining up out front to whisk away the important folks. Chelsea held her smile despite her disappointment. Showing the trophy to Dad without the applause wouldn't be nearly as exciting. She handed her limo card to the valet who whistled to her driver to have the car pulled to the front of the line.

She slipped into the back of the car with her trophy in hand.

The glass between the driver and the back of the car slid down.

"Looks like you had a perfect evening."

She glanced at the trophy in the seat next to her. "Looks that way, doesn't it?" She couldn't hide her disappointment any longer. "Thank you."

"Congratulations." The driver then raised the glass window between them leaving her alone with her thoughts.

She twisted in her seat, with her back to the trophy, and stared out the window the whole ride home, never feeling lonelier.

CHAPTER TWENTY-SIX

Chelsea placed the prized trophy on the living room mantle and stepped back to let it all soak in.

Despite the sparkle of the lead crystal, somehow, it didn't seem as exciting as she'd hoped it would be. It was pretty, and the applause had been exhilarating, but now that it was over, it was over. If it was any consolation, at least Dad wasn't sitting in the living room watching poker on TV. He must have had something come up at work. Didn't he always?

It was times like these that she missed her mom the most.

She let out a deep breath and stepped out of her designer stiletto heels and tossed them toward the doorway to her room, unzipping her dress as she walked. Then, kicking her shoes the rest of the way to her closet, she didn't bother to clean them and place them back in the box like she usually would. Her dress slid down her shoulders and fell to the floor around her feet. She kicked it aside and reached into a drawer for her oversized Redskins tee shirt. Pulling the top over her head, she leaned toward the mirror and wiped away smudged eyeliner. Then she plopped down on the bed.

It's no fun celebrating by myself.

She wondered if they'd even let her bring the trophy into that place to see Mom. So many rules.

She punched her pillow and then turned over, staring at the ceiling. *What could have been so important that Dad would miss tonight? Is there really anything that important?*

Not happy with the unanswered questions, she pulled herself up and scuffed into the kitchen. The pantry was full, but nothing looked good. She opened the refrigerator door. She could hear Dad now, "Is there a movie playing in there?" It didn't hurry her along though. She needed comfort food.

A smoothie would be good.

She pulled out a container of fresh strawberries and yogurt, and then grabbed the vanilla ice cream from the freezer. After capping and washing the strawberries, she pulled the blender over closer to the sink. First went in the fruit and yogurt, then a generous scoop of ice cream. She put the top on and held it as she flipped the switch and let the blender do its magic. Bubbles frothed along the top, and the strawberry seeds dotted the pretty pink. *Ahhh, this is going to be good.*

She pulled down a large glass, then put it back and took a straw out of the drawer and dropped it right into the blender carafe.

Now, that's perfect. She took a long sip and then licked the milkshake mustache from her lips.

"Cheers to me," she said.

Then she grabbed a dust cloth from under the sink and headed to the living room.

She wiped away the fingerprints until the crystal and silver plated trophy gleamed.

CHAPTER TWENTY-SEVEN

Ronnie could overhear a couple of the police officers talking outside the interrogation room. They thought he was linked to a string of crimes.

Thank God I have alibis for the nights in question. Chelsea can clear this up easy.

He knew she was excited about the awards dinner. Crappy timing, for sure, but the officers doubted his connection with her now that she'd barely acknowledged him when he called. Somehow, he'd convinced them to let him call her again now that the dinner was probably over.

Please come through for me, Chelsea.

A guard came and got Ronnie out of the holding cell. He was led to one of the interrogation rooms where a detective was already waiting for him.

"Press 9 to get an outside line," the detective said.

Ronnie punched in Cheslea's cell phone number from memory.

"Chelsea. It's me Ronnie."

"Ronnie? Do I even know a Ronnie? Look, I shouldn't even be speaking to you after standing me up." The straw made a slurping noise as she sucked on the smoothie.

"You know I'd have been there if I could have. You've got to help me." He leaned his arms on the wooden table in the tiny room. The light green cinderblock walls seemed to be closing in on him.

"How can *I* help you?"

"Those stories you wrote. The front page news. They think I'm somehow involved with those crimes."

"Stop! Are you telling me what I think you're telling me? Where are you?"

"I'm in jail," he mumbled into the phone.

"Ronnie Wright! Tell me you didn't do something stupid to help me get a story."

"No." He blinked to process the comment. "You know I wouldn't do that. Besides, you're my alibi. I was at your house waiting on you during the time frame of one of these crimes they're talking about. You have to tell them it couldn't have been me. Friday the 13th. Remember? I do because I thought it was bad luck that I was standing there waiting for you."

"Your alibi? Oh, I don't remember that."

"You have to remember. It's not like we had that many dates. You were late to half of them."

"I'm never late. Well, maybe I am a little but that's beside the point."

"You were with me, remember? And what about the university schedule you asked me to get for you?" he reminded her. "That puts me at the university just before that professor wrecked."

"I didn't ask you to do that."

"Yes you did! You asked me to do that as a favor. I brought the schedule to you on Saturday morning."

"What have you done, Ronnie?"

"Nothing!" He explained as quickly as he could, the circumstantial evidence and links to his website.

"You're upset. I'll come by there tomorrow and we'll figure it out."

"Tomorrow? I can't stay here all night. You've got to come and help me tonight. You've got to get me out of here. I can't be in a cell. You know that."

She half listened, trying to decide how best to respond. A reporter can't make promises, just report the facts. "I really don't know what I can do to help you. I'm sorry." She pressed the off button on her phone and slid it into her purse.

Ronnie replaced the receiver and dropped his head in his hands.

How am I ever going to get out of here?

***

An officer came to get Ronnie. "You've got a visitor," he announced.

Ronnie fell in step behind the officer. Maybe Chelsea had come to help straighten things out. When he stepped into the room, Tiffany and her mom sat at a small table. Another officer was in the room with them.

He sat down at the table.

Tiffany's mom reached across the table and touched his arm. "Ronnie, I'm so sorry I can't get you bailed out yet. I'm working on it. Are you okay?"

He nodded.

Tiffany's eyes welled. "I can't believe they've got you in here."

"Don't be upset. It'll get straightened out. I didn't do anything. You know that, right?"

"Of course!"

"I tried to call Chelsea. She's my alibi. She can clear this up," Ronnie said, but even he wasn't feeling a hundred percent certain about what Chelsea would or wouldn't do at the moment.

Tiffany's mouth pulled into a tight line. "Don't be such a jerk. She's the reason you're here. I know it. I can't totally prove it, but I will."

Ronnie blinked.

"Don't look so surprised. I don't think your attraction with her was so misplaced. She's a psychological oddity and you'll probably learn all kinds of stuff from her, but it won't be all lovey dovey like you'd hoped."

"Tiff..."

"Don't Tiff me. You're so obsessed with her you didn't even pay attention to the red flags that were snapping so loud they should have deafened you!"

The officer stepped over to the table. "Ma'am, please remain calm."

Tiffany let out a loud breath, and nodded. She cleared her throat and spoke slower, more calmly. "Here's what I know so far."

She laid out all the details that she had gathered.

Ronnie closed his eyes and shook his head. "How could I have been such an idiot?"

"You're a guy," she said. "Now tell me what else I can do with what we have to figure all this out."

They talked through the details until the officer told them their time was up.

Tiffany and her mom stood and watched as they led Ronnie back down the hall.

"You okay, honey?" Tiffany's mom hugged her daughter close. "I love you."

"I know. I love you, too, Mom."

"You know you need to talk to the detective. You can't keep digging around."

Tiffany wiped the tears from her cheek and nodded.

"It'll work out. The truth always comes out."

"Hey guys. There's some girl in the lobby wanting to talk about that kid you've got back here. Ronnie Wright? She refuses to leave."

"You talk to her," said the cop with the northern accent. "You're more patient than I am."

Busby shrugged. "That's cool." He was always getting ragged by the old timers. He didn't care. He wouldn't be the youngest guy on the force forever. "What's her name?"

The desk clerk smiled. "Tiffany. And she's as pretty as her name."

"My pleasure," said Busby. "Bring her back to my desk."

The desk clerk escorted Tiffany to the detective area. "Tiffany. Here's the guy who can help you. Name's Busby."

"Thanks." Tiffany pushed her hand out toward him.

He shook her hand and sat back down. "Hello."

"Hi. I need your help. My best friend has been arrested. I think I can help prove he's innocent."

"Who is your friend?"

"Ronnie Wright. You've got the wrong person. You've got to help me. I've been sitting out here for hours and no one will talk to me."

"Sorry. I...we didn't know. We've been working the case."

"I've found out some things myself. He's innocent. I know he is. I know him better than anyone."

Busby straightened. "I'd love to hear what you've got. First things first. I'll need some information about you."

Tiffany provided all the information he asked for, and was beginning to relax a little.

"Okay. Great. Now tell me what you know." Busby flipped his notebook to a clean sheet.

She eyed the green binder they'd taken from the apartment. "First off, I told you that's not his."

Busby looked at the binder and then Tiffany. "I believe you."

"You do?"

He nodded, and she relaxed into the chair a bit.

"Thank goodness," she said, and then she let every shred of evidence and every theory she had considered roll out of her mouth, barely taking a breath.

"I know this is going to sound crazy to you," Tiffany explained. "But Ronnie is brilliant. He's been building algorithms and models that have actually been right on target with some of the crimes that have taken months and months to solve. Please don't tell anyone about this. He'll kill me and it's confidential, but it works. I mean it really works."

Busby didn't look completely sold, but Tiffany wasn't surprised by that. It did sound a little crazy.

"So anyway, here's some examples." She pulled a spreadsheet out of her purse and started walking him through the data points. "See here. This is a list of the people who complete inkBLOT quizzes that came up as 'potentially dangerous'. Now, look here."

She flipped to a second page.

"These are ones that have been arrested." Tiffany laid the two sheets side by side. "It's a pretty staggering success rate."

"Wow. That's pretty awesome." Busby looked genuinely impressed.

"Okay. So, I was able to pull in Chelsea's results and look. This is her profile."

Busby sat back in his chair looking dumbfounded.

Busby said, "Okay. I'm listening. You've definitely got my attention. I mean police use psychics all the time. I suppose data is at least tangible. What else you got?"

Tiffany straightened. "Chelsea dated that guy that died in the explosion."

"Are you sure?" Busby scribbled as fast as he could while he listened intently, jotting down his own notes as she spoke.

"Yes. The lady running the Appliance King Showroom confirmed it. I also found out that she has ties to a pretty impressive musician who could be the owner of that flute ya'll found at the pumpkin-dagger scene."

"I remember that case. That was weird." Busby nodded. "You know that guy that was the target. He's a musician, too. Maybe that's another connection."

He pulled a thick folder out and opened it in front of them. Ronnie's cell phone had been processed. The list of incoming and outgoing calls from the SIM card was only a couple of pages long.

Busby turned the report toward Tiffany. "Recognize any of these?"

She glanced it over. "Yeah. Most of them are to me."

She held her hand out for a pen, and he placed one in her hand. She circled the other numbers on the list. Most were to one common number, there were only about half a dozen outliers. "Here you go. This will narrow it down. I bet that's Chelsea's number."

Busby picked up the handset and tried the other numbers. A florist, a restaurant, the Daily Banner and a pizza shop. Then he dialed the number that Tiffany thought was Chelsea's. She picked up on the first ring.

"Chelsea?" asked Busby.

"Speaking. Who's calling?"

"Hey there. It's Busby." Busby raised a brow in Tiffany's direction. "I was wondering if you wanted to get together tonight and discuss those questions I had." He set up the time and ended the call.

Busby stared at Tiffany with a smirk. "That proves she lied about how well she knew Ronnie. You know, she's kind of manipulative. Can't say that I'm surprised."

Tiffany leaped from the chair and gave Busby a hug. "Thank you for believing me. For helping me." Tears of relief fell to her cheeks.

"Whoa. Hang on there. Nothings settled. We still have to find the proof or get a confession out of her."

Tiffany lowered her eyes. "I know you probably don't care, but Ronnie had a tough childhood. His parents used to lock him in a closet. That cell. It's going to be like torture. Can you at least let him know you're looking into things? That we're making progress?"

Busby felt the hurt in her voice and saw it in her eyes. He placed a hand on her shoulder. "I'll make sure he knows. Don't worry."

Tiffany left knowing she'd done what she could to help. Now it was in the hands of the police. She prayed Ronnie wasn't going to kill her for sharing some of the confidential data from inkBLOT, but she'd really had no choice. If Ronnie was convicted inkBLOT would be history anyway.

Tiffany left the station feeling pleased that someone acted interested enough to at least look into things. All she could do is pray for him now.

Busby sat on the edge of his partner's desk.

Rimarksi said, "She was cute."

"She's a kid," Busby said.

"And you aren't?"

"Funny." Busby rolled his eyes. "She has some interesting details. Smart kid."

"What did she say?"

"It's not what she said. It's what she can prove. She's put more together in the last few hours than we have since we started looking into all these crimes."

Rimarski nodded. "Well, then maybe it's your place to do a little checking around for yourself. Stranger things have happened. Could be that we have the wrong person sitting back there behind bars? Wouldn't be the first time at this early stage of an investigation."

Busby chewed on his lip. "You know, she's been playing me for months. Asking for tips and help. She's a smooth operator."

"The Pressman chick?"

Busby nodded.

"You think you can handle it on your own?" asked the older cop. "I mean if she's into you and all."

"It's not like that, but yeah. Give me the chance."

"Go for it kid."

Busby tried not to let the "kid" comment bother him, but it always did a little. He grabbed his jacket from the back of his chair and left to pay a visit to the Pressman residence.

When he arrived at the address there was only one car in the driveway. It was her car. He pulled the cruiser up behind it to block her in.

Slamming his door, Busby glanced up at her windows as he rang the doorbell and waited. Either she wasn't home, or she was hiding. Maybe he'd go park down the street and see if anyone showed up later.

Just as he turned to head back to the squad car, the door opened.

Busby turned to head back to the porch. "Hey Chelsea? Is that you?"

"Do I know you?"

"It's me Busby." He pulled off his hat. She looked good, even in her pj's. "We talk mostly on the phone, maybe the hat threw you." He flashed his badge, and handed her his card. "May I come in?" he asked, now looking down at his feet, still feeling the sting of discomfort at seeing her rather sensual appearance. "I have some questions I'd like to ask you."

"Hey there. Sorry I didn't recognize you. You're always such a big help to me. Sure thing. Come on in," she said with a sweep of her hand. Shutting the door behind him, she gazed back at her papers strewn across the kitchen table.

"Yeah. That info I gave you about the boa murder was your first front page story wasn't it?"

She nodded. "Yeah. My first break."

"Good. Good." He nodded. "I bet that felt great. I mean to be on the front page. All that attention, you being so young and all."

She nodded again, but she looked less enthusiastic now. "Is this an official visit, Busby?"

"We placed Ronnie Wright under arrest earlier tonight. I understand you know him."

Chelsea pulled her hands into her lap. "Well, sort of. I mean I don't know him, know him."

"We suspect he had something to do with some of the stories you've covered recently."

Chelsea's mouth dropped wide. "Really? How so?"

Busby noted the Emmy-award acting. He knew Chelsea knew that Ronnie was arrested. He'd listened in on Ronnie's call to her. "How well did you know him?"

"He was kind of smitten with me I guess. He dropped a thousand bucks to get a date with me at the Diabetes auction. Did you hear about that?"

"No." Busby leaned back trying to appear casual and get Chelsea to relax. "Wow. That's a lot of money."

"I know. I was shocked."

"But you don't have a relationship or anything?"

She shook her head. "No. I mean he was kind of interested in me, but it wasn't like we were dating."

"So, if I told you that he said he was waiting for you at your house during the time of the incident on Friday, October 13th, you'd tell me that wasn't true?"

"Waiting? At my house? For me? No way. I was with Hallie Davison that evening."

"Detective Hallie Davison?"

"Yes. We've worked a few of the stories together. Actually, ever since you gave me that information on the boa murder she and I have been doing a lot of work together. I guess I have you to thank for that."

"I see." *Was Hallie involved? Oh Lord, I'm not experienced enough to tangle with that kind of thing. Maybe I should've had Rimarski come with me.* Busby got up and walked toward the mantle. He motioned toward the trophy. "Wow. That's nice."

"Thanks. Just won that tonight."

"Congratulations."

She smiled, relaxing a little.

"Things are really going great for you." Busby picked up a picture off the mantle, then glanced her way. "Where was this taken?"

"Oh gosh. I hate that picture. My dad insists on keeping it up there. I was employee of the month at Animal House the first month I worked there," she laughed. "All I did was clean out snake cages. Really, not so impressive. Feeding them mice and scooping poop pellets."

"Snake cages." He faked a shiver. "That would scare me to death."

She shrugged. "You have to be careful around snakes, especially poisonous ones."

She looked quite proud of herself. Busby made the connection to the professor who'd died of the snakebite immediately. Chelsea seemed to have no idea how that statement could incriminate her.

"Isn't that how that Professor died that you wrote about? A snake bite?"

A flash of panic, then movie star innocence came over Chelsea. She pulled her arms across her chest. "Yeah, I think so. I write so many I forget."

"You sure you don't know more about these crimes than you are letting on?" He gazed at her pensively, waiting for a response.

Chelsea looked as though she'd been caught off guard, and she was carefully selecting her next words. "Maybe I've been doing a little investigating on my own. It's part of my job, you know. Maybe the cops haven't done the best job in uncovering all the clues," she said with a defiant look on her face.

"How about filling me in on some of those details. We're friends, right?"

"How about coming back tomorrow. I'm not feeling so well. I hope you don't mind. I've been having some trouble with my back and I need to get some rest."

He stepped toward the foyer door. "I suppose this can wait until tomorrow." On his way out of the apartment, he spotted a notebook lying on the table next to her purse. At that moment, the phone rang and Chelsea turned her head. It matched the other notebook they'd taken from Ronnie's house. The one Tiffany swore didn't belong to Ronnie. He couldn't resist. He flipped it open flat on the table so she wouldn't notice and scanned the entries.

Chelsea spun around and mouthed, "It's my boss."

He gave her a thumbs up and pointed to the door that he'd let himself out.

Chelsea took in a deep breath. It was way too late for her boss to be calling for anything good.

"Congratulations again, Chelsea. I hate to be calling so late, but I heard something not so good about that kid who bid on you at the diabetes fundraiser. I sent Scott out on the story."

Great. The last thing she wanted was for Super Scott to get the story. "If there's a story there I should get it."

"Scott said you're involved with that guy," he said, his breath catching in his throat. "Is that true?"

"We're not involved, and you don't need Scott to cover this. I can do it. It's my story."

"Well, I'm going to let Scott run with this. Why don't you take a few days off until things settle down? We sure don't need any bad press about you being involved with him."

"Days off? I barely know him. Please believe me."

"I can't risk the paper's reputation," said Wadsworth as he hung up without a goodbye.

CHAPTER TWENTY-EIGHT

Busby pulled out a copy of Chelsea's cell phone records and spread the six pages across the desk. He'd contacted Tiffany to come in to see if she could help him sort through any of it.

Busby explained what he'd already done. "See. I ran a crosscheck against the numbers. Most of them are to the newspaper and to her voice mail, but these I highlighted in yellow, they may have significance to this case. They align with the dates of the crimes."

"That's Ronnie's number!" Tiffany held her hand to her mouth. "He hates contracts. He uses a pre-paid phone. That's his number." She pulled her own phone out and pushed a few buttons and then showed Busby. "See. He's in my speed dial."

"We have his phone. Remember?" said Busby. "I'd already marked his home phone number and all these calls and texts to his cell confirm what he says about them knowing each other. This text from Chelsea corroborates his alibi for Friday the 13th!"

"Thank goodness."

"He's not in the clear yet," he warned. "Hallie's pretty confident she's got the right guy, but I'm going to take this information to her and see if I can get a warrant for Chelsea's arrest."

"Can I wait for you?" asked Tiffany.

Busby paused. "Yeah, sure. I'll be right back."

Tiffany watched Busby. When he entered Detective Davison's office, he started speaking immediately. His hands were moving all around as he spoke. She watched him lay out his evidence across her desk. Hallie looked it over and when she straightened, she pulled her hands to her hips, and then nodded. In agreement, hopefully.

Tiffany looked away, in fear they'd catch her peeping.

Busby walked back to his desk.

She couldn't tell by his face if it was a victory or not.

"Well?" asked Tiffany.

"Detective Davison does not like being played the fool. Not one bit. She's working up the papers right now."

Tiffany raised a hand for a high five, and Busby slapped his palm against hers.

"It'll take a while. It has to go up the chain of command. Then we have to investigate the lead," explained Busby.

"You mean you can't let Ronnie out right now?"

"Sorry. No, we still have some things to connect before that happens." Busby reached for her arm. "You're a good friend to him. He's lucky. Be patient. We're making progress."

"Thanks. I know. I know you're right." Tiffany stood. "I guess I better get back home then."

"You're a good partner, too." Busby gave her a wink. "You ought to think about going to the police academy. We need smart thinkers like you."

By the next afternoon, Hallie had the paperwork she needed to begin getting the detailed information on Chelsea's personal records. She assigned that work to Busby since he'd done the other footwork on his own.

Busby hunkered down at his desk going through the lists looking for correlation to the recent events. He looked up, and Tiffany was standing at his desk with a brown paper bag.

"Hope I'm not interrupting," she said.

"Hi Tiffany. I was just working on the case."

She set the bag down on his desk. "I hope it's going well. I brought you some dinner. Chicken and dumplings. My specialty."

"Homemade?"

She grinned. "Grandma's recipe."

He dug into the bag and retrieved the plastic bowl. "Man this smells good. I'm starved, too."

"I don't know how I can thank you for helping Ronnie."

"You're crazy about that guy, aren't you?" said Busby.

"We're best friends. We share everything."

"And..."

"And yes. I'm crazy about him," Tiffany admitted.

"Hallie and I are meeting with the chief about the warrants in a little while. I think I've got everything we need. Looks like it doesn't stop there. Bank records show a purchase at Animal House, plus she used to work there. They have all kinds of snakes. That gives her access. She also paid the maid service that cleaned the home of the man who'd died from peanut allergy before he met his fate. A lot of circumstantial evidence."

Officer Busby continued. "Crenshaw died from a snakebite, that's what caused that car accident. If she planned that...well, she's a sick puppy. That really creeps me out. You hear about this kind of sociopath on TV, but you never think it would happen in your own backyard. It would be like a weatherman making it snow so he could report on extreme weather. Weird, huh?"

Tiffany took in a deep breath. "The details on our inkBLOT report gave her information that would have told her things like that guy's obsession with snakes, and the other guy's fear of nuts. I swear we never intended that data to get into anyone else's hands and it was all being used for serious research. I still can't imagine how she got it. We are always so careful."

"Probably innocent information until it falls into the wrong hands. It's not your fault. Things happen sometimes that we'll never understand." Busby stood and walked Tiffany back out to the front. "Thanks for dinner. I appreciate it."

"You're welcome. Thanks for listening to me," Tiffany said with a wave as she headed out the door.

Busby stopped to consider the scenario of Chelsea Pressman back there behind bars. That orange outfit wouldn't be as striking on her as the gray skirt and boots she wore the last time she came by to get the scoop on a story.

"I'm telling you. I've got to get to the bottom of this case," he told a cohort sitting near his desk. "I know what happened. Now, I need to make the case rock solid."

Busby knew he'd have to clear his head of her if he was going to work on this case successfully. Chelsea's charm had a way of making him forget what day it was, what time it was or even his own name for that matter. But now he knew what Chelsea was really made of.

An hour later, Hallie and Busby were in the chief's office going over the case and the evidence they had in hand so far.

Busby had the green binder with him.

"See here. These are all the names and addresses of the involved parties," Busby showed him. "This is the list that Chelsea Pressman stole from Ronnie Wright. Look, each victim is listed here. I confirmed with Tiffany that the data in the file was not in this order. Chelsea manipulated it to meet her plan. One by one, she created her own front page news."

The chief nodded. "The victims' families were relieved that we had the culprit behind bars. This won't look so good for us. How can we be sure he didn't have anything to do with it?"

"I know we're right on this, Sir," Busby said lifting his chin.

"Then, prove it." The chief crossed his arms. "What we've got on that boy is circumstantial. Get me hard proof. Evidence that will hold up."

Busby and Detective Davison exchanged a glance.

The chief cleared his throat and ran a hand through his hair. "My buddy down at the paper, Wadsworth, is going to go nuts if you're right. She's the paper's little darling. We better get this right."

"Yes, sir," Busby and Davison said in unison.

"Get it right." The Chief handed over the signed warrants to Hallie. "Good job, Busby. Things don't always turn out as we predict. Justice will prevail."

Officer Busby and Hallie Davison mapped out a plan on the board in Hallie's office to be sure they got everything they needed, and a plan B just in case.

The first step was to question Ronnie again, and then put the witnesses through another round of questioning.

Across the white board they had Chelsea's name with

> Motive – Career Advancement.
>
> Opportunity – the inkBLOT report and that press badge.
>
> Cell phone report conflicts with her statement

Notes under each event date crossed from one end of the board to the other. A copy of each story was taped below each one.

The detective assigned to re-interview Animal House confirmed that Chelsea had been previously employed there and that she'd been at Animal House under the guise of a story the day before the snake incident. The store handled quarantine and lodging arrangements for customers who traveled. One customer, a specially licensed exhibitor with licensing to handle rare and venomous breeds, had recently quarantined a snake and that snake had turned up missing. A rare and venomous reptile. The one from the accident.

The next few reports came in and confirmed what Tiffany had found. These official reports were stacking the case against Chelsea quickly.

Following the right leads also validated that Chelsea paid for the cleaning at the "nut" house. This was all under the guise of a "Chelsea's Job" series she was going to do that Wadsworth had never heard of.

And then everything seemed to fall right into place.

Officer Busby called Chelsea to get the ball rolling on the final sting.

Busby called Chelsea's number from Hallie's office on his personal cell phone.

"Hi, Chelsea. It's Busby. I was wondering if you wanted to get together? I have something I think you'll find interesting."

"You got a lead on something?"

He thought he detected a sexy breathy tone in her voice. Was that designed to throw him off track again? No way would that happen again.

"Yeah," said Busby. "Can I meet you?"

"When and where?" asked Chelsea. "Oh wait. Can you hang on? Someone is at my door."

She started to answer the door, but something didn't feel right. She wasn't expecting anyone and she rarely had visitors here at the house.

Banging came from the door again. She sprinted like the wind to the side window to peek out. Just as she pulled back the blinds, they announced themselves.

"Chelsea Pressman. This is the police. Open up!"

How could this have happened? I've always been so careful. I can't leave them standing there, it would look worse. She took a breath and put on her award winning smile and cracked the door open.

"Hi. Can I help you? Is something wrong?"

"Can you step outside please?" said an officer.

"Of course. What's the matter? Is Dad okay?" *Work it Chels, work it.*

Two other officers pushed past her into the house.

"Wait a second," cried Chelsea. "What are you doing?"

The officer pulled Chelsea's arm behind her back and handcuffed her in one half turn. "You have the right to remain silent. Anything you say can and will be used against you in a court of law. You have the right to an attorney present during questioning. If you cannot afford an attorney, one will be appointed for you. Do you understand these rights?"

"Wh-wh? Wait. Why are you arresting me?" Chelsea's eyes looked like a cornered animal. "You've got the wrong person." She helplessly looked from one officer's face to another. Feeling herself grow red with anger and embarrassment, she glared at the policemen who restrained her.

She spotted Busby standing next to Hallie on the curb.

"Help me." Chelsea tugged away from the officer. "Hallie. You know me. What's going on?"

Hallie turned her back.

Chelsea was led to the squad car in handcuffs. She slumped low in the back seat. The police car pulled out of the neighborhood and as it rounded a curve, a ray of sunlight reflected off a store window and flashed onto her. Alternately, she had a ray of realization.

I can make this work for me! A close up look at life in jail could be a bestseller.

The officer eyed Chelsea from the rearview mirror. One side of Chelsea's mouth was turned up in a wicked grin.

A few minutes later, the police car carrying her pulled into the station.

The drab building wasn't a welcome sight.

Officers walked in and out in their uniform blues.

Chelsea straightened in the seat at a familiar sight. She'd know that silhouette anywhere. Ronnie stood on the police station steps.

They've released him?

He had a tortured look. She'd had a part in that. She briefly looked away when he noticed her staring, then she looked his way again. She held his gaze as the policeman pulled the cruiser around back to take her in to process.

Chelsea's mind swept in a swirl of conflicting thoughts. *I'm sorry, but you'll never know that. If you'd have cared you'd have helped me. Why did you succeed and I didn't? I hate you for your success.*

There was a pang of remorse. Maybe she should have put love before success. He would have loved her, if he hadn't already.

I could have loved you.

So many things ran through her head. Hanging her head down, her eyes stung with guilt. Chelsea looked down at her hands. The ones that so eagerly pounded the keys just yesterday. So many stories, so many lives.

Her life would never be the same again.

Never.

CHAPTER TWENTY-NINE

Chelsea sat on the edge of the cot in her jail cell flipping the ugly prison pen between her fingers like a baton. Who knew there were special pens just for jail? She collected ink pens, but she'd never heard of it. A potentially dangerous weapon in the hands of a prisoner, and she was a prisoner now, the bendy prison pen was her only option. She crinkled her nose at the rubbery scent of it.

If I was at home, I'd be using a fancy pen. One of at least fifty that sat in the pink pencil cup with her initial, C, on it.

Chelsea ran a nervous hand through her hair and bounced the bendy pen against her leg. She wondered if Mom had to use these kinds of pens. The psych hospital had so many rules. She'd never thought to ask.

Well, at least nobody can get stabbed with these things. The only stabbing that's going to be going on around here is taking a stab at good behavior, hoping to get out earlier than sentenced. I'm smarter than they are. I'll be out of here in no time with a platform that will skyrocket my fame.

Chelsea leaned forward and began to furiously scribble in the notebook they'd given her. Four pages of words, scratching through and starting over, she stretched across her bed and tore the last sheet out.

She re-wrote the entry neatly, careful to not make any mistakes. Then she tucked the pen behind her ear, raised the notebook in front of her and read it aloud.

An inkBLOT image
a twist of fate
they never knew what hit 'em.

The test, of course
was multiple choice
but did they have one?

Art follows life
or life follows art
dark as an inkBLOT.

Fame has a price
sometimes not nice
Just see what I got.

I promise you this,
You'll see this Miss,
Right back at that spot.

Count on it...

A single tear fell slid down her cheek, settling between her dry lips.

Daddy, why haven't you checked on me or asked for my side of the story. I know you're disappointed in me. Again. Tell Mom I'm sorry I can't visit her at the hospital.

She laid back and pondered her options.

Maybe they won't convict me. That's always a possibility. I've only been charged, not sentenced yet. I can sit here and sulk and count the days, or I can start working a plan for success when I get out.

Plan A was the wimpy way to go. She'd stick to Plan B, and she knew exactly what path she was going to take. She folded the next page in her notebook and wrote in bold, straight letters across the center of the top of the page:

Little Women –Behind Bars Not In Them.

The book with an inside look at jail life of a young woman barely old enough to go into a bar, ending up behind them would end up a best seller. She licked the end of the pen and started writing.

CHAPTER THIRTY

Ronnie stood in front of the police station feeling mixed emotions.

On one hand he was glad they finally realized he was innocent, on the other he felt foolish. How had he let himself get in that situation to begin with? Obsession is a tricky thing. It takes on a life and purpose all its own. One more facet to consider as he plodded through the analysis of the human mind and thought process. Hopefully, the experience would strengthen his studies.

His car had been impounded so he had no wheels.

He wanted to call Tiffany, but he was embarrassed. He'd been so stupid. She was his best friend though, and Busby said she was key in his getting out of there. He had to trust Tiffany to forgive him.

Ronnie pulled his phone from his hip and stared at it for a moment. Then he hit the number one speed dial.

How could I have been such a poor judge of character? I never even saw it coming. She had everything going for her.

The phone rang again on the other end. Tiffany finally answered.

"Are you ever going to forgive me for being such an idiot?" he asked.

"I'm thinking about it," she giggled, and Ronnie knew she was teasing. He ran a finger under his nose fighting back the urge to cry—something he never did. Then, he wiped at the mist that clouded his vision. Tiffany was always there.

Ronnie swallowed back the emotion. "Thank you, Tiffany. I'm out, and they arrested her."

"Thank goodness."

"You knew, didn't you? All this time, you knew she was up to no good."

"I never liked her from day one. Call it a woman's intuition. Call it jealousy, whatever, but I did have a feeling."

"Well, I've had one heck of a wake-up call. I've been an ass."

"Yeah. You're a guy. It happens. Don't worry, you're forgiven. Where are you? We need to talk," Tiffany said softly.

"I'm walking, headed away from the police station. I'm on the corner of High and Court Streets. My car's still impounded."

"Stay put. I'll be right there," she said.

Ronnie lingered at the corner, pacing and looking into the store windows but only seeing the scenes replay in his head. Ten minutes later, Tiffany pulled up to the curb in her mom's Buick. The driver's door swung open and she ran toward him.

As soon as he laid eyes on Tiffany, his heart told him what he should have known the whole time.

Ronnie's heart swelled at the sight of her.

The right one's been in front of me all along. No one else knows me better. No one else sticks beside me through thick and thin. No one else laughs at my jokes like she does. I love her laugh, her smile. How could I have been so blind?

Tiffany slid to a stop right in front of him.

"I'm so glad you're okay." She wrapped her arms around his waist and hugged him. "Thank God, things can get back to normal."

"Normal is good," he agreed.

"Hey, do you know what today is?"

He threw his hands in the air. "Freedom!"

"Yeah, and a new beginning."

He paused for a second. "Yeah. That too! A happy one thanks to you. I'm sorry Tiffany. So sorry I've been such a jerk. Our relationship. It's way more than friends. It could be, couldn't it?"

Ronnie put his hand on the side of her face, stroking her jaw line. "Are we suddenly moving a step forward?"

She moved her shoulder to snuggle his hand against her cheek. "Oh, I think it's more than a step," she said, smiling.

Ronnie felt clarity he'd never felt before. "I almost screwed this up. I'm sorry if I hurt you."

"Love hurts Ronnie. Sometimes it can even leave a scar."

He put his hand to his shoulder where King had tattooed him. "I made my own scar. What was I thinking?"

"Scars are like tattoos only with better stories." She stood on her toes and planted a kiss on his lips. "No more tattoos, okay?"

"Deal."

THE END

If you enjoyed this book, we'd love to hear from you.

Share your thoughts with us on twitter, on the **inkBLOTtheNovel** facebook page or by email to streetteam@inkblotthenovel.com

About the Author

Johnson Naigle is a pen name for the writing duo of Phyllis C. Johnson and Nancy Naigle. inkBLOT is their first novel together.

Phyllis Johnson calls herself a Renaissance woman whose interests include acting in detective shows, writing for newspapers and national magazines and hosting slam jams. Yeah! A poetess, she has four poetry books to her credit, including Being Frank with Anne, a poetic interpretation of Anne Frank's diary.

inkBLOT was conceived one day while Phyllis was taking an inkblot test online and she wondered what potential evil could be done by some wicked person with the personal information she was keying in. How scary is that?

Like Ronnie in inkblot, she and her hubby have a black lab who has not yet learned to catch a newspaper midair.

Learn more about Phyllis at www.phyllisjohnson.net

Nancy Naigle writes love stories from the crossroad of small town and suspense. Her debut novel, Sweet Tea and Secrets, came out in May 2011. Sweet Tea and Secrets climbed to the top 100 Kindle Romantic Suspense within the first three weeks of its release.

Nancy is an award winning writer who is as good at weaving edgy techno into novels as she is at weaving the baskets she likes to make. Adding to her list of attributes, this surprising writer not only raises suspense in her novels but she also helps raise goats on a farm with her husband in southern Virginia.

Learn more about Nancy at www.nancynaigle.com